DARK HORSE

Five years have passed since former jockey Mark Presley chose to stay silent about the hit-and-run accident that left a beautiful young woman dead. But when his wife is killed in an incident with cruel echoes of that earlier tragedy, it seems justice has come calling. A broken man, he is driven by grief to clear his conscience at last.

The truth is about to come out. Or is it? Mark has nothing left to lose—but there are others he'd implicate by confessing. In the world of flat racing everything rides on reputation, and some people will do anything to keep theirs intact. Anything. Even murder...

DARK HORSE

John Francome

WINDSOR
PARAGON

First published 2007
by
Headline Publishing Group
This Large Print edition published 2007
by
BBC Audiobooks Ltd by arrangement with
Headline Publishing Group

Hardcover ISBN: 978 1 405 61978 3
Softcover   ISBN: 978 1 405 61979 0

British Library Cataloguing in Publication Data available

Printed and bound in Great Britain by
Antony Rowe Ltd., Chippenham, Wiltshire

With thanks to Katie Byam-Cook
BVSc MRCVS for her veterinary advice

PROLOGUE

The blonde girl with dishevelled hair drove carelessly along the rutted track. It was a hot autumn day and the trees were still heavy with leaves. Ahead, among a collection of buildings which sprawled across the valley, stood a redbrick Victorian mansion, her weekly destination.

A tubby man in a T-shirt with a grey-flecked ponytail was waiting by the front door. She knew that he had been alerted to the arrival of her dusty Golf by the guard at the lodge gate back on the road. Dr Huntley was the Director of Grovelands, and he always made a point of seeing Alice on her visits.

'How is Edwin?' she asked as Huntley led her across the tiled floor of the hall to the basement stairs.

'Very busy,' was the reply, which was no surprise. Edwin was always busy.

They descended to the suite of rooms below, where lights blazed and the smell of paint thickened the air. The weather was glorious and the other residents were pursuing their own salvation in the sunshine. But in all the years she had been coming here, Alice had never been able to persuade Edwin to set foot outside.

They passed down a corridor hung with impenetrable abstracts of purple and black— Edwin's work. The double doors at the end opened into an artist's studio where the wooden floor was spattered with paint and littered with rags. A stained and grubby porcelain sink ran half the length of one wall and easels and stools stood jumbled in a far corner, next to canvases stacked against the wall.

On his knees in the middle of the room a stick-insect of a man in a once-white overall contemplated a canvas lying face up on the floor. In one hand he held a brush. Pots of paint surrounded his work in progress. He did not turn at their approach but seemed lost in a distant world.

'Hello, Edwin,' said Alice.

There was no response. Instead, Edwin loaded his brush with paint and flicked a fine line of black drips across the canvas.

'He's still in his Jackson Pollock phase,' said Huntley.

Hardly, thought Alice.

'You can leave us, if you like,' she said. 'I'm sure you've got things to do.'

He smiled. 'True enough. But I want you to know that Edwin is an honoured member of our community. We care for him very much.'

'Thank you, doctor.' It wasn't the first time he'd made this speech but she appreciated it all the same.

She waited till he'd gone and then she knelt on the floor too.

'Hello, Edwin,' she said again but more softly than before.

He did not appear to hear but this time his brush dipped to the canvas and described a line across the surface. In a few quick strokes, quite unlike the movements he'd made before, he made a familiar shape. A horse's head—bold-eyed and noble, full of life—appeared on the canvas. Then, as swiftly as it had been conjured up, he obliterated it in a swirl of paint. A figure of smoke blown away in the breeze. But it had been there and she had seen it as he had intended.

'Thanks, Dad,' she murmured.

The stick-insect man ignored her and continued to flick with his brush.

CHAPTER ONE

'Eh, Turk. Ever driven one of them?'

Turk—real name Barry Marshgate—followed the direction of his friend, Scabby's, gaze.

In the car park of the estate opposite sat a parked van, its engine idling. The driver's sliding door was pushed back and the waffle of some fake bastard on Radio Two carried across the street to where the two lads sat on a wall.

If he had to put money on it, Turk reckoned the vehicle was a Vauxhall Vivaro but it could as easily be some kind of Ford. Not that he was much interested in delivery vans. Hot hatchbacks were more his kind of thing—Clios, Colts, Peugeot 206s—nippy little numbers you could hammer the crap out of. On the other hand, it was only Scab who was asking.

'Yeah. Loads of times.'

Scab popped another can. 'Bet you never.'

Turk could have wished for better company but the scabby one was the only kid wagging it today like him. Turk had gone over the wall at the back of the playground in morning break. He'd only stuck it out that long because the day started with DT, the one subject he was good at. A couple of other mates had said they'd be bunking off too and he'd mooched around waiting for them to show. In the end he'd given up—they must have chickened out. It was turning out to be a right manky day.

He'd run across Scab in the shopping centre hanging around the doors of H & M. 'All the top totty comes by here,' he'd explained.

1

Turk had swallowed the laughter that welled up inside. The notion that any lass, top or bottom totty, would look at Scab's spotty face with favour was ludicrous. What planet was he on? Planet Pustule, that's what. If any of the others had been around they'd have had a good giggle.

But the others were elsewhere and Scab was all he'd got to help face down the boredom.

'Look, Les,' he'd said, 'I've got a better idea.'

Scab had brightened at the unaccustomed use of his Christian name and Turk had instantly claimed an ally. If he'd put a gun in Scab's hand and told him to rob Barclays, the silly prat would probably have tried it on.

Turk's idea wasn't quite so spectacular, worse luck, but you had to know your limits. They'd shoplifted a six-pack of Carlsberg Export and a litre of Strongbow from the Indian seven-eleven on the corner of Barrow Hill—Turk doing the lifting while Scabby made a meal of buying a Mars bar and a bag of jumbo crisps.

'Did you have to get prawn cocktail?' Turk had complained as they'd picnicked on the wall over the road from the new housing development. 'I can't stand fish.' But he'd eaten them all the same and he had no complaints about the Mars. The cider and the beer had helped, of course. And then Scab had really come up trumps, pulling a hand-rolled cigarette from his back pocket.

'Nicked it from my brother,' was all he'd said by way of explanation as he'd fired up.

'Cheers, Les,' Turk had muttered as he'd accepted the spliff. Hanging out with the scabby one had compensations.

They'd been sitting there in the sunshine,

2

discussing which of the lasses at Barrow Moor school they wouldn't mind shagging, when the van had pulled up. Turk hadn't taken much notice, his thoughts having moved on to the staffroom talent and the new DT assistant, when Scab had pointed across the road.

The van was a bright azure blue with a legend in yellow scrolling across the side: Blue Sky Express—Safe in Our Hands. A poxy delivery van.

A large carroty-haired fellow emerged from the open door holding a clipboard and plodded round to the back of the vehicle. He wore an overall the same shade as the van with 'Blue Sky' lettered across his back.

Scab sniggered. 'Looks a right prat.'

Turk felt his lips stretch tight across his face—he must be grinning like a loony but he couldn't help it. The laughter that he'd been bottling up since running into the scabby one gurgled softly from his mouth.

The driver reappeared holding a brown package under one arm, tossed the clipboard back inside the van and turned for the passageway which led to the internal courtyard and the apartments at the rear. He looked like a great shambling cartoon figure, with his blue jacket and red hair. Like a character off *The Simpsons*.

Turk felt Scab shaking by his side and laughed louder. It wasn't funny but he couldn't help it.

The driver's head swivelled in their direction and he hesitated. For a moment Turk thought he was going to walk over and give them a mouthful but instead he returned to the van and slid the door closed. Then he disappeared down the passage.

'Stupid twat,' said Scab. 'Bet he's left the keys.'

For a moment Turk didn't get it. They couldn't see into the van. Then he registered the sound of some tedious old rock record, muffled now but still plainly coming from the van. The radio was still on. The key might still be in the ignition.

'Come on then,' he said, jumping down. 'I'll show you how fast one of them can go.'

He didn't look back as he scampered across the road. He knew Scab would be right behind him and even if he wasn't he didn't care. This minging van might not be the car of his dreams but it was better than nothing.

He yanked the door open and vaulted into the driver's seat, searching with his right hand for the key. His fingers scrabbled blindly across the strange fascia, his eyes on the passageway ahead, looking for a shock of red hair and a sky-blue jacket. As his hand closed on a dangling fob of metal, he saw only empty pavement and, beyond, the muddy brown grass of the inner court. The delivery man was round the corner and out of sight, doubtless still hunting down the right door.

This was going to be easy—provided Scabby didn't screw it up. He was tugging at the passenger door, the stupid arse, trying to open it like a hinge. Turk leaned across and shoved the door back on its runners. Scab lurched into the cab, sending a coffee carton tumbling from the dashboard, soaking Turk with cold smelly liquid. Turk just laughed. This was more bloody like it.

He had the van moving, ramming the stick through the unfamiliar gearbox with a painful screech. Scab's door was still open and, as he manoeuvred the vehicle round the tight little

4

parking area, Turk had an uninterrupted view of a blue jacket thundering down the passage towards them like an express train through a tunnel. Jesus, the big bastard could really move!

For a second Turk thought he'd stalled the flaming thing. The engine was grinding, his foot ramming on the accelerator and the gears squealing and the van man was in the doorway, gripping the sill, shouting something incomprehensible. He wasn't happy, that much was obvious. He looked like he'd pull Turk's head off, if he got the chance.

It was at that moment Scabby entered legend. He picked the clipboard off the floor and rammed it, end first, across the bridge of van man's nose. He squealed like a girl and fell back onto the ground, clutching face.

Turk scraped the side of the van against the gatepost as the lurched onto the road, sending a shower of blue paint chips into the air.

Perhaps it wasn't such a manky day, after all.

*   *   *

Luke's experience as a jockey was still limited. He'd only been getting regular rides for a couple of years and had been an apprentice well into the last season. But even though he could no longer claim a weight advantage, owners and trainers seemed as keen to put him on their horses these days as he was to ride them. Now he could honestly believe he was making a success of the one career he'd set his heart on and he loved it. So, the emotion that overwhelmed him as he strode into the parade ring at Beverley was foreign to his nature. He could see his mount being led round the far curve of the ring—Don't Touch, a well-built chestnut four-year-old with white fetlocks. He'd never admit it to anyone else but he couldn't lie to himself. He didn't want to ride that horse.

He'd tried to duck the job when Ivan, his agent, rang him with the news.

'I thought I was going to Newmarket,' he'd said.

'You were, son,' Ivan explained. 'But the horse has knocked its joint and doesn't run so now you're on one for Peter Lloyd at Beverley. Make sure you give it a good ride.'

Peter Lloyd was among the best trainers in Yorkshire, both Flat and jumpers. Luke had never ridden for him before. He and Ivan had even discussed how he might attract Lloyd's attention and here was an opportunity to do just that.

The problem wasn't Peter Lloyd or his horse. It was the man who owned Don't Touch—Alan Scott. Luke had never met Alan and knew him only by reputation. He ran a veterinary practice which catered to many Yorkshire yards and was well thought of throughout the racing business. In addition, Alan owned a handful of racehorses.

Luke spotted Scott now, standing next to the barrel-shaped form of Peter Lloyd. He recognised him from photographs occasionally glimpsed in the press—a tall, broad-shouldered man in his mid-forties with a head of wiry dark hair flecked with grey. You couldn't miss him. As he got up close, Luke became aware of the girl standing by the owner's side, her untidy blonde thatch blowing in the breeze, her eyes a startling green. Scott's daughter? Luke wondered. Surely she couldn't be his girlfriend. She looked about the same age as

6

himself.

The owner's angular face was cracked open in a welcoming smile and he enveloped Luke's hand in a warm grip as he introduced his companion.

The green eyes flashed as she, too, offered her hand.

'Alice is my practice manager,' Scott said. 'She works too damned hard. The only way I can get her to take a day off is by dragging her to the races.'

So, neither his daughter nor his girlfriend, Luke realised. That was a relief—not that it was any of his business.

'I've been following your career, young man,' the vet was saying, 'and I'm thrilled you're riding for me.'

'Thank you, sir.'

'Call me Alan, for God's sake,' cried the older man. 'We're all equals here. Except, of course, for the horses. They're superior to humans, in my book. Especially this one. I've got big plans for him.'

Luke knew all about those plans. Peter had briefed him when he'd paid a trip to the yard to ride out.

'Mr Scott sponsors a race at Doncaster at the end of October,' the trainer had explained. 'It's not worth much but he'd rather win his own race than the Derby, I reckon.'

This wasn't news to Luke but it was reflex to pretend he knew nothing of Alan Scott. 'Why's that?' he'd asked.

'It's in memory of his wife. This year's the fifth anniversary of her death.'

God, was it that long? You'd think a man would

7

have buried his grief after five years.

'Anyhow,' Peter had continued, 'Mr Scott's convinced that this is the horse that's going to pull it off. So you do a good job on him at Beverley and he'll not want to swap riders for Donny. Alan Scott's a good man, never forgets a fellow who's done right by him.'

Now, as Luke stood in Scott's shadow, waiting for Don't Touch to be led round so he could mount up, he reflected on the trainer's words. If he performed on Don't Touch here and then won the race at Doncaster that had so much significance for the owner, would he, in some small measure, make up to him the wrong that he had done him? And might he in consequence feel better about himself?

The answer to both questions was an emphatic no.

*　　　*　　　*

Jeannette was in a quandary. The day at the Marshgate yard south of York wasn't working out as planned which, given the nature of her governor's operation, should not have come as a surprise. It was virtually a one-man-and-his-dog training set-up and since the man was off at Newmarket, it was up to the dog to sort things out. No guessing who that dog was.

She wouldn't have minded so much if she hadn't aimed to make a swift exit from the yard to get ready for a celebration with her husband. It was to be their first slap-up night out for some months, since their honeymoon back in March in fact, and they both deserved a hassle-free day. Chance

8

would be a fine thing.

She didn't like to disappoint Mark. He'd had enough disappointment in a life of blighted hopes—of chasing glory on a horse's back, of making money in business, even of finding a woman he could make a home with. Well, she'd put a stop to his run of failure by proving to him that last dream was his for the taking. Unfortunately, she'd not been around to ease the pain of the chronic ankle injury which had put paid to his career as a jockey; nor to help him avoid the Valium addiction that had scuppered his ambitions to get into the horse transport business. But he'd bounced back now. Their future was bright—brilliant, in fact—provided he kept the faith. And she would see to it that he did.

All the same, she didn't relish the prospect of calling Mark to say she was running late. Unnecessary hiccups were to be avoided at all times and especially on a man's twenty-fifth birthday. She would cope at the yard. She always coped.

Her problem this afternoon was Kingmaker, a strapping two-year-old who had shown some promise at the start of the season by winning his maiden race at Thirsk. Since then, unfortunately, he'd shown more interest in the fillies trotting round the yard than in extending himself on the racecourse. As a result, he'd finished his treatment with the vet the day before less of a horse than he'd started. The possibility of Kingmaker making any kings or queens in the future had now been surgically terminated. In Jeannette's opinion castration was a drastic solution to the problem of a randy male. Though one she would happily have

9

recommended for a few humans of her acquaintance.

As a result of this procedure, Kingmaker needed to be walked regularly to keep the swelling down. But the track they usually took away from the yard was wet and muddy from heavy overnight rain and Jeannette didn't want to risk getting dirt in the horse's wound. The other route, which was dryer, was also a no-go because the farmer had turned some pigs into the field and Kingmaker, like all horses of Jeannette's experience, wouldn't walk past them.

In these circumstances, the alternative was to use the horse-walker but it had broken down yesterday and despite several phone calls and some tinkering of her own there was no chance it would be fixed for today.

Jeannette pondered her final option—to take the horse out along the lane that led up to the main road. It was never used for horses because the road was a narrow single carriageway with high hedges and few passing points. Meeting traffic with a skittish horse in your charge was not good for anyone's nerves.

On the other hand, the surface underfoot would be firm and the road was little used, except by locals who were aware of its dangers. And, in any case, what choice did she have?

*   *   *

The van was heavier to handle than Turk had expected and the gears were a bastard. He got stuck in second as he shot through on amber over Barrow Hill. A granny with a shopping trolley

10

recoiled in horror from the crossing and he gave her the finger through the window as he flashed by. That woke the old girl up.

Scab was honking away in the passenger seat. He had the weirdest laugh but for once it didn't get up Turk's nose—it only added to the crazy thrill of the day. He'd nicked cars before, dozens of them, but only at night and never a wagon like this. And he'd never left the driver sitting on his arse in the dust behind him before. This was special.

They were out on the dual carriageway now, leaving the suburbs of York behind.

'Where we going?' shouted Scab over the radio, which was still blaring Radio Two.

Turk didn't have a clue. Did it matter? 'Barnsley,' he yelled. They were heading south and Barnsley was south, he knew that much.

'Can't you go faster?'

Turk had been barrelling along the inside lane, getting used to the feel of the van. The gears were OK now provided he stamped hard on the clutch. Mind you, they still screeched in protest when he got it wrong but who gave a stuff about that? It wasn't his motor.

'Come on, Turk, it's not a bloody milk float.'

Turk shot the other a look of venom. The scabby one was getting above himself. All the same he yanked the wheel to the right and pressed his foot to the floor. They shot out into the overtaking lane, interrupting the progress of a navy saloon and eliciting a blast of horn.

Scab gave the driver a V sign out of his window. 'Stick it up your arse, shithead,' he cried and then he pointed ahead excitedly. 'Look up there! It's a bleeding school coach.'

11

Turk doubted that, though the familiar name 'Hawley's' across the back of the long vehicle in the inside lane made it a possibility. Half the schools in the area used Hawley's for trips.

'Get alongside,' yelled Scab but Turk needed no urging, he was already level with the coach's back bumper.

'There's lasses!' Scab was bouncing in his seat. Above them a couple of pink smudged faces framed by dark hair stared down disdainfully.

Scab waved both arms. 'Gizza kiss, angel!'

One girl said something to her friend. The friend laughed. It was plain the remark was not flattering.

'Snotty little bitches,' murmured Scab and began tugging at his belt. 'I'll show 'em.'

Traffic was piling up behind the van as Turk held its position alongside the coach. A horn sounded but he ignored it. He could guess what Scab was up to and he had no intention of spoiling it.

Scab was up on his seat now, his kecks around his ankles, his naked rear thrusting out of the open window. Turk craned forward to see what the girls were making of the sight.

Many more faces pressed to the coach windows now and shock and disgust were fixed on all of them. Turk wasn't surprised—he knew for a fact that Scab's rear end was as spotty as his face.

The chorus of horns from behind grew louder and the girls were now shouting unheard obscenities and making gestures that were unmistakable.

Turk savoured the moment, dragging it out for a full minute before finally putting his foot to the floor and shooting ahead.

Scab wobbled around dangerously as he rearranged his clothes, peering back out of the window as the coach disappeared in their wake.

'I just wish I could have seen their faces,' he said. 'What do you reckon they made of that?'

'They loved it. Be dreaming about you for weeks, guaranteed.'

Scabby beamed and fished another spliff out of his pocket. 'Celebration time,' he said as the cab filled with thick sweet smoke.

Turk poured on the gas. He'd get this big bastard up to a hundred if he could.

Just one thing was spoiling the day's perfection.

'Eh, Les,' he yelled. 'Change the sodding music, will you?'

*   *   *

Going down to the start on the top side of the course, Luke tried to put his misgivings about Alan Scott out of his mind. He'd been hired as a professional to do an honest job and that's what he would do. He had enough to think about for the moment with the race ahead. Beverley wasn't an easy place to ride, with its up-and-down track and tight bends. If you weren't drawn close to the rail on the sprint course you might just as well stay at home. On the round course you needed plenty of luck in running, unless you were drawn high and on a front runner—but even then you had to be careful to judge the pace right.

Luke's experience here so far was limited to sprints, and this race, over a mile and a quarter, was the first time he'd be taking on the round

13

course. He'd walked it an hour ago and he'd talked the race over with Peter and Ivan and others whose opinion he valued, but none of that would count for much when the stalls opened.

Just ahead of him, heading for the melee of horses at the start, was Sebastian Stone on the race favourite. Seb was often to be found on the favourite, which was as much to do with his reputation as the horse's. Champion rider for the last two seasons, Seb was the weighing room's all round top man—top with the punters, top with the press and top with the ladies. Every sport needs a standard-bearer and Seb carried the flag for racing with style. Also, as the winner of five Classics in four seasons, he was swiftly becoming very rich.

Luke counted Seb as a friend, for which many considered him fortunate. As a wet-behind-the-ears sixteen-year-old, Luke had attended a racing school near Doncaster and had been amazed to find himself sharing a room with Seb Stone. Back then, five years ago, Seb was already on his way to the top but he was too heavy-handed with his whip and, as a consequence, had been sent back to school to mend his ways. That in itself had been a lesson worth learning for Luke.

Seb was one of those whose advice Luke sought and the older man had always been helpful, even when they were riding in the same race. All the same, it wasn't often Luke finished in front of him.

Luke wondered how Seb would feel if he were in his position, riding for Alan Scott. Would he, too, feel conscience-stricken at accepting employment from a man he had wronged?

Of course he wouldn't. Luke thought it was likely that Seb Stone didn't have a conscience at

14

all.

*   *   *

Before she took Kingmaker out onto the lane, Jeannette called Mark. She always called him at this time, just after lunch. It wasn't that she was checking up on him, though if a man was to have a drink, it might well be with his lunch—or instead of his lunch, as it had been when she'd first met Mark. But he wasn't like that any more. She felt it in the warmth of his body when he knelt by her side in church and she read it in his eyes when they made love. He'd sworn it to her as he begged her to marry him. Alcohol was in his past. They'd go out tonight and indulge their appetites in a restaurant, go to a club and let their hair down, come home and satiate themselves in bed. All without the help of booze.

But if there was any tiny chance Mark's resolve might slip, it would be at lunchtime today, when he told the guys at Yarridge Farm that it was his birthday. Peer pressure, the urge to be one of the lads, the salesman's instinct to please—those would be the factors that could undo him.

'Yes.' His voice was clipped. She knew at once something was wrong, though not in the way she feared.

'Hello, birthday boy.'

'Oh, it's you,' he said, his voice softening. He was in the car. She could tell from the background noise and the hands-free hiss on the line. 'I'm on my way home.'

'Is everything OK?'

'Yarridge has got a new supplier. I've lost the

15

contract.'

That was a blow.

'What a shame,' she said. 'Did he give you an explanation?'

'The other guy offered better terms—that's what he said. But Yarridge has never liked me. He's been looking for a reason to blow me out.'

She could hear the anger in his voice. She knew he would have sworn and cursed except that he'd learned she didn't like profane language. Who said wives couldn't change their husbands?

'Don't take it personally, Mark. It's the name of the game in selling, isn't it?'

'I suppose.' There was a short pause and Jeannette listened to the sound of the traffic on the line. She could picture the set of his chin as he digested his disappointment and the white-knuckled grip of his hands on the wheel. Big square hands, strong but capable of such gentleness. He spoke again. 'Who wants the poxy Yarridge contract anyway? I'll be glad not to flog all the way up there again.'

'I'm sure there's nicer people to deal with.'

'You bet. I'll have a ring around when I get home. Chase up some new leads. And tonight we'll paint the town, eh?'

That was better.

'I can't wait,' she said.

'Any chance you could get away early?'

For a moment she was tempted to say yes. She could skip Kingmaker's walk, say it had been too wet on the track and blame the broken horse-walker. Or she could get Lucy to do it. But the horse's welfare came first and Lucy was just a kid. Jeannette was not a woman to duck her

16

responsibilities.

'I'm sorry, Mark.'

The silence on the phone was eloquent. But she knew how to cheer him up. She began to sing 'Happy Birthday to You'. Her Marilyn Monroe impersonation wouldn't win prizes but it was the way she'd sung it to him early that morning when she'd woken him with her leg hooked over his hip and her tongue in his ear. He'd liked it then and she could tell he liked it now.

'You'll get back as soon as you can, won't you, Jeannie?'

Of course she would.

As she walked poor old Kingmaker gingerly up the lane, she reflected on what made Mark the right man for her. He wasn't the most eligible, her mother had made that clear enough. But he was a fighter. He'd been knocked down often in his life but he'd always got up again. She could help him get what he wanted, she was sure of it. She'd carry them both if she had to but she knew it wouldn't come to that. Jesus wouldn't allow it.

He was all she'd wanted. A good man at heart who needed her help. That was it, over and above everything else. He needed her. And she wouldn't let him down.

*　　　*　　　*

'Come on, Turk, when we going to get there?'

'Where?'

'Barnsley. Like you said.'

'I dunno, man.'

'I thought you knew where you were going.'

'I do.'

17

'When we gonna get there then?'

'You're like some little kid, you know? Are we there yet, daddy? Relax, we'll get there. Trust old Daddy Turk.'

Scabby looked far from mollified but he shut his trap for the moment. Turk had seen another side to Scab on this trip. The little creep had more balls than he'd thought—the way he'd decked that driver! And he had to respect the guy for flashing the coach. The looks on those girls' faces.

The fact was, Turk didn't have a clue where they were going. He'd only done a journey in this direction once and that was with his dad, which showed how long ago it had to be. It was six or seven years since the miserable git had buggered off for good. He couldn't remember much about their trip to see his grandma in Barnsley except his dad had cried on the way there and had bought him Coke and two lots of chips. And his nan had stuffed him so full of cake that he'd been sick all over the front seat on the way back.

Why was he thinking about his dad? Bloody typical. The bastard had been gone half his life and he still couldn't get him out of his mind.

'Oh shit, Turk. Look!' Scab was gesturing to the other side of the carriageway. 'Police.'

Turk hadn't seen them but he looked in the mirror and just saw a glimpse of red and white disappearing into the distance.

'So what?'

'If there's one on that side, there could be one over here. They'll be looking for us, won't they?'

That was true. And the blue van was too bloody obvious. Might as well wear a sign saying, 'We're over here.'

Turk stared at the next set of road signs and knew at once what he had do. The sign said 'Marshgate.' Like his surname. It made perfect sense.

He pulled over into the inside lane. The turn-off was just ahead.

*　　　*　　　*

Don't Touch was drawn fifteen out of sixteen, one off the rail of the right-handed track. This was an advantage at Beverley, giving the inside runners a shorter distance to travel than their rivals on the outside. But this was little comfort to Luke when Don't Touch missed the break at the start and he found himself stuck behind a wall of horses. It was the worst possible start, especially as Peter Lloyd had impressed upon him that Don't Touch was just a stayer.

As the ground rose and then began to fall away downhill to the first bend, Luke began to pick his way through the field. Progress was difficult. Gaps opened ahead and then closed too swiftly for him to take advantage, and the runners on the inside clung tightly to the rail, blocking off the shortest progress through the field.

All the same, Don't Touch was travelling well. He was neat and powerful and had the ability to win. Putting him in a position to take advantage of it, however, was another matter.

The runners were bunched together round the bend, a flowing river of horses and riders. Luke was still trapped in the middle, up against the rail, as the track bottomed out and began to climb to the next bend. From here on it was uphill. He just hoped that the gradient and the sticky ground would begin to take its toll on his rivals.

In front, a group of four blocked his progress. He waited, hoping for a gap to appear, just as he'd been waiting all the race. But now, for the first time, there was room to get out and go round them.

He steered Don't Touch wide to the left, away from the rail. He didn't have a hope of winning the race as there were horses further ahead of the pack but at least he'd give his mount a chance to stretch out.

Don't Touch seemed to relish the challenge, finding another gear despite the ground and the gradient. They pulled away from the four on the rail and set off in pursuit of the three runners ahead. The last of them was four lengths away entering the last furlong and Don't Touch caught him comfortably. Now he was just a length down on the animal placed second and poised to swoop past him when Luke felt the horse beneath him falter. It felt like a car about to run out of petrol. Luke could hear the horse gasping for breath. He put his whip down and pushed him towards the line but they were going nowhere and another horse came from behind to deny him second place.

'Sorry,' he said to the reception party who had seen him off. 'I missed the break.'

But the owner was smiling. 'Never mind. You got him in the frame and that's good enough for me.'

'I thought I would win but when I had him in top gear he started choking.'

All eyes were on him, including the big green ones of Alice.

'We'll have him home and check that out,' Alan Scott said. Peter nodded—Luke could see from the trainer's expression that the news wasn't a complete surprise. 'I've no complaints,' Alan added and clapped Luke heartily on the back.

Luke would have preferred not to find himself liking the man so much but, as he basked in Alice's smile of congratulation, he reflected that riding for Alan Scott had turned out all right after all.

*   *   *

Jeannette reckoned she'd taken Kingmaker far enough. They'd walked about half a mile from the yard along the narrow road, which was sufficient for both their needs. When they got back to the yard she'd turn the horse over to Lucy and make a quick getaway. Maybe she wouldn't be that late after all.

She turned the horse round and the pair began to amble homewards.

The horse heard the sound first. He pricked his ears and began tugging on the reins. Then she picked it up—a car engine, sounding clearly now— coming from behind them, back up the lane in the direction of the main road.

The vehicle must be travelling fast. She could hear the screech of tyres and clash of gears. Some of the locals did drive fast down the lane but they knew the road and when to put the brakes on. Visitors tended to motor gingerly along the twisting route. There were several signs alerting them to the possibility of horses on the road.

All the same, Jeannette felt vulnerable. They were on a bend and the hedges were too high to see over, it was impossible to tell what was coming along. But the sound of a car engine being thrashed was unmistakable.

Kingmaker was twitching with nerves. He seemed to have forgotten his operation and it was all Jeannette could do to hold him. She knew she had to get him off the carriageway, which was barely a car's width wide. If she could reach the farm gateway they could pull off the road.

The roaring of the engine and squealing of tyres on wet tarmac grew louder by the second. Jeannette was beginning to panic. What on earth was this idiot driver doing?

Kingmaker wasn't going to wait any longer. His instincts told him he had to run. Jeannette clung tight to the rein, yelling to the horse, but she couldn't hold him. As he tugged the rein from her grasp and bolted down the road, she toppled forward and fell face down across the lane. The racing engine was almost upon her and she jerked her head round to see blue metal hurtling round the bend.

*   *   *

'Shit! Look out!'

Scab's warning was redundant. Turk could see the woman for himself sprawling across the road, trying to reach the bank.

He slammed on the brakes and jerked the wheel away from the silly cow. The van hit the opposite verge and veered back across the carriageway straight towards her.

*   *   *

Jeannette thought she was going to make it. She'd somehow scrambled out of the road onto the steep grass of the bank. But as she tried to pulled herself clear, her footing gave way and the howl of the terrible engine was in her ears. 'Poor Mark,' was the last thought that flashed through her mind as the van hit her.

CHAPTER TWO

Some people lost themselves in music or the movies, or even in a good book, but Robin Scott only escaped from himself when he had a scalpel in his hand and a life at his fingertips. Even as he gave orders to the nursing team and kept his eye on the hundred and one details that were essential to the success of the operation, his mind was entirely focused on the body of the animal that lay partially dismembered before him.

There are approximately sixty feet of small intestine in the guts of a horse and, in the colic operation he had just concluded, every inch had to be removed from the body and unravelled. He had discovered the blockage, excised the blackened section that prevented food from passing freely, and carefully—very carefully—reconnected the gut. They had laboriously replaced the coils of intestine into the body of the sleeping animal. The entire operation was a procedure that required the precision of a watchmaker and the strength and stamina of a labourer. Robin loved every minute of the four hours it took to complete.

The fact that things could go wrong—terminally wrong—was what heightened his senses and made him feel like a king when he pulled off a tricky operation. He'd never admitted it to anyone but himself but he enjoyed the power he wielded with his scalpel. Life or death—it lay in his hands. Often, in his job as a vet, he had to choose death and he'd never shrunk from putting an animal down when he had to. But suppose his patients were human? The only reason to terminate a horse's life was illness or old age; the same did not apply to men or women. There were some people who deserved to be put down. He reckoned he wouldn't shrink from that task either, if it came to it.

As he cleaned up after the operation, he reflected, as he often did, that he had nearly missed his vocation. Missed it because he'd never been able to control his personal life as he could an operating theatre and because he'd resented living in his brother's wake. Alan was six years his senior and the age gap had been hard to bridge. His brother's successes loomed over him like a father's shadow. When he'd all but given up on his vet's studies, only Alan's bullying had kept him going. And the time he'd spent two nights in a French jail after a fight, Alan's intervention with the court saved him from a longer stay. Then when Alan had recognised Robin's potential as a surgeon, he had given him the chance to become someone of worth. Thank God, he had taken it.

Thank you, brother, Robin murmured to himself as he scrubbed his hands. He owed him just about everything.

Alice Young swore under her breath as she worked her way through the list of calls Liz had left for her in the office. It was all right for Liz. She had the cast-iron excuse of picking her kids up from nursery school. There was no one dependent on Alice—apart from the patients, customers and staff of the Silston Equine Hospital, that is. Three vets, four nurses, half a dozen part-time 'consultants', and the so-called 'admin team'— which meant her and Liz. On top of that there were the stable staff who were always roping her into their problems as well.

She'd never intended to be some office manager, even if it was for a horse hospital. She'd been to art school and her father was a painter. Inside, she knew she was a bohemian with a creative path to follow, if only she could discover where it lay. And then there was her race riding. She rode out regularly at Peter Lloyd's yard where Alan kept his horses and she managed to get seven or eight rides a season. But, however well she did, she was hardly going to make a career out of that either. She was a dilettante, that was her trouble— dabbling here and there without committing herself to one path.

In the meantime, while she was making her mind up what to do with her life, she was here organising men of brilliance but no common sense, consoling and cajoling unsentimental country people who were soppy about their animals, and generally being the glue that kept Alan Scott's practice together. That's what he said anyway, the cunning bugger, whenever she lost it and threatened to leave. And so, here she still was, five and a half years after starting as short-term help.

She heard the rumble of wheels out in the yard. Through the small office window she recognised the middle-aged woman getting out of the driver's seat of the Space Wagon but not her passenger, a teenage girl in school uniform with a tear-streaked face. She guessed this was Jemma Price whose pony, Mudlark, was currently undergoing an operation for a twisted gut. The animal had been rushed in that morning in some distress and the procedure had been shoe-horned into a schedule already disrupted by the absence of the head of the practice. Alan Scott was 'ill' and it was all hands on deck in his absence. Thank God for his brother, Robin, the other partner in the business.

After Alice had made the last two urgent calls marked on her list, she made her way to the reception area to see how Jemma and her mother were holding up. As she approached, she could see through the window in the door that the girl had undergone a transformation and was now beaming. There could be only one reason for that—Mudlark must have survived his operation.

She stepped into the room to see that the good news was being delivered by the surgeon himself.

Even in green scrubs and a silly surgical cap pulled tight over his dark curling hair, Robin Scott cut an impressive figure. He had his brother's square features but there was a warmth in his face that was all his own. He was slimmer than Alan but just as tall and the look in Jemma's eyes as she gazed up at him was familiar. Alice had seen it in the faces of countless females as they'd listened to his words of comfort or commiseration. They adored him. She'd adored him too, in her way, but she knew too much about his ex-wives and current mistresses to be numbered among those kind of admirers; just as he, she suspected, knew too much about her own minor dalliances with young men who never seemed to quite measure up.

Not that she and Robin hadn't been tempted. There had been occasions when he'd sought a shoulder to cry on when she'd suspected that a shoulder was not all he was after. And once or twice she'd rung him in the early hours to pour her heart out, looking for more tangible comfort than a voice down the phone. But they'd always drawn back and, in the cold light of day, they both knew that was best.

The sight of Mudlark's schoolgirl owner gawping at her saviour roused a pang of jealousy in Alice. Give it a couple of years and pretty little Jemma would be just Robin's type—for a month or two. He was probably filing her features away for the future. Alice put her resentment down to the fallow patch in her own love life. It had been ages since an interesting admirer had come her way. The most excitement she had these days was riding her horse, Henry, and looking forward to her next race.

The next half-decent guy who asked her out was going to be in luck, she decided.

'You and your mother have been very brave,' Robin was saying to the schoolgirl. 'Obviously we made the right decision to go in at once.' He made it sound as if the initiative had all belonged to them.

Jemma started to say something but the words wouldn't come. Instead she threw her arms around him clumsily and planted a fervent wet kiss on his cheek. He held her gently in a fatherly hug and rubbed her back, much as he did to the animals in his care. Horse or human, Alice thought enviously, they all loved his touch.

Mrs Price turned to Alice—looking much more relaxed than when she had accompanied the injured animal to the surgery earlier. 'I can't thank you all enough,' she said. She added softly, as Jemma found her voice and began to jabber excitedly to the vet, 'I must say I was disappointed when Mr Scott Senior wasn't available but his brother is a genius.'

Alice could only agree, though she could have elaborated on how close the brother had come to missing his vocation—but that would hardly have been appropriate.

After the Prices had been ushered away to peek at the recovering Mudlark, Alice fixed Robin a cup of coffee. She made it strong. With his brother out of action, Robin's day in the operating theatre was far from over.

'We were damn lucky,' he said as he took the mug from her. 'Ten more minutes getting to the operating table and he'd have been a goner.'

'I doubt it was luck. You're gifted, like Alan.'

'Do you really mean that?' His eyes flashed at her; they were an earthy brown but alive with light.

'I wouldn't have said it otherwise, would I?' She suspected him of fishing for further compliments but as she saw him register the rebuke she reminded herself how long he had lived in Alan's shadow.

'Sorry,' he said and took a final gulp of his coffee before tipping the remainder into the sink.

'I'd better get on with it.' He turned for the door. 'Any idea whether he'll be back tomorrow?'

'Haven't you spoken to him?'

Robin shook his head. 'Do me a favour, will you?' Alice knew what was coming. 'Go up to the house and talk to him. He might listen to you. I mean, we all understand the way he feels but he'd do himself more good by being useful to the living instead of moping around over someone who's dead.'

There was a sting in his tone that took her by surprise.

He saw the look on her face and reached for her hand. 'Oh God, I'm sorry, Alice. I didn't mean to be rude about Claire.'

'It's OK.'

'It's just that you get on with your life. He can't see past . . . well, you know.'

'Forget it, Robin. I'll talk to him, I promise.'

It wouldn't be the first time she'd talked Alan Scott out of the hole he hid himself in when the grief for his dead wife Claire was too much to bear. And only she could do it because she shared that grief. She had more right to it than him in many ways considering Claire had been her sister.

*   *   *

As he sat by himself watching the last of the sunny afternoon bleed into the evening, Alan heard the crunch of footsteps on the path at the back of the house. Silston Hall was a large dwelling for one man and he'd long ago turned half of the building over to accommodation for selected staff at the hospital. But their entrance was through the front;

29

his quarters were at the rear, overlooking the private gardens and the woods beyond. No one came this way by accident. So who had they sent to flush him out?

It would be one of two. He hoped it wasn't Robin. Much as he loved his brother and, these days, depended on him, there was no room within him at present to feel guilt and make apologies. He'd left Robin in the lurch today. His brother would have borne the burden manfully, and he wouldn't utter recriminations, justified though he would be. All the same, his presence would be a reproach Alan would rather not face right now.

Below, the door closed and he heard a light tread crossing the wooden floor of the hall, far too light for Robin. So it was Alice. The curtain of the day's depression lifted a little further. His sister-in-law was the only company he could tolerate at the moment. She brought a little touch of Claire back into his life. And though she was young enough to be his daughter, only Alice had an inkling of how he felt on days like this.

The bottom tread of the stairs creaked. Alice would know where to find him—in the first-floor sitting room that Claire had created. His wife had made many changes to the rambling old mansion, all of them for the better. And who knows what further improvements she might have made to his life if she hadn't died? One, certainly, that would have transformed his world. Silston Hall was a fine place to bring up children. And Claire had been pregnant when that evil little swine killed her.

God rot his soul, wherever he was. Alan poured his silent curse on the unknown head as he had done every day since Claire had been taken from him. He was not much of a bible-reader but his thoughts were expressed in Old Testament terms. For the joyriding scum who had murdered his wife he wished famine and plague, pestilence and suffering to the end of his days. Amen.

'Alan?'

He forced himself to return to the present. Alice was framed in the doorway of the pretty room, caught by the last shaft of sunlight. She was taller than her sister, and messier, more tousled, less polished. Claire had been petite and stylish, always aware of her appearance, with an acute eye for the presentation of things. That's why her refurbishment of the Hall and its dusty treasury of antiques had been such a revelation.

On the surface, her younger sister had none of this. Alice was an unstudied force of nature, carelessly dressed, clean but uncombed, rarely made up and styled on the through-a-hedge-backwards principle—so she claimed. But she had the look of Claire in her almond eyes and over-large mouth which tugged upwards at the corners in just the same way her dead sister's had.

To have Alice in the room with him was to have a little piece of his late wife back by his side.

*   *   *

Alice was relieved to find that Alan met her gaze. That was a good sign. And he was in here, not lying on the bed that he'd shared with Claire and which he now never used, with her clothes strewn across the room, as happened sometimes. Though unshaven and dressed in a crumpled shirt that she recognised from yesterday, he must be feeling better. She could tell from the brightness in his eyes and the quick movement of his hand as he gestured her to a seat that he wasn't physically ill.

All day she had puzzled over his absence. It was expected at certain times of the year—Claire's birthday, their wedding day, on the anniversary of the accident—but today's bout of depression was a surprise. Yesterday he'd come home from Beverley in excellent spirits. His horse had gone well—'Just held on to finish in the frame,' he'd announced with triumph, as if Don't Touch had performed some miracle—and he'd invited the late shift round for a glass of champagne. Yet he'd rung Alice at seven thirty that morning and told her in flat, lifeless tones to 'forget me today' and put the phone down without explanation.

Like Robin, she had supposed that as time went on Alan would find his wife's death easier to deal with. But if he was going to be struck out of the blue like this, it seemed the opposite was nearer the truth.

She sat in the easy chair beside him. It was where Claire used to sit and she knew that was why he liked her there—so he could look for his dead wife in her. It made her feel weird. But she could not object to his obsession when she could understand—who better?—exactly how he felt.

'So you haven't killed yourself then?' she said.

To her relief, a thin smile stole across his face. 'I don't have the balls.'

That was crap, to her way of thinking. Alan was not short of courage and, as a vet, the means were easily available. He could do away with himself as he had done to so many animals in the course of his veterinary duties. Then he'd be just another statistic. It was no accident, to Alice's way of thinking, that suicide among vets was four times the national average.

But they'd discussed his suicide once or twice and he'd sworn to her he'd never end his life. With so many depending on him at Silston—his patients, the practice and all the staff—his death would be a punishment on the living and she knew that weighed heavily with him.

Across the room the television screen flickered, the sound turned down. It looked to Alice like one of the rolling news channels Alan subscribed to. Now, as the picture switched to another story, he raised the remote control.

'They've found the vehicle,' he said.

Alice didn't know what he was talking about. Current events had passed her by in the hectic confusion of the day.

The picture closed in on the fire-blackened carcass of a van hidden amongst a fringe of trees by the side of a field. The news reader's voice burst into the room. 'A police spokesman has confirmed that the burnt-out vehicle discovered three miles from Selby in South Yorkshire is that of a Ford van stolen from a York housing estate just after one o'clock yesterday afternoon by two youths. It is believed that the vehicle was subsequently involved in the fatal accident that took place outside the hamlet of Marshgate. Police are appealing to drivers using the A19 between one fifteen and two thirty yesterday for sightings of a blue van on the southbound carriageway. They say they already have several witnesses to the van being driven in an erratic and dangerous manner.'

The screen changed to a shot of a dimpled,

33

smiling woman in her late twenties leading a racehorse. 'The family and friends of stable girl Jeannette Presley, who was hit by a vehicle and killed while walking a horse on the road outside the Marshgate stable owned by trainer Billy Powell, are today mourning the loss of a universally loved young woman. A friend confirmed that Jeannette and her husband Mark, whom she married in March, were expecting their first child early next year.'

Alice scarcely took in the rest of the report—a description of the two boys seen in the van and a request from the police that they come forward. The similarities with Claire's death sickened her. In Claire's case it had been a joyrider in a stolen Mondeo who had caused the accident—some feckless youth, high on drink or drugs, who cared for nothing but his own thrill-of-the-moment pleasures. At least, that's what she assumed. Whoever was in the car that had killed Claire had never been caught. And the burnt-out stolen vehicle had yielded no clues to his or her identity. She prayed that it would not be the same in this case, though she held out no hope.

At least now she knew what had caused the black dog of depression to seize Alan in its jaws. She slipped her hand into his and squeezed. He wasn't alone.

'I'm sorry for him,' he said.

He meant the husband of the dead woman. That's who he would feel for most.

Alice said nothing—what was there to say?

'You know,' he continued, 'if they ever catch the vermin who killed Claire, I'll find a way to get to him. I dream about it sometimes.'

She wasn't sure she wanted to hear what was coming next. She had enough nightmares of her own about her sister's death.

'We're in court and there's a lawyer speaking on his behalf. I suppose it's at the end of some sort of trial and he's been found guilty. The lawyer makes a good speech. He says Claire's death was a long time ago and his client has changed in those five years. His life has been blighted by guilt. The crash was just a moment of youthful madness for which he, too, has suffered. And now he's facing a prison term—a year or two, I can't remember exactly. Then he kneels at my feet and begs me to find within myself a morsel of forgiveness to heal the hurt.' He laughed, a wry, bitter sound.

'Go on.' She didn't want to hear but she couldn't allow him to stop there.

'I say that I'll show him the kind of mercy he deserves. Then I force my hand down his throat. I plunge elbow deep into his chest and pull his guts out onto the floor, searching for his heart. But he doesn't have one. He's not human, do you see? I tear him into bloody shreds all the same. I wake up with a smile on my face when I have that dream.'

Alice removed her hand from his. 'Did you have to tell me that, Alan?'

'I'll tell you one more thing. That poor fellow who's just lost his wife has got all this ahead of him. Poor bastard.'

*   *   *

Seb relished the curve of Martine's rear, showcased in tight riding breeches, as she bent to place the breakfast plates in the dishwasher. There was no denying she had a fantastic arse—or *derrière fantastique,* you might say, seeing as she was French. And for a rich kid she was pretty good around the house. Recently, he'd been considering asking her to move in permanently—the first time he'd ever considered such an arrangement with any woman. The notion of having his very own French maid on call twenty-four hours a day had a lot of appeal. Not that Martine could be considered domestically compliant. She was too fiery for that and it took a bit of wooing to get her to do what he wanted. And sometimes she simply told him to get lost. No British girl had ever treated him like that. Maybe that was her appeal, he mused, aside from her *derrière,* of course.

'What are you laughing at?' Martine had caught the smirk on his face as she turned round and, naturally, she wanted to know the cause. She didn't miss much.

'I'm simply smiling with contentment, my darling. You make the best coffee in the world.' You wouldn't catch him spilling the beans about her arse. Such comments tended to get lost in translation.

Her sexy little bow of a mouth pulled down in a sombre curve, and sighed. 'I cannot help thinking, when we are so happy, of your poor friend.'

For a split second he wondered who she meant. It was Mark, of course, poor fellow. He nodded in agreement.

She sat next to him and laid her head on his shoulder. 'He will never sit at breakfast like this with his wife any more. It is so sad.'

Guiltily, Seb slipped his arm around her waist. It seemed wrong that she should be on the verge of tears when Mark was his friend and she barely knew the lad. He supposed it was a female thing.

'Yeah,' he said. 'It's a bad business, all right.'

'Would you like me to come to the funeral with you?'

'That's kind but there's no need.'

'But I don't mind. I should like to go. I will cancel my plans and come with you.' Her small pointed chin jutted with determination. He knew that look. For all her petite prettiness, Martine was hard to throw off the scent when she had made her mind up.

He'd better come clean. 'It's all right, sweetheart. I'm not going.'

'What?' She jerked away from him.

'I can't. I'm riding at Haydock.'

'What does that matter? I heard you promise him on the phone that you would go. He needs you there.'

Jesus. He felt bad enough about that without Martine calling him to account.

'Look, if I could then I would. But riding comes first.' And that was the God's truth. He'd sweated blood to get to the top of the tree and he couldn't afford to relax his grip. Short of broken bones, nothing would stop him fulfilling his duties in the saddle. 'I committed myself to these rides weeks ago and I stand by my commitments.'

With most girls that would have killed off the topic. But not Martine. That sultry little mouth spat back with venom. 'The only commitment that matters is to your friend. You owe it to him, Sebastian.'

He met her furious glare without speaking. To her mind, she was right, he could see that. But she

37

wasn't champion jockey.

She changed her angle of attack. 'He's your best friend. You grew up together.'

'That's not exactly true. We both come from Belfast but I didn't get to know him till we went to racing school.' He squeezed her hand. 'God's truth, I feel bad about it but I can't just back out of my rides. What would my owners say? And one of them, I may remind you, is your father.'

'Pooh! He would understand. He could easily find someone else to ride for him. Or is that what you're afraid of?'

He snatched his hand away in irritation. Of course he didn't want any other jockey stealing his ride but that wasn't the point. He may be the country's top jockey but he had to go out every day and prove it. Each ride was important to him, though the outing on Jean-Luc Moreau's colt Chartreuse was of particular significance. The horse had been an expensive purchase at the sales and was making his racecourse debut. Maybe Jean-Luc's beloved daughter could get away with reneging on a promise but Seb wasn't convinced the French owner would be so forgiving in his case.

Martine's black eyes were still blazing at him, trying to shame him into submission. But she had no chance. His thoughts were already on the day's racing. Riding races came first and always had done.

Mark would understand why he had to skip the funeral.

*   *   *

Mark Presley had never much liked to be

touched. Back-slapping, arm-round-the-shoulder camaraderie left him feeling awkward; wet, aunty-ish kisses and unnecessary hugs from female relatives were always to be avoided. Girlfriends who had turned out to be clingy hand-holders had been dumped in short order. His mother's touch had been an exception, of course—how he'd longed for her arms about him, even at the end in hospital when she was so brittle it seemed she might break. Since then only his wife's embrace had been welcome.

But they all manhandled him today, squeezed his hand in meaningful grips and clutched him in bear hugs, kissed him fervently on both cheeks and pressed soft damp palms to his pale cheeks. They meant well but he wished they would keep their distance. No one had a right to lay their hands on him, even on this occasion.

He bore it stoically. Forced himself to respond, to press the fingers and proffer the cheek. A funeral was no time to shrink from sympathy sincerely offered, though the stench of unsuppressed emotion in the air made him sick. He had no time for tears either and the sight of Jeannette's tribe of aunts and cousins grizzling into their bunched-up Kleenex turned his stomach.

Notwithstanding the gratitude he owed his in-laws for organising the funeral, he had no doubt that he and they would soon be going separate ways. He knew they'd always viewed him with scepticism, which was understandable. Despite their admirable Christian principles, it was hard for any family to wholeheartedly accept a recovering alcoholic with a chequered employment history into their ranks. He had to hand it to them, however, they had been as mindful of his anguish as of their own. He didn't think he'd be standing outside the church today, clean-shaven and suited, without the assistance of Jeannette's brother, Neil, and his wife, Sarah.

'Are you OK, Mark?'

Sarah had stationed herself by his side as they welcomed the mourners filing into the church, ready no doubt to leap to his assistance with a paper handkerchief and a bracing exhortation to keep his chin up should he show signs of crumbling. But Mark never cried these days, not since he'd quit drinking, and he wouldn't let Jeannette down by caving in here.

The church was large, which was as well. The mourners kept coming and he could imagine that a moment might soon arrive when they'd have to close the door on the solemn queue snaking down the path.

He scanned the line anxiously. Though there were many racing folk here, most of them were friends and former colleagues of Jeannette, though one or two had come to lend their support to him. Like Luke Eliot, who had cancelled his rides that afternoon to attend.

'Thanks for coming, mate,' Mark said as Luke stepped up. 'I appreciate it.'

Luke just nodded, lost for the right words, and who could blame him? The poor lad looked as if he were bereaved himself yet he'd only met Jeannette a couple of times.

Behind him came a face which seemed out of context here. But the tall thin frame of Detective Inspector Giles, the man in charge of the hunt for Jeannette's killers, had become familiar to Mark

40

during the past few horrible days.

'My sincere condolences, Mr Presley.' His fingers were slender and delicate yet his handshake was firm.

'Inspector.' Mark wondered if he was meant to be grateful that the policeman had turned up. He'd rather Giles was out catching the scum who'd run over his wife.

'Have you found them?' he asked, aware he was probably breaking some kind of protocol in bringing it up at this moment but not giving a damn.

Giles shook his head a fraction. 'There's no fresh news,' he said. 'I'm sorry,' and he stepped into the church.

Mark felt a tug on his elbow. Sarah said, 'I think we should go in now.'

There were only a handful left in the line. He realised the group by the churchyard gate were press, TV and news reporters. The story of the callous hit-and-run death of the smiling stable girl had claimed national exposure.

Where then was Seb Stone? Luke had made the effort so why hadn't Seb, his long-time mate, his best man at his wedding? Seb was the only one he'd called personally and asked to attend. And Seb had promised that he'd be here—if he could.

Mark knew what that meant.

'OK, Sarah,' he said.

Obviously Seb had more important things to do.

*　　　*　　　*

Out of four rides at Haydock, Seb rode two winners and a third, not bad for an afternoon's

41

work; it justified his decision to duck the funeral. His only regret was that Jean-Luc Moreau had not been present to see him bring Chartreuse home in triumph after a storming late run in the mile-and-a-quarter handicap.

'There's been a change of plan—Monsieur cannot be present today,' Marsha Hutton, the horse's trainer, had told him as she'd accompanied him on a walk around the course before the meeting began. Since Moreau ran a chain of hotels across five continents, that was not entirely surprising. He was based in London but he could as easily be called away to Boston, Hong Kong or Sydney at any moment.

Marsha did not look like a horse trainer, being slender and elegant with an extensive wardrobe for all weathers—even her rainwear looked as if it came with a designer label. According to Martine, who was boarding at Marsha's yard, Moreau and the glamorous trainer were 'close'. Certainly Marsha was reaping the benefits of their friendship in training several of his best Flat horses.

'However,' Marsha had gone on to say, 'he is sending Mademoiselle in his place.'

So it was Martine who had seen Seb off from the parade ring ahead of Chartreuse's race. Evidently, her orders to attend had been last minute for she barely made it in time. Seb greeted her formally for Marsha's benefit. As yet the precise nature of their relationship was not known to Martine's father and he didn't want premature news of their intimacy getting back to the Frenchman. That event would have to be handled carefully.

In any case, from the frosty scowl on Martine's face as she'd seen him legged up onto the horse, any such disclosure might turn out to be academic.

After the race, however, it was a different story. As he'd dismounted in the winner's enclosure, Martine had thrown herself into his arms and kissed him with considerable enthusiasm.

Marsha raised an elegant eyebrow and said, 'It looks like the owner will get a good report on your riding.'

He should bloody well hope so too.

*   *   *

Mark talked to Jeannette throughout the service. It was a habit he'd started way back, long before the nightmare of this week. When she'd gone off to work and he was left alone with his doubts and inadequacies he'd just talk to her as if she were with him. At home, in the car, even if he was in a shop or standing in a queue at the bank, he would murmur softly to her. It helped him keep his life on track. To face up to the things that scared him. And he needed that courage now more than ever before. So, as he stood in the packed church, he addressed her quietly in the privacy of his mind.

He apologised for thinking uncharitably of her family. He would do his best to stay close to them for her sake. And he thanked her for helping him ignore the devilish thought that a drink—just one small drink—would make the horror of all this more bearable. With her help, he promised, he would stay on the side of the angels.

Then he told her how much he wished he could change places with her. What had she ever done in her life but be a force for good? Whereas he— he'd been a screw-up throughout his rackety, irresponsible existence. Compared to her, what right did he have to go on living? There were things he'd done which he deserved to pay for. It made no sense that his blameless wife should be taken ahead of him.

Unless it was a punishment. He'd thought, living his new life with Jeannette and with the baby on the way, that he'd escaped his past. That he'd atoned for his sins and been forgiven. What a fool he'd been. This was a new and crueller consequence. He was cursed. The future gaped at his feet like a bottomless pit. There could be no happiness in its depths.

Suddenly, he didn't care about the angels. The first chance he got, away from the simpering pity of Jeannette's relatives, he'd have that small drink.

He stood up straighter. He concentrated on summoning Jeannette's face and listening for the soft lilt of her voice as she urged him to stick to his pledge. 'You don't need alcohol,' she used to say to him in his moments of weakness. 'Not now you've got me.'

But he didn't have her any longer.

*   *   *

As Seb was coming out of the weighing room at the end of the afternoon, a journalist from the *Racing Beacon* asked him for a word. Seb didn't believe in saying no to the media—it stood to reason you had to keep the press on your side—and, anyway, the reporter had always seen him right over the years. As he answered a few regulation questions about the afternoon and his prospects at Ascot next week, a thought took root.

44

'Can you say about Chartreuse that I dedicate the victory to Jeannette Presley? You know, the stable girl that died in a hit-and-run.'

The journalist had already registered the name. 'Did you know her?'

'She's married to my old mate Mark. We're both lads from Belfast and started out in racing together. If he hadn't been forced to quit through injury it might well be him riding winners instead of me. It's tragic that he's lost Jeannette, especially like this. When they catch the nasty little sods who killed her, they should put a rope around their necks—give me half a chance and I'd do it. Perhaps you'd better not quote me on that though.'

'I don't know, Seb. It's only what everyone feels even if they don't have the guts to say it.'

He supposed that was true. He prided himself on giving the press boys a punchy quote.

'To be honest, I should have been at the funeral this afternoon and it's eating me up that I had commitments here instead. So I'd like the victory to be in memory of Jeannette and I shall be donating my riding fee and share of prize money to a charity in her name.'

As he strode to his car, Seb felt a bit better about Mark. Though he might have broken his word, he reckoned he'd made it up to his friend in some measure.

*   *   *

At the reception after the service, Mark kept an eye on Giles. The policeman was being grilled by a succession of family members.

'Why haven't you caught the little bastards?'

45

Jeannette's Uncle Thomas was putting the question. 'It can't be that difficult—you've got dozens of witnesses including an entire bloody girls' school hockey team.'

The policeman answered his interrogator patiently, doubtless regretting that certain details had found their way into the press. His words were placatory. The search for the two joyriders was their number-one priority, extra officers had been drafted in to help, descriptions had been issued to the public and he had every confidence of finding those responsible within the next couple of days.

Mark had to give Giles one thing—he had the nerve to look everyone in the eye and say his piece. He sounded sincere enough.

Finally he shook hands all round and made for the door, catching Mark's eye as he did so.

'Is there really no news?'

They stood on the garden path. In the afternoon sunlight Mark could see the fatigue in the policeman's features. Facing bereaved and angry relatives must be among the worst parts of his job. Mark guessed that Giles was in his early thirties but right now he looked a damn sight older. Too bad. This man was paid to take the grief.

'I can't tell you anything definite, Mr Presley. I wouldn't want to get your hopes up unfairly.'

'But these kids should have been at school. Can't you check attendance registers and things? See who was there and who wasn't.'

Giles nodded and Mark read the sympathy in his soft brown eyes. It occurred to Mark that the copper felt sorry for him, which only sharpened his anger. God, how he hated being the object of everybody's pity.

'Rest assured, Mr Presley, we are checking the schools but you must bear in mind that if these youths are of school age they could have travelled to York from anywhere within, say, a fifty-mile radius. That's a lot of schools and a lot of pupils but we are getting round them. And also responding to the thousands of calls we've had from the public. And viewing the many hours of CCTV footage. As you know, we've got enough to put out a couple of descriptions.'

'But they could be any kid between twelve and twenty in jeans and a hoodie!'

'Our best bet is some neighbour who's had enough of the hooligan next door. Or a conscience-stricken relative. They do exist, Mr Presley.'

He offered his hand in farewell and, despite himself, Mark found himself clinging on to it, as if detaining the policeman would elicit some tangible comfort. But how could that be?

'We're trying our damnedest,' Giles said. 'I promise you.'

Mark watched him walk to his car. He had no doubt that what the man had said was true but it wasn't enough.

He stood there long after Giles had driven away. He did not want to return indoors where, he could tell from the raised pitch of voices and, just occasionally, the sound of laughter, the wake was taking a traditional turn with the arrival of wine and beer. Devout though they may be, Jeannette's family had healthy appetites and a capacity for enjoyment. Though they mourned her passing, soon the many friends and cousins would be celebrating her life in a glass or two. But he

47

couldn't do that.

The alternative was his empty house, the poky two-bedroom cottage with the half-decorated nursery that would never be used and cupboards full of Jeannette's clothes and possessions. At least he could talk to her there.

He heard footsteps behind him. Sarah's voice cut into his thoughts.

'How are you doing, Mark?'

He shook his head. It was impossible to answer.

'I saw you talking to the detective. He seems a good man.'

Was he? Mark supposed so. It took a good man to volunteer for a job like his.

'It was kind of him to come,' she went on. 'And Gary too.' She was referring to the family liaison officer assigned to keep an eye on the grieving relatives.

Frankly, Mark could do without his hand being held.

'They're nowhere near catching those lads,' he said. 'They've got no idea.'

'I don't think that's right. These are just stupid kids. They always get them in the end.'

Mark said nothing in reply; he knew from his own experience just how wrong she was.

CHAPTER THREE

Billy Chesil finished his morning chore of ringing numbers from the Sits Vac column and surveyed the pad on which he'd scrawled the results. Three definite interviews for the afternoon and the prospect of a couple more later in the week if he got a call-back. He supposed it was a decent return for an hour and a half on the blower. Face it, he'd spend all bloody day on the phone if he thought it would do any good. He had to get a job. Sleeping on his sister's sofa was doing his head in and God knows what it was doing to Annie. Putting a crimp in her love life that was certain—he'd seen no sign of her yuppie boyfriend since the night he'd arrived and they'd all got rat-arsed. He should have kept his mouth shut about Everton now he was in enemy territory.

For the hundredth time that morning—well, it seemed like it—Billy stopped himself from lighting the cigarette that had magically come to nestle between his lips. Perhaps the worst thing about dossing down at Annie's was her ban on smoking in the flat. She'd turned into a fag fascist since she'd crossed the Pennines and Billy blamed the yuppie.

He went into the tiny kitchen, shutting the door behind him, and opened the window. Leaning on the sill, ignoring the thin drizzle that blew into his face, he cupped his big hand round his mouth and lit up.

Oh, thank Christ—what a relief. Nicotine was all he took these days—and beer, of course. But they couldn't put you inside for that. Billy Chesil was a reformed citizen, legal narcotics only and not even his sister could forbid him those little pleasures. Anyhow, she'd never know. He'd squirt the air-freshener about before she got in from work.

He flipped the butt out of the window but not before he'd lit a second. It was necessary. He had to think.

How long could he keep going here, beholden to his younger sister, bumbling around her tidy, well-scrubbed home like some big shaggy dog who'd escaped from the rain? He made mess wherever he went, disrupting her social life and, though she wouldn't say so, costing her money. He'd been on her sofa for a good ten days before he got the job with Blue Sky and then he'd managed to get the sack before the first week was out. He'd been lucky they'd at least coughed up some cash.

It was ironic but he, a hard man from Knowsley with a list of offences from theft to drug-dealing on his CV, should be existing here in bloody Yorkshire as a victim of crime. He wasn't familiar with the sensation of being a victim but there was no getting over it. And, like most other victims he'd encountered when the boot was on the other foot, it was his own fault.

If only he'd not left the keys in the van. He'd even spotted the two poxy little scallies sitting on the wall opposite, eyeballing him. So why hadn't he locked up properly? That's what the Blue Sky governor had asked him. And the police, and the reporters and every bleeding person who'd had a go at him since the whole sodding business kicked off last week.

But not Annie, thank Christ. She'd just said, 'Don't you dare blame yourself for what happened to that girl. You didn't run her over. Don't let them tell you otherwise, Billy. Stand up for yourself.'

And he had done, but it was bloody hard. The police had given him a real grilling, kept him for hours going over and over the description of those two lads and then turned him loose for the newspaper people to chew over. And he'd blurted

50

out his side of it without thinking. If he'd kept his mouth shut maybe he could have made some money—exclusive interview, that sort of thing. But he was proud he'd not done that. He had some standards—and he'd never have heard the last of it from Annie if he had.

He chucked the second fag away half smoked and filled the kettle. Time to tidy up the flat and have a shave. Think how he was going to convince some hard-eyed bugger that he could be trusted with a company vehicle. It wasn't going to be easy, not given his criminal record, lack of references and the events of last week. Even if he lied, it would soon come out and then he'd be worse off. He'd been passed over for four likely positions so far this week.

He could go back to Liverpool, of course. His friends and family were there—but so was his past and he wanted to get away from all that. He was going for a fresh start here in Yorkie land. It had sounded like a good idea when Annie put it to him. But maybe he'd be better off back in Knowsley after all. If something didn't come up soon, what choice would he have?

The kettle was whistling on the hob but when he turned the gas out, the sound continued. Funny. Then he realised it was the doorbell. God knows where his brain was at these days.

*   *   *

The moment the door opened on a red-headed fellow in a singlet with a bruise across his face, Mark Presley knew he'd come to the right place. He didn't think the family liaison copper would have given him bad information but it wasn't guaranteed he'd find anyone at home in the middle of the morning.

'If you're looking for Annie, she's not in,' the man said in a thick Scouse accent.

'No, Mr Chesil, I'm looking for you.'

The big man stared at him, his immovable bulk filling the doorway. 'I'm not talking to any reporters.'

It would be very easy to turn round and go away. The thought was quickly dismissed. 'I'm Mark Presley.'

Mark saw the name register. The man nodded his head, as if he'd made a decision, and stepped back, holding the door. 'You'd better come in.'

The interior was pastel prettiness, flower pictures on the wall and photo frames in a regulation row on the mantelpiece. A bundle of sheets and blankets on the sofa made it clear that this was not Chesil's own home.

The man made no reference to the domestic arrangements, just scooped up the bedding in his arms and thrust them out of sight. 'Sit down.'

Mark wanted to get straight to it but first he apologised for barging in. He didn't feel like apologising to anyone, least of all this great hulk, but he made himself.

Chesil nodded again but said nothing.

Was he simple? That might explain how he came to leave his van with the key in the lock, gift-wrapped so two murderous little scrotes could lift it. On the other hand, and it came to Mark in an unlikely jolt of memory, people were often careless with their vehicles.

'Hey, lads, will you look at that?' A finger pointing

52

at the navy Mondeo, a key fob dangling from the lock on the driver's door. 'Looks like we won't be needing that taxi after all.'

He softened his voice as he spoke. 'You saw them, Mr Chesil. I just want to know what they're like. The scum who killed my wife.'

'I told it all to the coppers.' The big man's pale eyes engaged with him fully for the first time. He wasn't simple at all. 'Over and over. And the papers, too.'

Mark knew all of that stuff—the two boys in hooded vests, one blue, one charcoal grey, and dark jeans and trainers, the unreal photofit faces, a bony one and a jellyish blob, neither looking like a real human being. Whatever, it wasn't enough to identify the two youths. It was a week now and there'd been no arrests. Giles had done his best to sound upbeat when Mark had managed to get him on the phone but there was no denying the failure of the inquiry. The papers had moved on and so had the police. The van kids were still wanted of course but there were other sensations on the front page and other investigations demanding urgent attention. Mark was painfully aware that the chances of catching Jeannette's killers were slipping away like water down a drain.

He couldn't allow that to happen. Even if he had to go after them himself.

Perhaps Chesil sensed the unspoken desperation within him. Finally he began to speak.

'I was parked up on this new estate to make a delivery. I saw two lads across the road. They were sitting on a wall sharing a fag, eating crisps. Kids of about fourteen or fifteen, I'd guess. One was scrawny, all elbows and shins. The other was a spotty-faced lard-arse. I didn't think much about them. I'd only been on the job a few days and I was concentrating on getting the paperwork right. Hand over a package without a signature and you can get the sack.' He pulled a mirthless smile. 'Turned out I got the sack anyway. I went off to make the delivery round the back of the block when I heard the van being put into gear. I'd left the key in the ignition.'

He looked at Mark, as if challenging him to make something of it, but what would be the point?

'I just dropped everything and ran back. One of them was hauling on the passenger door, like he couldn't get it open. I couldn't see the other but when the door went back he was behind the wheel. I was screaming at them, hoping they'd give up and run off but they didn't. I thought I was going to get there in time and I nearly did. I had a foot in the doorway and a hand on the doorframe when the spotty one hit me in the face. My own bloody clipboard. He rammed the end of it across my eyes, here—see.'

Mark could see all right. It still looked painful.

'If he'd hit me anywhere else it wouldn't have mattered but I just fell back. I thought he'd blinded me. They made a pig's ear of getting the van out of the car park. I thought they were going to run me over, the little bastards.'

Mark felt he was expected to sympathise but he didn't have any sympathy going. Just a vague satisfaction that someone else had suffered.

'Look,' said Chesil, 'I'm dead sorry I left my keys in the van. I'll never forgive myself for that.'

Mark wondered if the man felt sorrow because

54

he'd been thumped in the face and lost his job. But he shouldn't be uncharitable.

'Would you know these boys again, Mr Chesil?'

'Please call me Billy.' He sounded like it mattered to him. 'Of course I'd know them. I see their bastard faces in my sleep, laughing at me while I'm lying on the floor and they're nicking my van. And I've got my eyes peeled everywhere I go round here. They won't be laughing if I catch up with them.'

Mark had no doubt about it. The big fellow didn't look like the right man to make an enemy of.

He took in the neat, well-coordinated surroundings. Everything in the small space, from the peach-pastel sofa he sat on to the stripped-pine table, looked new, if cheap, and carefully chosen. Probably by a woman. And, judging from the bundle of bedding in the cupboard behind him, a woman who was not romantically connected to Billy Chesil.

'I'm stopping with my sister for now,' said Chesil, catching the direction of Mark's glance. 'I'm from Liverpool way.'

Mark had guessed as much from the accent. 'Are you going to stay?'

The other man shrugged. 'Depends. I'm not having much luck finding another job. And I dunno how long I can stick it on that titchy sofa. I might not be cut out to live in Yorkshire.'

A stab of anxiety lanced through Mark, surprising him with its ferocity. So he could feel things after all. He'd thought that since Jeannette's death he was numb to everyone else's cares. But this was not to do with some Scouser's failure to find a job. It was about finding those responsible for killing his wife.

It was very important that Billy Chesil did not up sticks and bugger off back to Liverpool. He was the only person who'd got a good look at the scrawny kid and the spotty one. The drivers on the A19 didn't count, they'd not got a proper sighting up close—close enough to be thumped in the face. The police had made appeals and circulated descriptions but would that be good enough? This big tough-looking man had really seen these boys—and would break their bones like matchsticks if he got his big hands on them.

Mark leaned forward. 'Billy, would you do me a favour?'

*   *   *

Billy smoked another cigarette out of the window. He'd been making the packet last but there was no need for that now, thanks to Mark Presley.

He'd been half paralysed with shock when he'd realised the slip of a fellow at the door was the dead stable girl's husband. He'd half expected a knife in the ribs or, at least, an earful of bitter recriminations. He'd known it was foolish to let him indoors but, in the circumstances, what else could he do? He'd been feeling pretty sorry for himself recently but in comparison with this guy Mark it was nothing. Common decency required that he hear out whatever Mark wanted to say. Decency and the fact that if he hadn't left his key in the van this man's wife would still be alive. Jesus. So he'd had to let him in but he could never have predicted how things would turn out.

Since Mark had been gone, Billy had counted the money several times, as if there had to be something wrong with it. Why would a stranger walk off the street and put five hundred in notes into his hand unless there was something dodgy going on? Especially in these circumstances.

Only, perhaps the circumstances were responsible. Who knows how the death of your wife might affect you? You might go a little crazy

The money was real, all right. Mark had said he didn't have a use for it any more—he'd been saving it for the baby that was coming but now there was no need to flash out on car seats and buggies and all that other gear. That was proof of his craziness in Billy's eyes, for what man had no use for five hundred nicker? No one Billy knew.

He shouldn't have taken it or, at any rate, allowed the feller just to leave it on the table, next to the phone pad where Billy had been making notes. And now, under that morning's doodles, was a mobile phone number and Mark's address.

'I don't want you to leave York,' he'd said. 'You're the only one who can identify those lads. Can't you stick it out a little longer?'

And he'd laid the money down and said it was to help Billy settle in. Look on it as a loan if he wanted to—he could pay it back when he'd found a job. No rush, no strings. It might just help.

Billy should have snatched it up and shoved it back in the other man's pocket. But he hadn't and now Mark was gone and he knew he'd never have the will power to put the notes in an envelope and post them right back.

There was a bedsit round the corner. Annie had sussed it out but the landlord wanted two-fifty key money and a month's rent in advance. She'd offered to sub him the two-fifty but the rent had been a problem.

Not now.

One of these interviews this afternoon wasn't out of the question. It wasn't what Billy would have chosen—working security. It was a world he knew a fair amount about and it had got him into trouble last time round. But maybe it would be different in this town.

He wrote out Mark's number carefully in his address book. Could be he'd be paying him back sooner than either of them thought.

Billy didn't like to be beholden to anybody. Especially not in these circumstances.

*   *   *

Guilt wasn't a regular part of Seb's make-up—he didn't hold with beating himself up over things he couldn't change—and neither was social obligation. To be a jockey required single-minded dedication and that, for better or worse, meant being selfish. But it was getting to the point where he couldn't put off seeing Mark for much longer and he wasn't looking forward to it. It was going to be a stressful occasion.

If he were honest, seeing Mark hadn't been a bundle of laughs for some while, not since Mark had met Jeannette and bought into her straight citizen values. Or was it when he gave up the booze? Not that there was any distinction between the two events. Mark had sworn off drink when he'd fallen for Jeannette and a lot of what made him a great guy to hang around with had disappeared at the same time. This was fact, though it wasn't politic to admit it to anyone.

Well, there was somebody who understood his point of view and Seb reached for the phone. Time to give Eddie Naylor a call.

He realised that Mark had done the sensible thing in giving up the booze. It made him more reliable, more employable and less prone to vomit over the back seat of your car. He could see what was in it for Jeannette to turn her husband into an upstanding member of society. But, looking at it personally, Mark turning into a sensible sad sack had done nothing for his social skills.

They'd enjoyed some rare nights out in the past, at casinos and nightclubs, getting pie-eyed and flirting with the girls. It seemed impossible that they'd ever had nights on the town but they weren't that far in the past. And, maybe, they could come back again—not immediately, of course, but some months down the track. He'd have to square it with Martine, of course, but it was plain she would be happy for him to play a part in his widowed friend's life. He knew he wasn't good at handling the pain of the present but he'd make it up to Mark in the future. He'd organise some nights out—a few old friends, a few laughs, like the old days. That's when a mate like him would prove his worth.

For the moment, though, Seb would have preferred to leave Mark to handle his grief in his own way. But needs must.

The phone switched Seb to voicemail and he left a message. Eddie was unavailable, not a great surprise. The lad from Romford was a fly one, with his finger in plenty of pies. He could be flogging a fancy horse to a baronet, or bonking the baronet's wife or, more likely, bollocking one of the managers of his little business empire, which was on the way to cornering the equine bedding supplies in the north-east, according to him anyway. Even though he'd failed in his attempt to be a jockey—he'd grown too big, for one thing—Eddie Naylor had already gone a long way in life based on not much more than cheek and charm. That charm had been especially effective with the ladies. It had been Eddie who had introduced him to Martine, for example. He owed him one for that.

The call was returned five minutes later.

'How do, champ?' Eddie liked to call him that and Seb had no objection. 'Saw you on the box yesterday. Peerless riding, mate. In a class of your own.'

It could be a sincere piece of flattery or simple bullshit, you could never tell with Eddie, but it was delivered with warmth and Seb was hardly going to take issue.

'Have you been in touch with Mark?' Seb asked, getting straight to the point.

'I went to the funeral, chum. Didn't see you there.'

Seb ignored the dig, he wasn't going to start making excuses to Eddie. 'How was he?'

'He wasn't cracking jokes, if that's what you mean. He looked out of it, poor sod.'

'Out of it? You mean pissed?'

'No. Like he was in a trance. When I went up to him afterwards, he was saying some funny things.'

'How do you mean?'

'He was muttering about being cursed. He's in

60

deep shock, I reckon. I didn't really know what to say.'

It was rare for Eddie to be lost for words. He was talking again now, describing the funeral.

'Jeannette's clan were out in force, half of them in tears. They can't half sing, though, and they know how to hold a wake and all. Decent people. They're keeping an eye on Mark.'

At least that was good news. Maybe he should have gone to the funeral after all.

'I'm about to give Mark a call,' Seb said. 'I thought I'd just see how he was doing first.'

'He's doing bad is the answer. But that's hardly surprising, is it? I think you ought to get off your arse and get over there sharpish.'

For once, Seb didn't defend himself.

'You're right, Eddie. I'll go this evening.'

'And keep me posted, eh? We've got to stick together at times like this.'

Seb pondered on that as the call ended. What did Eddie mean by 'we'?

But it slipped from his mind as he dialled Mark's number.

*   *   *

Seb had only visited Mark's place once before, for a dinner party with Martine in tow a couple of months after the newly-weds had moved in. It had been a pretty dire evening, with Mark and Jeannette playing the teetotal hosts—'though *you* must have a glass'—and Martine prodding the steak and kidney pie on her plate as if she'd been served dog turd. It had been just the kind of suffocating occasion that gave Seb the creeps as,

61

once upon a time, it would have done for Mark.

The place was just as horrible as he remembered—a cramped cottage with a whiff of damp where every floorboard sang its own tune. It was full of Jeannette-style homely touches—a hand-crocheted rug in front of the sofa, a dried-grass flower arrangement in the fireplace, a kitchen with a mug tree. Worst of all, upstairs was a half-decorated boxroom with a cot in it—the so-called nursery. And existing in this dog kennel with just a TV for company was his Mark, once an up-for-it, life-and-soul kind of guy, now reduced to a shell of man. The TV wasn't even on. On the table, however—a low-slung glass-and-wicker coffee table with an unwatered African violet and a coaster rack—was an item that drew Seb's eye like a magnet: an unopened bottle of vodka.

He leaned in close as Mark offered him a coffee. His friend's stormy grey eyes were cloudy with anguish but his words were unslurred and his breath was clear. And when Mark returned from the kitchen, the hand that held out the mug did not shake. It didn't look like Mark hadn't fallen off the wagon. Yet.

Seb tried his best but it was awkward. After apologising for not making the funeral (twice) and asking for progress in the hunt for the lads in the van (none) and hoping Mark was managing OK (yes—the brother-in-law's wife came round nearly every day), Seb fell back on cliché. Mark had to keep his chin up, get through this nightmare, in time things wouldn't look so black. But he soon dried up—it all sounded pretty lame and it was all too easy to put your foot in it. He really, really wasn't good at this. He should have brought

Martine.

There was a pile of racing papers on a chair, all neatly squared away by someone—probably Sarah, the sister-in-law who came round—but he could tell they'd been read. He wondered if Mark knew about the race at Haydock he'd dedicated to Jeannette. If so, he hadn't mentioned it.

'I've brought my chequebook,' he said. 'Who shall I make the money out to?'

Mark looked at him as if he were speaking some foreign language.

'From the win I dedicated to Jeannette,' he added.

'Give it to the church up the road. St Mary's restoration fund. She was a big supporter.'

So Mark did know. He might have said something before. At least he added, 'Decent of you, Seb,' as he took the cheque and put it on the mantelpiece.

Now he'd run out of things to say, and with Mark apparently not in a talkative mood—for which he didn't blame him—Seb wondered if he dared suggest they watched the television for a bit. That was the kind of thing mates did, after all. Maybe just sitting by Mark's side through a long and dreadful evening would help somehow. Being there for him—that's what people called it. He'd earn some Brownie points off Martine when he told her. He surreptitiously turned a page of the local paper, looking for the listings.

Mark finally opened his mouth.

'I'm going to come clean about the accident.'

Seb didn't understand for a moment. 'What do you mean? I didn't think you were there.'

'Not Jeannette's accident. The other one.'

'Sorry?' Seb still played dumb. As if wilfully misunderstanding might somehow close the subject.

'You know what I'm talking about, Seb. That woman. Claire Scott. We killed her just like they killed Jeannette.'

Oh shit. He should have listened to his instincts and stayed away. Whatever was coming next, he didn't want to hear it.

*   *   *

Mark watched the blood drain from Seb's face. It was petty but it gave him a buzz of satisfaction to see his friend's discomfort. Seb had been twitchy ever since he'd arrived. It was plain it was a duty visit, an attempt to make up for failing to make the funeral despite his promises.

Some might wonder why Seb had bothered to make the effort at all. He was champion jockey, a pampered young man with a beautiful girlfriend and a circle of wealthy new acquaintances with whom he could let his hair down. Why was he bothering with an old connection like Mark, who lived a mundane existence in meagre surroundings? Even before Jeannette's death, Seb had been edging away from him, reluctant even to talk on the phone and too busy with his hectic, successful life to give much thought to his old friend.

Mark was well aware of the gulf that now separated them. But there was a link between them that could not be broken—and would never be, no matter how much either party wanted it. This, as much as the crumbling bonds of friendship, was the reason why Seb sat uncomfortably in his front room looking at him in pale-faced alarm.

'We didn't kill anybody,' Seb protested.

'We were responsible.'

'No way. I don't accept that. We happened to be in the car but it wasn't down to us. We weren't driving, for a start. It's nothing like what happened to Jeannette.'

It was funny how blind a man could be when he was trying to wriggle himself off the hook. Mark recognised every wilful squirming word of self-justification because he'd uttered them to himself often enough. And he'd have repeated those words right up until a week ago, until Jeannette's death. But that event had changed everything, shining the light of truth on his past conduct.

'Let's not fool ourselves, Seb. These kids stole a vehicle and got into a road accident which killed my wife. You and I got into a car knowing it had been stolen and were involved in an accident which left a woman lying by the road. We drove off without reporting it and she died. I don't see any material difference, do you?'

'But it wasn't like that—not exactly.' Seb jumped to his feet. He was agitated. 'It wasn't just you and me anyway. And it was five bloody years ago!'

Mark did not respond. These things might be true but they didn't alter the essential truth of the matter.

'I'm going to talk to Alan Scott,' he said.

Seb's mouth flapped like a landed fish. 'Can I have a drink?' he said.

Mark watched him fetch a glass from the kitchen and pick up the bottle. The sound of the

65

seal being broken echoed in his ears—and the splash of liquid into the glass. He fancied he could taste the metallic spirit as Seb drank and feel the burn in the back of his throat.

He'd bought the bottle as he'd walked home after the funeral. He'd been able to resist its call though he'd not had the strength to throw it out. And now someone else had opened it.

He'd pour it down the sink after the jockey had gone.

The drink seemed to calm Seb down. He set the empty glass beside the bottle but did not resume his seat.

'What are you going to say to Scott?'

Calmly, Mark proceeded to tell him.

*   *   *

Seb leant on the sink in the grotty little bathroom and stared at his reflection in the mirror. He looked as God-awful as he felt. There were two toothbrushes in a glass by the sink and, next to it, a woman's razor. It probably still had the dead woman's hair in it. His skin crawled.

He splashed water on his face. Jesus Christ, what was he going to do?

Why on earth had he ever got involved with Mark bloody Presley? He didn't recognise the man downstairs as the guy he'd spent happy-go-lucky times with not much more than a year ago. He'd gone mad. Or the death of Jeannette had driven him mad, it didn't matter which.

He'd spent the last half an hour listening to stuff which made no sense—though it did chime in with what Eddie had told him. Mark had enumerated

66

the ways his life had gone downhill since that night—the end of his career as a jockey, his troubles with alcohol, the failure of his business and now Jeannette's death in a hit and-run.

'I reckon I'm cursed because of what happened with Claire Scott. And there's only one way I can put it right.'

Seb had tried to tell him that these things were just a terrible coincidence but Mark wasn't having any of it. He'd said it was a punishment, an eye for an eye, and that's how Jeannette would have seen it too.

Seb had reminded him about the other car that had come along. So it wasn't all down to them.

'But we left her to die. We should have owned up,' Mark had said. 'We should have gone to the police and faced up to the consequences.'

It was all very well for Mark to say that now but they'd agreed back then, the three of them—and Luke—to stay silent and keep their heads down and hope it all blew over. And they'd been lucky—so far.

The thing was, Mark was in a deep hole. The poor bastard was depressed and, the way he saw it, had nothing left in his life worth preserving. That wasn't true for Seb. Christ, if Mark started blowing his mouth off now, he could see his entire future going up in flames. He could go to prison and who'd use him when he came out? The likes of Jean-Luc Moreau and Marsha Hutton wouldn't give him the time of day, let alone a ride. And all his dreams of future victories at Epsom and Newmarket and Longchamps would vanish from his life. Not to mention Martine. She'd be gone in a flash.

Mark had said he just wanted to make his own peace with that poor sod Alan Scott. He'd keep everyone else's name out of it.

'I'll say I was in the car on my own.'

'But your foot was in plaster. That's why we were in the car in the first place.'

'I won't tell him that. It'll be OK.'

No, it wouldn't. Seb had met Scott. He was an affable enough guy on the surface but he was obsessed with his dead wife, that was well known. If Mark put himself in the frame, Scott wasn't exactly going to pat him on the back and say it was water under the bridge. Mark would find himself in a police interview room in a heartbeat. And then the whole sorry tale would be dragged out of him. Mark might think he could stick to his version of events but he wouldn't stand a chance.

And then where would the rest of them be?

'Seb?' Mark's voice came through the bathroom door. 'Are you OK?'

He looked at his watch. God, he'd been in here twenty-five minutes wrestling with this nightmare.

'I'm all right. Just got a bit of a headache.'

'You'll find some pills in the cabinet.'

'Thanks, mate. I'll be right out.'

He listened to Mark's footsteps receding and opened the tiny mirrored cupboard over the sink. There were pills, all right. Lots of them. The mad sod was probably existing on medication these days. He found a packet of Anadin Extra and wondered what the hell he should do.

He'd plead for time. Get Mark to hold off getting in touch with Scott for a few days while he considered his options.

Then he'd call Eddie. Perhaps he'd be able to

come up with something. After all, he had more incentive than anybody to keep quiet about Claire Scott, since he'd been driving the car that killed her.

* * *

Mark listened to the sound of Seb's car disappearing down the road. He'd seen the fear and horror in his old mate's face and listened to all that he'd said. The conversation had been heated. At first Seb had been shocked and bewildered, then he'd been angry and desperate. He'd pleaded and ranted and finally he'd run out of words. He'd barely said goodbye as he left.

Their friendship would not recover from this. But Mark could see now—as Jeanette had always told him—that it was not much of a friendship in any case. He'd promised not to act in haste, to give Seb a chance to warn the others no doubt, but that was just a sop. He'd already written to Alan Scott, so why hadn't he heard from him yet? Waiting to hear was killing him.

He'd never told Jeannette about Claire Scott. At least, not until now. Sitting here in the days since the funeral, in the front room of the house where they'd planned their future, he'd made his confession to his dead wife's spirit. And that's when he'd realised what he must do about his past crime. Confession was owed to the living, whatever the consequences.

The vodka whispered to him from Seb's glass on the table next to the bottle, a faint medicine-like aroma. People said all vodkas were the same but Mark could remember the tastes of all brands with crystal clarity, from burning rubber to faint oily apple, smooth and clean on the palate. Not that the taste was the point.

He ought to get up and pour the stuff away right now. It was what he'd promised himself he would do once Seb had left.

In the past, when he'd been confronted by difficulty, he'd had a shot of vodka to see him through. He used to take a nip back in his riding days. When he was quitting Valium he'd carried a flask. And he'd downed three neat fingers of Stoli before he'd got up the courage to propose to Jeannette—and that had been the best thing he'd ever done in his life.

He reached for the bottle.

*   *   *

Robin was alone in the clinic—which was not unusual. Unlike everyone else, it seemed, his life did not march to the beat of the nine-to-five drum. Even Alice conformed to office hours although she, too, lived alone with no family commitments. But she, of course, had a comfy little set of rooms in Alan's mansion and a horse to attend to and her art and her racing, not to mention a circle of friends to keep up with.

And what did he have? A rented flat above a newsagent's with barely room for a decent sized bed. It wasn't exactly smart—cosy was the best adjective he could summon to describe it. All the same, it hardly impressed his women friends and he liked to pretend it was his private crash pad, handy for the clinic (which it was), and not his main residence. The fiction didn't fool them for very long.

It didn't, for example, fool Gloria, his current female companion—part-time, of course, since she was married to a Rotherham travel agent. Their children had left home and her husband appeared to do a fair amount of travelling, which left Gloria with time on her hands to indulge her hobbies, such as running countryside protests, supporting the hunt and breeding from her two mares. Robin had met her during an awkward foaling back in February and had been added to her list of pastimes. Entertaining and enthusiastic though she was, he had been thinking for a month or two that he should scratch himself from the list. But he wasn't convinced Gloria would let him go without a fight.

It had been a gruelling day and he didn't have the energy to go home yet. He was out of booze and, embarrassingly, didn't have enough in his pocket to stop at the off-licence. He could have touched Ahmed, the newsagent from downstairs and his landlord, for a tenner but it would have entailed a long conversation about the Premiership and tomorrow's card at York. Ahmed was a good fellow—he hadn't raised the rent in three years—but Robin didn't feel up to it.

But the situation was salvageable. Alan kept a drink's cabinet in his office for moments such as this—at least, that's how Robin looked at it. He rooted out a bottle of Highland malt and was savouring his second peaty snifter when the phone on the reception desk burst into life.

His first thought was of Gloria. Had she tracked him down here? He certainly didn't have the energy to tussle with her at present.

But it might be something more pressing. A medical emergency, for example. A recorded message would give the caller an out-of-hours number but there had been some complaints recently about the late-night service.

He reflected that he might be feckless and disorganised in his personal life but when it came to his job he knew the right path to take. And he picked up the phone.

'Mr Scott?'

The voice was low, urgent. He didn't recognise it.

'Yes?'

'Mark Presley. Did you get my letter?'

'No.' The name rang a bell though—had he received a letter from a Mark Presley? He'd been so busy today he'd scarcely glanced at his post. 'At least, I don't think I did. What did you write to me about?'

There was a pause. Robin could hear breathing down the line, as if the man on the other end was struggling to control his emotions. When he next spoke, the words came slowly and with deliberation.

'My wife was recently killed in a road accident. Just like yours was, Mr Scott. A hit-and-run accident. So now I know how you must have felt all these years.'

Robin was fully awake suddenly, all fatigue vanished in an instant and the whisky buzz dispelled. This man was the husband of the girl who'd been killed by joyriders. Presley—he could place the name now. And Presley thought he was speaking to Alan.

Robin felt sympathy for the man, of course, but

72

his overwhelming emotion was that Presley must not be allowed to bother his brother. Alan had been pretty fragile since this nasty incident had hit the news and it wouldn't do him any good to become directly involved.

Maybe this misunderstanding was fortuitous.

'All of us here are very sorry about what happened to your wife, Mr Presley. We've followed the story on the news and you have our sympathies.'

'That's kind, thank you, but that's not why I called. I—I wish you had received my letter.'

Robin wondered where it had got to. He'd better find it once this call was over and get rid of it.

'You see,' Presley was still talking, 'it's not just that we have this terrible thing in common but I know about your wife's accident. That is, I have personal knowledge of the circumstances.'

Good God. Robin couldn't believe what he was hearing.

'I should have come forward at the time and I deeply regret it. I'm not looking for your sympathy, Mr Scott. I want to tell you what happened on the night your wife died. If you want to hear it.'

'I see.'

He didn't see at all. As far as he was aware there were no witnesses to the accident—certainly no one had ever come forward to the police. And now this fellow had popped out of the woodwork. Had his own tragedy disturbed his mind? Was he looking to share his grief with someone who had been in his own terrible situation?

Whatever it was, Robin realised he must stop Mark Presley getting to Alan—at least until he had got to the bottom of this.

'I'm ringing, Mr Scott, to see if we can arrange a meeting. We must talk properly, face to face. I can come to your office if you like.'

'No.' That couldn't be allowed to happen. 'Where do you live? I'll come to you.'

Presley gave his address and Robin scribbled it down. It was the other side of the M62, about half an hour away. They agreed Robin would drive over the next evening.

Once Robin had put the phone down, he examined the pile of post waiting in Alan's office. Then he went through his own in-tray and looked on Alice and Liz's desks. He found no letter from Mark Presley. Maybe it had got lost in the post—or simply hadn't been delivered yet. As long as he got to it before his brother, it wouldn't matter—that's if his brother was even coming in tomorrow.

He cleared away his whisky glass and turned out the light as he went. Home, food, bed, that was what he needed. He must face this crisis with a clear head.

*   *   *

Mark's hands were shaking as he emptied the vodka bottle into a tumbler. He'd laid himself on the line to Scott—not completely, but enough so there would be no going back. He couldn't change his mind now. He'd thought the die was cast with the posting of the letter but actually speaking to the man he had wronged seemed more significant.

And tomorrow he would look Scott in the eye and confess. He didn't mind what happened to himself after that. They could lock him in a dungeon for ten years and he wouldn't care. He wouldn't have to face the world and Jeannette would be proud of him.

He drained the glass and reached for the bottle but it was empty. It didn't matter. He had another in the kitchen.

CHAPTER FOUR

Alan was sitting down to breakfast when Robin showed up. It wasn't altogether unexpected. His brother had become a good judge of when to leave him alone and they'd not had any kind of heart-to-heart since—well, since the day he'd ducked going to the clinic. Of course, that hadn't been the only day.

'You might have told me you were coming,' Alan grumbled. 'I can put more eggs on, if you like.'

Robin shook his head. 'I've already eaten. Been up since six. Had a run along the river.'

Alan larded a dollop of butter onto his hot toast and watched it melt. He plunged his spoon into the first of his eggs, displacing a thick dribble of golden yolk which he caught with his finger. He grinned at his brother as he licked his finger clean. Delicious.

'Schoolboy comfort food,' Robin said. 'Bad for the arteries.'

When had his brother turned into a clean-liver? Feckless Robin, chucked out of three schools for smoking and boozing—and running a betting ring, mustn't forget that. And he'd almost screwed up his degree. Got a girl pregnant, dropped out, doped up, buggered off on a gap year that looked like turning into a gap life. (Did they call them gap years back in the eighties?) And all the while he himself had grafted at building his practice. Hard graft.

And now his baby brother had the nerve to sit at his table and make snide remarks about him eating an effing boiled egg.

'Bad for the arteries,' Robin repeated, 'but good for the soul.' He leaned across the table and gripped Alan's shoulder. 'You're looking better.'

Alan felt better. His brother's touch through his shirt was comforting, firm and warm. Reassuring. All his irritation melted away in an instant.

He mustn't forget the way Robin had turned his life around, at the point when Alan really needed him. After Claire's death, Robin had devoted himself to his cause—he owed him everything. Without Robin at the helm, the business would have failed. Just when Alan had been incapable of doing anything to save himself from grief, despair and the bitter, burning desire for revenge, his brother had stepped in, showing the kind of leadership Alan had never known he possessed.

They'd talked about it often, of course. But Robin always found a way of deflecting his achievement. The disaster of Claire's death had given him an opportunity to escape from his own failures, so he said. He'd been bumbling along at the clinic, behaving like an employee rather than a partner, on the brink of divorce and weighed down by the cost of putting two children through the schools his soon-to-be ex had chosen. Debts and importuning women had been the theme of his life. Alan and Claire had regularly discussed Robin's failings, wondering whether he'd ever grow up. It

76

was ironic that it had taken the death of Claire for Alan to see the best of his brother.

'Sorry,' he said. He didn't really need to explain what for. It could refer to his dilatory efforts over the past week or the way he'd treated his burdensome brother back in his troubled past, or even his indulgent diet. He was out of shape these days and his brother's lean frame across the table was something of a reproach.

Robin chose to put his own interpretation on it. 'Don't worry. The ship's all in shape. Alice got in a locum to cover and juggled appointments. She's the one who's done all the work.'

Alan wasn't surprised to hear it, not only because it was true but because diverting credit in Alice's direction was another of Robin's tricks.

'Alice is wasting her life working for us,' he said. 'She should be bringing up children and painting works of genius.'

'Couldn't agree more.'

'So what are you doing about it?'

Robin did not rise to the bait—it was too familiar. He'd made it all too plain many times that, much as he treasured her, Alice was not for him. 'No fear,' he'd said. 'I could do without any more wives or children.'

Alan took the point, though personally he was disappointed. If Robin had another family he could be a proper uncle this time, which was more than he'd ever been to his nephew and niece. He saw them about once a year, as often as Robin did—though he knew very well that the bills for their maintenance came in on a more regular basis.

It wasn't appropriate for a middle-aged man to feel broody, but that was how Alan often felt. He'd longed for children with Claire and for years it had looked as if it would never happen. Finally, she'd become pregnant and then . . . Then she'd got killed.

That was the aspect of the stable girl's death that had so upset him. He'd not been able to get it out of his mind—her being run down by joyriding thugs, just like Claire. And being pregnant.

He shook his head, as if trying to clear it. He couldn't allow himself to go under to this kind of obsessive thinking.

'This Presley business has really got to you,' Robin said.

Presley? For a moment Alan was confused, then he remembered. Jeannette Presley was the stable girl's name.

'I'm afraid so. Ridiculous, isn't it? Five years and I still can't control it.'

Robin shrugged. 'You can't help how you feel. It's like the weather. Yesterday was foul and wet but today is sunny. It just passes through.'

Alan had never thought of it like that. 'You're right.'

Robin was grinning at him as he slyly buttered a cold piece of toast. 'And today is going to be sunny.'

'Is it? Excellent.' Alan snatched the toast from his brother's hand and got to his feet. 'I'll make you some fresh.'

'Don't forget that I'm doing Don't Touch's tie-back op this morning.'

How could he have forgotten that? But he had. He'd been moping around here for too long.

'I'll come down with you then. You sure you wouldn't like an egg to go with this?'

78

'Actually, I'd love one.'
Alan whistled as he put it on.

*   *   *

Alice should have smelt a rat. She'd just stepped into the yard for a break from the office hurly-burly when Liz insisted she return and take a call. With ill grace, she picked up the phone.

She didn't recognise the voice.

'Hi, Alice, it's Luke Eliot.'

She didn't recognise the name either. 'Yes?' Why on earth had Liz interrupted her for this?

'We met last week at Beverley Races when I was riding Don't Touch for Mr Scott.'

The penny dropped. It was the jockey. She did remember him: a lean boy who rode as if he were moulded to the horse's back. He'd fondled the horse's ears as he'd talked to them after the race and, beneath his riding hat, his pale face had looked no more than sixteen. Why was he calling?

He answered the unasked question. 'I was wondering how the operation went.'

Don't Touch had been admitted the day before to address his breathing problem. After cantering him on the treadmill with an endoscope down his throat, Robin had discovered that the left side of the animal's larynx was partially paralysed and didn't open fully. As a consequence, the horse wasn't getting the optimum amount of air into his lungs. The operation was tricky, requiring a high degree of skill. If the muscle flap was held back too tightly there was a chance that food could pass into the lungs, which would trigger all sorts of complications, such as pneumonia, and Don't

Touch could easily die. Unlike humans, a horse can only breathe through its nose.

'Don't Touch is fine,' she reported to Luke. 'He had the op first thing and should be back in training in a few days.'

'That's great news.'

She was surprised he'd bothered to inquire. Then she remembered that Luke had been responsible for spotting the animal's problem in the first place, which made her regret her abrupt manner.

'I reckon that calls for a celebration,' he continued. 'How about a drink? Or dinner if you prefer.'

This was the point where she finally identified the rat. That sly cow Liz. That's why she'd insisted on her coming back to take the call. Alice thought she'd given up trying to pair her off with likely lads. But Liz wasn't the type to keep her nose out of other people's business.

The pause stretched out awkwardly as Alice rearranged her thoughts. Luke spoke again.

'Just say no if you don't want to, Alice. I shan't take offence.'

She laughed. 'I wouldn't want to offend one of our most promising jockeys.'

'You're saying yes?' He sounded surprised.

'Absolutely. Just tell me when.'

'Tonight?'

She supposed she should play hard to get and pretend she was booked up for weeks. Frankly, she couldn't be bothered. And, though this Luke looked like a skinny schoolboy, he did have an engaging grin.

*　　　*　　　*

Alan sighed heavily and grumbled to himself as he contemplated the chaos of his desk. This was always how he behaved when he was spending the morning catching up on paperwork. To Alan, the worst kind of work was on paper. He'd rather be up to his knees in horse muck or pulling down an old cowshed or even sticking a thermometer up some stroppy animal's rectum than wading through a mound of overlooked correspondence. For a successful businessman it was surprising how much he loathed the conventional requirements of office life.

He worked quickly. He had a spare half hour before he must leave for Birmingham where he was due to give a lecture on pain management to a room full of other vets. He enjoyed the lecture circuit, which always included a convivial lunch with old and new faces. And today, thank God, he felt in the mood for socialising. Fortunately his in-tray held nothing of significance to detain him. He knew Liz would have weeded out anything urgent and either Alice or Robin would have dealt with it.

Just as he tossed the last letter, with a scribbled reply, into the basket, Liz entered.

'I've finished,' he announced with satisfaction.

'Not quite,' she said and held up another envelope. 'It came while you were away, marked Personal, and I put it to one side.'

She hovered for a moment, plainly keen to find out what it contained. But Alan was wise to her ways and asked her to leave it on the desk. He waited till she retreated through the door to answer the phone before picking it up.

81

It was probably just a thank you from a grateful customer, though why anyone should mark that for his personal attention he couldn't think. The way things were shaping, he was the guy round here who did the least. He ripped it open impatiently.

But it wasn't what he expected.

Dear Mr Scott

This is a letter I should have written five years ago, but didn't through lack of courage. Sadly I now know exactly what you have gone through when losing your wife and understand the anguish of having no precise knowledge of the moments leading up to the accident itself or for having anyone to blame. It is for those reasons that I am now writing to you. If you would like to know what happened the night your wife died and who was responsible for her death, please contact me.

Yours sincerely,
Mark Presley

As Alan sat puzzled and still at the desk, he became aware of his heart beating in his chest. He'd sat here many times over the years, longing for a letter such as the one he had just read—something that might shine a light into the black mystery of his wife's crash—and he'd long ago given up hope of receiving it. But you must never give up hope, that's what people said. It just went to show that there was a kernel of truth in every cliché.

Who was Mark Presley? The name was familiar—he'd heard it recently but couldn't place it.

Presley. Robin had said the name over breakfast. That poor girl who'd been run over had been called Presley. Was there a connection? There was one way to find out. He reached for the phone.

*   *   *

'What's the big deal?' Eddie had said when Seb called him after his evening with Mark. But this was not a matter that could be discussed over the phone and Seb had ended up driving to the back end of nowhere to meet him. Black Croft Equine Supplies turned out to be an old asbestos-clad barn behind a rash of rundown farm buildings. As Seb parked, Eddie emerged wearing a pair of shabby brown corduroy trousers and a frayed shirt with a torn collar.

The jockey was not used to seeing his friend in such a state. He looked far from his usual dapper self. But it made sense when Eddie ushered him inside. Pallets of old newspapers were stacked from floor to ceiling and the air was alive with dust and the rattle of machinery. A forklift truck grappled with polythene-wrapped bales. The driver, a man of advanced years, raised a hand in greeting as he manoeuvred along the row. Beyond the truck, Seb was aware of movement, of paper piles being shifted along a conveyor belt. He wished he'd changed into the old shoes he kept in the boot of his car, for the floor was inches deep in paper and shreds of plastic and God knows what other kind of dirt. Eddie was grinning at him, enjoying his evident surprise and distaste.

Seb had never interested himself in Eddie's

various business operations. He knew Eddie had got into supplying bedding for horses—the reason for all this paper—the moment he'd quit trying to become a jockey. But recently Eddie had emerged as a bit of a dealer in thoroughbred horseflesh; he'd brokered a sale to Jean-Luc Moreau a few months back. Seb had thought the kind of industrial grind he could see in this barn was no longer a part of Eddie's life.

'I didn't know you still got your hands dirty,' he said.

'Old Joe does the day-to-day.' Eddie pointed to the forklift driver. 'But I pop in to keep an eye on things. Joe's getting on a bit.'

Seb didn't bother to pretend interest he didn't have. It wasn't why he'd come. But his obvious impatience only prompted Eddie to insist on showing him around.

'We load the paper on here and it goes along the belt into the shredder.'

The shredder was about three foot square, in which whisked a set of the most terrifying knives Seb had ever seen.

'Then the paper goes along this belt and drops down there, see?'

As directed, Seb looked through a perspex covering at a chute which tumbled a stream of shredded paper into a pit.

'Now watch—this is the good bit.'

Suddenly, with a metallic rumble, the side of the pit seemed to heave inward, as a ram shot across the space, thrusting the paper into a tunnel on the other side.

'Hydraulic press,' Eddie explained with a touch of pride. 'It pushes the paper into bales and they come out down there, wrapped in polythene. Job done.'

Whack! The ram thrust across once more, jamming another bale together with hideous force.

'Damn near took Joe's foot off once,' Eddie said cheerfully. 'Some wood fell in and jammed it. Instead of stopping the machine, Joe thought he would kick the wood free, only he didn't move his foot back fast enough. Bloody near thing.'

Suddenly Seb had enough of being polite. 'Can we just go somewhere and talk about Mark?'

Eddie sighed. He obviously wasn't looking forward to the conversation.

*   *   *

'What do you make of that?'

Alan was standing by Alice's desk, thrusting out a sheet of notepaper.

She took it from him and read the letter with shock and increasing unease. The name at the bottom teased her with distant familiarity.

'Mark Presley?'

'The husband of the hit-and-run stable girl.'

She nearly said, 'But that's too big a coincidence.' But it wasn't a coincidence at all. Mark Presley and Alan had been dealt the same hand. Presley had racing connection—maybe he knew about Claire because of the memorial race each year.

But it was more than that.

'How can he know anything about Claire's accident?' she asked.

He fixed her with one of his piercing stares. When she'd first met him ten years ago, as a

85

teenager struggling with her GCSEs, she'd found these glares unnerving. She still did.

'That's what we need to find out.'

We—the word stabbed her.

She was not like Alan. She mourned her sister, missed her as keenly as a front tooth. But she'd got used to the gap in her life. She'd made herself get used to it because otherwise she'd never be able to face forward and get on with living. She couldn't bear to be like Alan, constantly looking over her shoulder, prodding the hurt so it never healed.

They'd talked about the accident often enough. 'Don't you want to know what happened?' he'd ask and she'd say no. She coped best by just blanking unpleasant events from her mind. A car had crossed the white line on the bend and knocked Claire off the road through a post-and-rail fence into a tree. Those were the facts according to the inquest and she didn't want to speculate further.

'But what about *him*?' Alan would demand. *Him*—the joyrider who'd hit Claire's car. The police had found paint residue from the impact which matched up with the burnt-out Mondeo discovered next morning in a field five miles away.

If only the Mondeo driver had stayed at the scene and called for help. Then Claire may not have died. But he'd run away. Driving off had been an admission of guilt and Alice agreed whole-heartedly with Alan on one point. She wanted whoever was in the other car to stand up and admit their involvement. She wanted justice for Claire.

Is that what this letter was promising? How on earth could poor bereaved Mark Presley be involved?

'What are you going to do?' she asked.

86

'I'm going to call him. In fact, I have been calling him but there's no reply. I've a good mind to go round there right now.'

Alan's face was flushed with a nasty purplish tinge just under the cheekbones. Alice knew that look and didn't like it.

'What about your lecture? Shouldn't you be on your way?'

'Sod the lecture.'

'But, Alan, you confirmed you were OK to go just this morning. And you're looking forward to it, I know you are.'

He chewed on the matter for a moment. 'Too bad. Someone else can get up on their hind legs. Claire is more important to me than talking a load of twaddle to a roomful of boozed-up quacks.'

Alice made her mind up. She got to her feet and tucked her arm through his. 'You know very well it's not twaddle and they'd be stuck without a speaker—you'd leave a lot of good friends in the lurch. People who've made space in their busy lives to come and listen to you. It's not like you to let people down, Alan.'

He flapped the letter in the air. 'But I've got to find out what this man knows!'

She pointed to the paper. 'Leave it with me. You keep your engagement.'

'You mean you'll ring him?'

'Don't look so surprised, Alan. I'll explain you're tied up and see what I can find out. After all, Claire was my sister, I've as much right to talk to Mark Presley as you.'

He opened his mouth and she thought he was going to refuse, then he snapped it shut again.

'Just leave me the number,' she continued, 'and

I'll see if I can catch him this afternoon.'

*   *   *

Seb followed Eddie across the barn to a cubbyhole of an office partitioned off from the rest of the space. The door was flimsy but at least it cut down some of the noise.

Seb took the rickety chair he was offered. 'You're right, Mark's flipped,' he said. 'He told me he was cursed.'

'That's what he said to me too.'

'And he thinks the only way to lift the curse is to confess to the car smash that killed that Scott woman.'

Eddie's face curdled like milk. 'What?'

'He wants to write to Alan Scott and set up a meeting with him. Then he's going to tell him all about us nicking the car and the accident.'

'We can't let him do that.'

'Well, how are we going to stop him?'

Eddie fell silent and Seb felt a perverse satisfaction that he'd managed to dump some of his burden. Serve Eddie right for giving him a guided tour of a barn full of poxy old newspaper.

Not that it solved the problem.

'Does Luke know about this?'

The question took Seb by surprise. He'd not considered talking to Luke about it, though the younger man would also be compromised by the disclosure. His first thought had been to tell the guy who was most likely to know what to do about it. And, let's face it, the one who was most responsible.

'I've come to you first. Do you think he'd be any

88

use?'

They'd always thought that if anyone was likely to spill the beans, it was going to be Luke, not Mark. It had taken maximum pressure to keep the kid's mouth shut at the time.

Eddie shook his head. 'Let's keep him out of it for the moment. See what we can do.'

Seb watched Eddie pick his car keys off the table and take his jacket from a hook on the wall.

'Where are we going?'

'Where do you think?'

A number of excuses rose to Seb's lips. He could think of several legitimate reasons why he couldn't drop everything and run off in search of Mark right this minute. They were all to do with his glittering career and his promising love life. But if he and Eddie couldn't persuade Mark to keep his mouth shut, it was unlikely he'd be enjoying either of them for much longer.

*   *   *

Alice almost failed to recognise Luke when he walked into reception at the end of the day. He seemed taller, certainly older; maybe it was the thick black hair down to this collar and the broad smile on his face. He hadn't been smiling after he'd failed to win on Don't Touch at Beverley.

Also, she was not expecting him. She'd thought she'd have time to go home and smarten herself up. Even if her hopes were not high for the evening ahead, she needed some time to prepare—it was part of what constituted a date, after all.

His unexpected arrival also prevented her trying Mark Presley's number again. So far she'd not got a reply and had intended to try when she got home—maybe he would return home at the end of the working day. But she couldn't call now. Tomorrow would have to do. After five years, what difference would another day make?

'I thought I could have a look at Don't Touch,' Luke said. 'You can pretend I'm not here and we'll meet up later, if you'd prefer.'

'Well, you're here now,' she said, not altogether graciously, but she did dash off to quickly run a brush through her hair and put on some earrings she found in the bottom of her bag. It was just as well she never bothered with much make-up. She'd have to do as she was, in jeans and rumpled blouse. Too bad if that wasn't what he was expecting.

She must have taken longer than she'd thought for she found Luke outside Don't Touch's stall, already deep in conversation with Robin, who had operated on the horse earlier.

The men were discussing the tie-back procedure which, Alice was aware, was a speciality of Robin's. He was among the top three or four in the country and horses would regularly be sent long distances to receive the benefit of his skill.

The pair of them dropped the medical talk as she approached and she was aware of both their eyes on her. Luke grinned, as if he wanted to say something complimentary but was unsure of his footing. Robin smiled lazily. She knew he'd noticed the earrings and the quick squirt of perfume. His eyebrows rose fractionally and she could guess the kind of sarcastic comment that might be coming her way the next day—'Baby-snatching now, are we, Alice?'

Well, she might be three or four years older than

Luke but so what? She didn't need Robin's approval.

To her surprise, Robin turned to Luke and shook his hand. 'Good to meet you, Luke. Have a great evening. She looks smashing, doesn't she?'

There was no sarcasm in his tone—it was all in her head. Alice felt a sudden rush of relief. It seemed she did need Robin's approval after all.

*   *   *

Mark's cottage looked just the same as before but, standing on the doorstep, Seb knew there was something different about the place.

They rang the bell and knocked loudly but there was no reply.

'He must be out,' said Seb. 'We'll have to come back.'

'That's his car, isn't it?' Eddie pointed to the maroon Toyota parked by the hedge. 'He can't be far.' And he disappeared down the side of the house. A moment later the front door swung open and Eddie reappeared. 'Back door wasn't locked. Let's wait in here.'

The moment Seb stepped over the threshold he realised what made the place different. The smell of booze must have oozed through the door; inside, it was overwhelming. The effect of alcohol on the household was apparent. On his last visit, the interior had been neat, whether tidied away by Mark or his minders he couldn't guess, but now things were starting to go to seed. The kitchen sink was overflowing with dirty crockery, fast-food containers littered the table and the front-room carpet was soggy with some kind of spillage. And there were bottles everywhere, most of them empty.

Eddie kicked a beer can across the hall. 'Maybe he's down the off-licence. Let's just wait.'

Seb nodded. There didn't seem much choice. 'Do you want tea or anything?' He didn't fancy poking around in the kitchen but who knew how much time they had to kill?

Eddie shook his head. 'I want the bog.'

Seb gestured up the stairs. As Eddie headed off, he turned on the TV. Then turned it off again. What the hell was he doing in this dump? He was due to meet Martine and her father this evening. The Frenchman was paying a flying visit and had invited Seb to accompany his daughter to dinner. After a lot of research, Martine had picked the restaurant but she feared it would fail to meet her father's exacting standards—she'd been stressing about it for days. Seb was not looking forward to calling to say he would be late. That's if he made it at all.

'Seb!' Eddie's voice rang out from above. 'Up here!'

He took the stairs two at a time. Eddie was in the so-called master bedroom beyond the pathetic little nursery room. He was bending over a figure lying prone across the pink candlewick bedspread.

Mark was fully clothed, his eyes closed, a fuzz of stubble covered his chin and his lips were rimed with a nasty white crust.

For one moment Seb thought, he's dead! Then the eyes flicked open.

He had to admit, terrible though it was, that for a split second he felt a stab of disappointment.

CHAPTER FIVE

Luke couldn't believe his luck. He'd liked the look of the green-eyed girl from the moment he'd seen her at Beverley but he'd not expected to be whisking her off for the evening just a week later. To be fair, he was often smitten with girls at first glance but when he'd followed up they either turned out to be ditchwater dull or dismissive of his attempt to strike up a friendship. He had a feeling that was the direction things were heading with Alice when he'd called but here she was, seemingly quite happy in his company. So far anyway. He hoped he wasn't going to balls it up.

They were sitting outside the Black Sheep, ten minutes down the road from the horse hospital, enjoying the late-September evening. She was drinking gin and tonic and he was just on tonic.

'Are you watching your weight?' she'd asked as he'd ordered.

He could have agreed, said he was down to do eight stone tomorrow at Chester, or he could have said that he never drank if he was driving. But he simply told the truth. 'I don't drink.'

He had friends who took the mickey out of him for never touching alcohol. A girl he'd asked out— one of those smitten-at-first-glance girls who'd deigned to let him buy her several Malibu and Cokes—had made fun of him for it. 'Pity they don't serve milk in pubs, isn't it?' she'd said.

But Alice just said, 'Good for you.'

If she'd asked, he'd have told her the reason he didn't drink was that he'd seen the kind of stupid things that alcohol made you do and he wanted no part of it. Not that staying sober necessarily kept you out of trouble.

'I've booked a table at the Cloisters,' he told her. It was the most expensive he knew—a restaurant on the river in the grounds of an old abbey—and the best place, he imagined, to take a woman he wanted to impress.

Her eyes widened and she shook her head. 'Do you mind if we don't? It's a bit formal, isn't it? I'm not exactly dressed for a place like that.' It looked like there were several other things she could have said. Instead, she just put her hand on his and said, 'Please.'

It wasn't that big a deal. As he called the Cloisters and cancelled, she finished her drink and stood up.

'I've just remembered something,' she said. 'Can we go back to the clinic? I've got to put Henry's rug on.'

'Who's Henry?'

'My horse. Alan lets me keep him in the stables. I'm really mucking up your plans, aren't I?'

Luke supposed she was, but he couldn't care less.

*   *   *

Seb admired the way Eddie took charge. Having concluded that Mark wasn't in a serious condition, just sleeping off a bender, Eddie had him sitting up in a chair and began a search for clean clothes which, from the niff in the room, were certainly required.

'I'll get him in shape,' Eddie murmured to Seb.

94

'You nip down to the corner shop and get some food in. We'll get some grub down him.' Then he turned to Mark with his broadest grin. 'Come on, mate, we're going to sort you out. Where do you keep your shaver?'

Seb was happy to get out of the room and follow orders. Thank God Eddie was a hands-on, can-do sort of fellow. He did what had to be done—which was useful when facing the kind of problem presented by Mark Presley.

As Seb watched Mark put away the bacon, beans and toast, washed down with coffee, eaten in silence, he allowed himself to believe that this was the first step in returning Mark to sanity. Sure, he'd fallen off the wagon but the teetotal Mark was dull and earnest and, since Jeannette's death, downright dangerous. Maybe now he was back on the booze he would come to his old self and see that, for all their sakes, Claire Scott's accident should remain buried in the past.

This illusion lasted up to the point Mark pushed away his plate. Till then he'd only muttered 'Sorry' a few times and begun a few stuttering explanations which Eddie had shushed like some mother hen.

Now Mark looked them both in the eye for the first time. 'I know why you're here.'

'We've come to see how you're getting on, mate.' Eddie reached across the table and laid a hand on Mark's arm. 'You need your old buddies around you at a time like this.'

Mark removed his arm. 'Bollocks. You're here because I told Seb I'd be getting in touch with Alan Scott.'

Eddie leaned back in his chair. Still affable but

mildly perplexed. 'What on earth do you want to do that for? It's taken the poor guy years to get over his wife's death. You don't want to go digging it up now.'

Mark shook his head, just an inch maybe but it was a firm gesture of dismissal.

'You don't understand what it's like. Scott needs to know what happened to his wife like I need to know about Jeannette. It doesn't matter how long it takes.'

'Come off it. You haven't got a clue how you're going to feel five years down the track. What's happened to Jeannette is terrible but you'll come to terms with it. And that's what she'd want.'

Seb knew Eddie had put his foot in it with that little speech.

'Don't tell me what Jeannette would want. I know what she wants. She wants the truth to come out and I'm going to make sure Alan Scott hears it.'

Ouch. That shut Eddie up for the moment. He looked across at Seb, as if asking for help but, frankly, Seb had no idea. He'd run out of them the other day.

'You do realise,' Eddie was having another go, 'that you are dumping the rest of us in the shit. You might feel like you've got nothing to lose but some of us aren't so bloody fortunate.'

That was another mistake. Telling a man who'd just lost his wife and unborn child that he was in any way fortunate was ill-judged, in Seb's opinion. And that was understating it.

However, Mark didn't rise to it. 'I'm going to keep you out of it. I'll say I took the car and I was driving.'

'But he'll go straight to the police and by the time they've finished you'll have spilled your guts.'

'I'll do my best. Anyway, I'm going to tell him about the other car and tell him it was an honest accident. He might simply be grateful to hear the truth.'

Eddie laughed, a snort of ill humour. 'He'll pull your effing head off your shoulders, mate. That's what I'd do in his shoes.'

Mark seemed to relish the thought. 'So be it,' he said.

*   *   *

After they'd settled Alice's horse for the night, Luke proposed dinner once more. Nothing fancy this time, but a return to the pub—the menu on the blackboard had looked quite tasty. But she'd ducked him again, saying she was in a mess but she could offer him something simple to eat at her place, if Luke didn't mind. Luke didn't mind at all, in fact he much preferred it. So she'd led him on a short walk back past the paddock and a wooded park, up a broad gravel drive to the Hall.

To Luke it looked like some kind of baronial mansion and he gathered that Alan Scott lived in half of it and the rest was divided up into flats for the staff at the clinic. The grounds were big enough to house the buildings of the equine hospital and the yard attached to it, together with a large paddock and the wooded gardens that surrounded the main house. Alice lived in a ground-floor annexe.

She led him down a long gloomy passage made gloomier by a succession of vast oil paintings,

97

oppressive abstracts in shades of grey and black and swirling purple. Happily, they soon emerged into a small suite of rooms at the back of the building, overlooking the garden. The place was disordered but cheerful, with overflowing bookshelves and clothes piled on chairs and an ironing board set up in front of the television in the sitting room. Alice had shut the door on the chaos and directed Luke to the kitchen while she disappeared to change.

She returned five minutes later in a denim skirt and a T-shirt, her hair tied back off her face, and apologised for not making more of an effort. Luke thought she looked fantastic.

He'd spent his time studying the wall space around the kitchen noticeboard, where more art was displayed. But this, thank God, was in a different vein to the horrors in the hall. Here were informal drawings and paintings of horses, in charcoal and watercolour and, Luke guessed, crayon, blu-tacked onto the wall in an overlapping haphazard fashion. Some were precise, as if they'd been worked and reworked, others were looser, just quick sketches, a few lines and blocks of colour. Luke liked them best of all.

'These are good.'

She blushed. 'They're just a hobby. I've got lots of free models down at the surgery.'

'Did you do the big ones in the hall too?'

'No, they're my dad's. He's a real painter.'

Not in Luke's opinion but he was hardly going to say so.

She rustled up some food. Luke hardly noticed it, he was too intoxicated by her presence. Things had not worked out as he'd anticipated. They'd turned out much better.

'Does all of this—the house and the grounds—belong to Mr Scott?'

'Oh yes. It's all Alan's.'

'Being a vet is more lucrative than I thought.'

She laughed. 'He's a good businessman but he didn't acquire all this through his practice. He was left it by one of his patients.'

'A patient?'

'Sort of. A wealthy widow who owned racehorses. She had no close family so she left the Hall to him.

'A wealthy widow, eh?' He drew the obvious conclusion.

A small frown furrowed her brow. 'It's not what you think.'

The conversation had been going well, light-hearted probing with just a hint of flirtation. He pushed on.

'Why, what am I thinking?'

'You're thinking that he slept with her to inherit her money. Everyone says that but it's rubbish. It's just envy.'

'I'm sorry, Alice.' He seemed to have put his foot in it.

'It's OK, I'm not having a go at you. But I hear it all the time and people are just ignorant. Mrs Markham believed in Alan. He used to treat her horses and she left him her property on the condition that he set up an equine hospital in the grounds—which is what he did. Anyway, from the photos I've seen of Mrs Markham, I can assure you she wasn't his type.'

'What is his type?' Luke was curious. He still didn't know the precise nature of Alice's relationship to her employer. She seemed to know a lot about his personal life. Maybe she had been his girlfriend after all.

But it wasn't that. Though he didn't like the idea, the truth was much worse.

'He likes small blondes who boss him about,' she said. Then, evidently reading the suspicion in his face, she laughed. 'Not me. He was married to my sister.'

'Your sister?'

'Didn't you know? My sister Claire. She was killed in a car accident in 2002. They'd only been married four years and he was absolutely potty about her. It's very sad. And he's never looked at another woman since,' she added, in a tone that rather suggested she wished he would.

Luke nodded and said nothing, hoping that Alice could not read in his face the dismay that now gripped him. Alice was Claire Scott's sister?

He'd been building castles in the air all evening. Apart from her intoxicating physical presence, he'd felt a sympathy with this woman. They could be friends—and more. He'd allowed himself to imagine a proper relationship.

But how on earth could he go out with Alice now? He was implicated in the death of her sister.

He got to his feet abruptly. 'I'm sorry, I've got to go.' God, he was't even able to put a polite gloss on it.

'Oh.' She looked surprised—and disappointed.

'I've got an early start tomorrow. I'm riding at Chester.'

She smiled. 'That's OK. I like a man who takes his responsibilities seriously.'

'I'll call you,' he said. 'It's been a great evening.'

He backed off down the path with a wave and a smile that would have fooled no one.

*　　　*　　　*

'He doesn't give a monkey's,' said Eddie as they drove off in Seb's car—an hour spent in fruitless argument. For all Eddie's ranting and raving, Mark had not budged an inch. 'He's not bothered whether he lives or dies, is he?'

The same thought had occurred to Seb. 'Maybe he'll drink himself to death before he gets round to seeing Scott.'

'Dream on,' Eddie said, then as Seb seemed about to overtake on a blind corner, he added, 'Are you in a hurry or something?'

Seb slowed down. It didn't really matter how late he was for Martine's dinner—it was already past the point where he could avoid a row.

'Did you see all those pills in Mark's bathroom?' he said. 'He's got enough to open his own pharmacy.'

Eddie grinned. 'Perhaps if we get really lucky he'll take 'em all at once then.'

Exactly what Seb had been thinking, God forgive him.

*　　　*　　　*

Even though Seb was more than an hour late and Martine's welcoming stare was chilly enough to freeze blood, the evening was not a disaster. That's if you didn't count the Mark situation, of course, but sitting in the gleaming glass interior of Martine's chosen restaurant, the meanness of

101

Mark's booze-soaked cottage seemed to exist in another world.

Evidently the restaurant was a hit or else Jean-Luc Moreau was simply in a benevolent mood. He greeted Seb with the warmth reserved for an honoured guest and shooed away his excuses.

'There is no need for apologies, Sebastian. Fortunately, you have only missed the hors d'oeuvres.'

The fourth member of the party, Marsha Hutton, gave Seb a sly smile and said, 'That'll save you an hour in the sauna then.'

Too true. Lavish dinners in restaurants were not suited to a racing regime. On this occasion, Seb didn't care. The events of the afternoon had not left him with much of an appetite.

With her father in such an evident good mood, Seb could see Martine relax. Beneath the tablecloth her hand found his thigh and squeezed, roughly at first, as if she wanted to punish him for his dilatory behaviour. Then her grip softened and her hand remained in his lap. What would Jean-Luc make of that? Seb wondered. He got the impression that he would not be too concerned.

Martine must have told her father more about their relationship than he'd thought. His welcome had been almost paternal. Jean-Luc must approve. That was a relief.

'And how is our mutual friend Eddie?'

Eddie had been acquainted with the Moreaus before him, by virtue of selling Jean-Luc a horse. And it had been on Eddie's arm that Seb had first set eyes on Martine. Though broad and round-faced and not exactly elegant in a dinner jacket, Eddie was as familiar with the upper crust as the dregs—it was like that in racing.

'I saw him this afternoon,' Seb replied. And, flushed by two glasses of champagne, he proceeded to give a graphic account of his tour round Eddie's paper-shredding plant. He took a perverse pleasure in dramatising its squalor.

'I had no idea Eddie had such interests,' said Jean-Luc.

'Nor me,' said Martine in a reproachful fashion. The French miss did not appreciate being reminded of life's less salubrious aspects.

Her father, on the other hand, seemed amused. Seb was thrilled things seemed to be going so well with the Frenchman. Suddenly they got even better.

Jean-Luc put a hand on his arm. 'Marsha and I have a proposition to make to you. If you are prepared to hear it.'

Of course he was. And it sent a current of excitement fizzing through his veins. He was being promised a selection of top rides for the rest of the season. If he performed satisfactorily—and how could he fail on the animals the Frenchman owned?—next year he would have a full contract.

His euphoria was so great that he forgot all about Mark and the problems that existed in another world.

Only as he walked towards his car, leaving Martine in the care of her father, did the other world become real once more. And the realisation hit home that if Mark carried out his threat, the golden future Jean-Luc had dangled before him in the restaurant would be the real illusion.

*   *   *

103

Luke was so deep in thought when he arrived home that he didn't notice the figure standing in the shadow. He'd virtually run out of Alice's door and now he was regretting it. Had he made a mistake? Was he being too sensitive? He wouldn't mind betting that if Seb had been in his position he'd never have seen Claire Scott's death as being any barrier to a relationship with her sister. It was five years ago, for God's sake. And it wasn't as if he'd been actively involved—only as an accessory after the fact, as a lawyer might say.

All the same, he had no doubt it would matter to Alice—if she ever found out.

But why should she find out? It was water under the bridge now.

Luke could see it boiled down to whether he was strong enough to put the road accident out of his head. It wasn't as if he was on the brink of marrying the woman. They'd spent one evening together. All he was asking of himself was the chance to spend one more, and then they could see how things progressed.

By the time he got home, all of a ten-minute drive, he'd convinced himself he'd march straight indoors and call Alice. Tell her those things he'd planned, about her owing him a proper chance to take her to dinner. He was strong enough to do that, wasn't he?

So that was the reason he didn't notice Eddie Naylor waiting for him in the shadows. And by the time Eddie had left, an hour later, he had no heart to ring Alice. What would be the point? It looked like all his future prospects, professional and personal, were about to go up in smoke.

*　　　*　　　*

Eddie was a half-full sort of fellow—one of life's optimists. But he left Luke's place with dread poisoning his every thought. He'd come to talk the Mark business through with Luke in the hope that somehow the younger man might offer a solution. And of course to spread the load. There were four of them in it, as there always had been. Though Luke had always been the most suspect link in their pact of silence, he wasn't any more. Now, he too had plenty to lose should the whole mess become public knowledge. Which seemed certain.

As Eddie had waited for the jockey to get home, he'd fantasised that Luke might somehow hold the key to unlock Mark's obstinacy. He didn't think there was a particular bond between the younger man and Mark. But he'd seen Luke at Jeannette's funeral. Perhaps Luke could get through to the poor sozzled bastard that blowing the whistle after all these years was no solution to his own grief.

Well, it had been a hope without foundation. Luke had not leapt to his feet to rush to Mark and persuade him to see sense. He'd not even volunteered to call him, though Eddie had made sure he had Mark's number.

Jesus, there had to be a solution to this. Eddie started his car engine and pondered where to go. There didn't seem much point in just heading home for a sleepless night stewing over the insoluble.

If only there was some way to stop Mark. He had as much to lose as anyone. If the case went to court, what would happen? After all, he'd been the driver. Would he go to prison and the others walk free?

He didn't want to find out.

*   *   *

In a perverse way, Mark was glad of the visit from Eddie and Seb. He was ashamed of the mess in which they'd found him, not for them so much but for himself. After all, they'd found him in similar states in the past. But he was well aware how much he had let himself down. 'You see how I'm struggling without you,' he said to Jeannette. With her by his side he'd been strong enough to beat the bottle—he'd kept it at bay till after her funeral. But not any more. If he didn't have Jeannette he must have something.

He cleaned the place up, sort of. Gathered up empties, washed dishes and carted the rubbish to the dustbin. He knew it wouldn't fool the observant—certainly not Sarah when she next turned up to check on him—but that was too bad. He was a grown man and if he chose to have a drink that was his business. Anyway, he'd come to a decision. Drink could return to his life but on his terms. No out-and-out binges, just moderate consumption—a lifeline to see him through. He'd cut out the beer and stick to vodka. It went with anything, even tea and coffee. Something to do the job without being too obvious.

Apart from the in-laws, he still had to deal with the police. Work could wait; his boss had told him to take all the time he needed, which, since his retainer was tiny, wasn't such a compassionate gesture. Whether he would ever return would depend on the outcome of the one appointment in his life that counted—the meeting with Alan Scott.

He'd meant everything he'd said to Eddie and Seb. He'd keep their names out of it if he could, but Scott had to hear a proper account of his wife's death. And maybe the personal consequences would be painful. His life might be ruined—but it was ruined as it was. And the only way forward that he could see was to confess. At least that would be one burden lifted and he could get on with the business of honestly mourning Jeannette. From a prison cell, if that was the price he had to pay.

He lit a candle in the front room, the aromatic kind that Jeannette used to sweeten the atmosphere. God, how his hand shook. It had been that way ever since Eddie and Seb had bullied him into life. He'd had to eat slowly and then he'd thrust his hands into his pockets so they wouldn't notice, willing them to say their piece and leave. He'd take another Valium, and another drink, of course, just to still the shakes. He brought the pills down from the bathroom and fetched the bottle from the kitchen. He washed the medicine down with a swig from a mug. Mugs somehow didn't look so incriminating.

He lit another candle on the mantelpiece. He had to disperse the smell of stale beer. He didn't want Alan Scott walking into a parlour that stank like a taproom.

The doorbell rang. He took a deep breath to steady himself before he went to answer it.

* * *

The man who opened the door was half a head

107

shorter than Robin and thin, though the hand that shook his was large and gripped firmly— unnecessarily so, as if Mark Presley wanted to impress on Robin's flesh the strength of his sincerity.

'Thank you for coming, Mr Scott.'

'It's not a problem.'

Presley had studied his face as he shook his hand. If Robin had read any confusion there he would have declared his true identity but evidently the other man took him for his brother. It was convenient not to disabuse him—at least until he had found out what it was he had to say.

'Would you like a drink? Tea or coffee or . . . ?'

The unfinished question hung there. Robin had caught the toothpasty whiff of mint on the man's breath as he passed and noted the deliberate way Presley ushered him into the small front room, as if he were concentrating hard on placing one foot in front of the other. His host was three sheets to the wind but determined not to reveal it. Too bad for him that Robin was a seasoned observer of the degrees of drunkenness in his companions. That Mark Presley was not a fanciable female did not undermine his judgement. The man had obviously had a few by way of Dutch courage and would doubtless drop his conversational knickers all the faster for it.

'Tea would be fine,' Robin said, 'though if you're offering me something stronger I wouldn't say no.'

Presley produced a tumbler half full of neat vodka and poured one for himself. Robin asked for something to mix it with and was offered flat tonic water. He resolved to be careful with his intake.

When it came to booze, Presley obviously didn't muck around.

No sooner had Robin settled into a corner of the lumpy sofa than Presley launched into a speech that he must have rehearsed in his head many times. He appeared to be saying that he was in the car that had hit Claire and forced her off the road but the words tumbled from his mouth so fast that Robin stopped him and made him start again.

'Sorry.' Presley took a breath. 'It's just that this has been bottled up inside me for so long.'

'Please take your time.'

'I can't tell you, Mr Scott, how sorry I am. It's been destroying me.'

But not destroying you so badly that you've wanted to tell the truth until your own wife was killed.

Robin kept that thought to himself and said, 'You were in the other car—the Mondeo?'

Presley lifted his glass and gulped an inch of the pale liquid as if it were water.

'Yes.'

'Who was with you?'

'No one. I was on my own.'

'What happened?' That was the key question, no matter how many people were in the car.

Presley drank again, draining his glass. He reached for the bottle and poured himself another generous hit.

'I was a few miles out of Doncaster. I'd had a drink or two but I wasn't drunk, probably not over the limit but I admit I was going fast. Another car—your wife's—came round a bend and I hit her. It was an accident.'

Robin said nothing, just waited for the other man to continue.

109

'I pulled off the road into a lay-by. I was in shock for a few minutes then I realised I should go back to see if anyone was hurt and get help if necessary. I reversed back till I could see the other car. It had gone through a fence and into some trees. It looked like it had turned over. I would have got out but there was another car already there.'

Robin leaned forward. 'There was another car?'

'Yes. It was never mentioned on the news. It was facing the same direction as your wife's car and so it must have come past me while I was sitting in the lay-by. I was so stunned I never saw it. And the driver must have seen your wife's vehicle because he'd stopped.'

'He?'

'I saw a man kneeling down and then I noticed a shape on the ground—the driver of the first car. There weren't any lights on the road but it wasn't dark and there were two sets of headlights. I could see the shape on the ground was a woman—she'd been thrown out of her car.'

'That's what they said at the inquest.' Without thinking Robin drank from his fizzless, lukewarm vodka and tonic. He registered that it was disgusting in a remote part of his brain. 'What did you do then?' he asked.

'I drove off. I knew I shouldn't have and I've regretted it ever since. But I panicked. Because I'd been drinking and the car wasn't mine, I could have got into a lot of trouble. But I'd never have driven off if it hadn't been for the other car. I mean, I honestly thought there was someone on the spot to get help. I couldn't believe it when it was on the news the next day that your wife was dead.'

Presley poured the dregs of the vodka bottle into his glass and downed it in one. He set down his empty glass and looked Robin in the eye. 'Are you going to call the police?'

'No. At least, I don't know yet. I want to ask you some questions.'

'Because I'm prepared to talk to them,' Presley continued, blundering on. He was starting to slur his words. 'If I go down for it then so be it. I'll take my punishment like a man. Now Jeannette's gone I don't care what happens to me.'

Robin did not allow himself to smile. The man's personal trauma had disturbed his wits. Even a couple of nights on remand in one of Her Majesty's prisons amongst society's dogs and dregs would knock such naivety out of him. And Presley would have to do it without the help of alcohol. Not that he was inclined to feel sorry for him.

'Tell me about the man in the other car.'

'I can't tell you much. He had his back to me and he was kneeling. He had dark hair, average length, and was wearing a sweater and jeans, I think. No jacket or coat anyway. That's all I can remember. There was nothing special about him.'

'So you wouldn't recognise him?'

'No chance. I might recognise his car though. It was one of those fancy sports jobs and you don't see many of them around.'

Really?

'It was a light colour, white, I think. I wouldn't know the make. I'm not a sports car fan but I could tell it wasn't an ordinary motor.'

Robin nodded, filing the information away. 'And the car you were in—you'd stolen it, hadn't you?'

Presley slumped in his seat. 'Yeah. I couldn't get

111

a taxi out of Doncaster and I'd missed the bus. I just saw this Mondeo with the keys hanging in the door and jumped in. It was stupid.'

There was no denying that.

'Where were you going?'

The question seemed to take Presley by surprise. 'My digs. A bit further on down the road towards Retford.'

'That's where you were living, was it?'

'I was working at one of the yards that way.'

'And what were you doing in Doncaster?'

'Just meeting some mates. Having a few drinks on Friday night, you know.'

'Do you remember which mates?'

Presley shot him a look of irritation. 'No, I don't. It's a long time ago.'

'You seem to remember plenty of other things and they were a long time ago too.'

Presley shrugged and reached for his glass. He put it down again when he realised it was empty.

Robin stood up. 'I'm just going out for a few moments. I need to think about what you've just told me.' He pointed at the empty bottle. 'I thought I might get another.'

Presley made no objection—why should he? He sat, crumpled and boozy.

Robin put his hand on his shoulder and squeezed. 'I really appreciate what you are doing,' he said and Presley stared up at him with gratitude in his eyes. 'It takes a lot of courage for a man to admit his mistakes,' Robin added as he walked to the door.

That ought to keep the pathetic little bastard sweet until he got back.

Mark sat in a daze after Scott had left. He felt—he didn't know how he felt. This confrontation with Scott was all he'd thought about for days, almost since Jeannette had died, when he'd realised the sins of his past were returning to haunt him. Confession was what he was bent on—real confession, not the tokenism of a religious ritual—and real absolution was what he sought. Whether that would take the form of physical punishment or prosecution, he didn't know, but it was important it was initiated by the man he had wronged. The man who, like him, had been shattered by the loss of his wife.

But Alan Scott had not responded as expected. He'd not offered Mark violence or contempt or passion of any kind. He'd listened to Mark's story without comment and then asked questions—sly, probing darts some of them—as cold-blooded as a fish. Even though they were antagonists—the situation demanded it—Mark had expected to recognise some kinship of feeling in Alan Scott. But there'd been none as far as he could tell. Was this what five years of grief did to you?

Or were his own perceptions too deadened by booze to be able to read Scott properly? Scott had laid his hand on his shoulder and praised his courage. Maybe he'd got the man wrong and he was a true Christian gentleman, strong enough to offer genuine forgiveness.

He wasn't much of a drinker though. Mark was keenly aware of his visitor's barely touched glass on the table by the sofa. Until Scott returned, it was the last remaining drop of alcohol in the house.

He rose cautiously to his feet, aware he mustn't move too fast or he'd overbalance. He picked up his glass, then Scott's and carried them slowly into the kitchen. The place didn't look too bad—just as well he'd cleaned up a bit. There was even space in the sink for the two glasses. First, though, he raised Scott's to his lips. Ugh—he'd forgotten Scott had watered the spirit down with tonic. But he'd drunk worse in his time. A heck of a lot worse.

As he filled the sink with hot water he reflected on how it had gone with Scott so far. If he were honest, getting things off his chest had not provided the release he'd expected. Some of that was due to Scott being so unemotional. But it hadn't helped that he'd not been able to be totally honest with the man. He'd had to lie about the others. But Mark couldn't tell Scott about Seb and Eddie. This was his confession, his alone, and it was up to the others if they wanted to do the right thing.

He'd thought that protecting the rest of them would be simple but it had implications beyond the obvious. 'Where were you going?' Scott had asked and he'd made up about having digs near Retford. Suppose Scott asked him for the address, the name of the landlord, even which yard he claimed to be working in? 'I can't remember' was going to sound pretty feeble after a while. Five years wasn't long enough ago to justify complete amnesia.

He dried the glasses and mugs he'd washed, then put them away in the cupboard over the microwave. Jeannette had always insisted on putting things away. She liked clean surfaces, tidiness. And now his life such an effing mess. He felt tears start to prick his eyes. No, not now—not when Alan Scott was about to return and he had to account for his sins like a man.

The doorbell rang and Mark turned blindly towards it, smacking his head on the open cupboard door. Shit! It was all he needed.

*   *   *

Robin stood on the doorstep, stone cold sober in the chill of the night, willing Presley to hurry up and let him in. He hoped the man wasn't incapable. Not yet.

In his hand he held a carrier bag containing two bottles of undistiguished vodka. Fortunately he'd had just enough cash on him to effect the purchase at a seven-eleven-style store ten minutes back on the main road. When he'd returned he'd parked two streets away, by a school playing field. He didn't see why anyone should have noticed him or his car.

He thumbed the bell again. Surely Presley hadn't changed his weird mind about his confession? He was pretty sure the promise of more drink, at the least, would ensure his re-entry.

'I'm coming,' he heard through the door and finally it opened. Robin stepped in smartly, anxious not to linger on the doorstep. He found Presley holding a piece of bloody paper tissue to his temple.

'What have you done?' he said.

'I banged my head on one of the kitchen cabinets.'

'Let me have a look.'

'It's OK. It's nothing really.'

115

Robin ignored him and made him sit by a light in the front room so he could examine the damage. There was a bloody gash where something had nicked the skin, doubtless bruising would follow.

'Have you got a plaster?'

'Yeah, somewhere.'

'Where?'

Presley shook his head. 'Does it matter? I'll be fine.'

'Look, I'm a doctor. Well, a horse doctor but, believe me, I know the best way to deal with cuts and bruises. Where do you keep your plasters?'

Surprisingly, Presley had a comprehensive selection of medicines in his bathroom, not what one might have expected of an alcoholic. Then Robin remembered the dead wife.

He fussed over the wound, superficial though it was. Then poured Presley a hefty slug of vodka.

'Here, take these.' He handed Presley some pills.

'What are they?'

'Syndol—paracetamol and codeine. I found them in your bathroom. They'll stop your head hurting.'

Presley obeyed orders, downing two of the small yellow lozenges. But he looked askance when Robin handed him two more. 'Don't you think two's enough?'

'Four's better. Trust me, you'll be fine.'

It was a lie, of course, but Robin wasn't bothered about lying to a man like Presley. What he hadn't mentioned was that the tablets also contained doxylamine, an anti-histamine which acts as a sedative. With luck, the double dose taken in conjunction with large amounts of alcohol would soon make Presley a very sleepy fellow.

It took more time than he expected, time in which he made Presley go over his story again and asked him questions, often the same ones, hoping to catch him out. There was something here that definitely wasn't right. Presley's recall was full of detail in some parts and hazy in others. It was haziest before and after the accident—where he'd been on his night out in Doncaster and where he'd gone after he'd driven away.

'How did you torch the car?' he asked him

'What?' His speech was slurry by now—the word came out as 'Wha?'

'How did you go about setting the car on fire after you dumped it?'

Mark thought about it. 'I put a match in the petrol tank. And it exploded.'

'Like in the movies?'

'Yeah. Boom.'

Robin didn't believe it. Cars didn't explode in the spectacular way that movies would have you believe—at least, not by dropping a match in the fuel tank. He suspected the flame would have been extinguished by the liquid before any damage took place. The best way to destroy a vehicle would be to light the soft furnishings of the interior with lighter fuel or burning newspaper, say. That was probably the way the car in question had been burnt and it was obvious to Robin that Mark had not been involved.

So, who was he protecting?

'Come on, Mark, tell me who else was in the Mondeo with you.'

Presley stared at him glassily. 'I told you. I was on my own.'

117

'I don't believe you.'

'Believe what you like, Mr Scott, I've told you all I can.' The words were slurred. 'I'm going to bed.'

Presley tried to stand, leaning heavily on one arm of his chair. His leg slipped from under him and he fell onto the carpet. 'Shit,' he said feebly.

Robin knelt beside him. 'Are you OK?'

'Yeah, yeah. Fine.'

He tried to get to his feet but failed. His limbs were no longer obeying the command of his brain.

'Don't try and move.' Robin took a cushion from the sofa and slipped it under Presley's head. 'Why don't you just rest there for a bit?'

The inert figure did not attempt to reply. It looked as if he was out of action for the night.

Robin perched on the sofa and considered his next moves. What evidence was there of his presence? Presley had taken his glass and washed it up, so that was one problem solved. He left the room and walked quietly up the stairs, retracing his steps to the bathroom. With toilet tissue he wiped the door handle and the cupboard above the sink where he'd found the plasters and pills. Then he returned downstairs and wiped all the places he could remember touching.

He felt pretty stupid doing it. His DNA would doubtless be all over the place if anyone should seriously look for it. But why on earth should they? It was just a precaution.

Presley was still fast asleep, breathing heavily. Robin doubted if anything he did would wake him but all the same he eased the cushion carefully from beneath his head and replaced it on the sofa. The man sprawled where he had fallen across the floor, his feet towards the door.

118

Robin had been eyeing the candles all evening, the one on the mantelpiece in particular. It was situated above a vase of dried flowers and grasses which masked the gas fire in the fireplace. It was an eye-catching arrangement—he could imagine Jeannette Presley fussing around to make it look just right. She'd evidently been a house-proud little body.

He shifted his imagination to Jeannette's sad apology of a husband. With her gone, his world had fallen down like a two-legged stool. He placed the diminished bottle of vodka further along the mantelpiece. To grasp it, Presley would have to reach past the candle and, in his unsteady state, it would be no surprise if he knocked it on its side. Like that.

Robin watched the hot wax dribble into the fireplace and the small round stub of candle with its orange-blue flame roll across the mantelpiece and fall onto the arrangement of dried flowers. It lodged in the brown web of stems and, for a moment, Robin thought he would have to lend a hand to accelerate the process.

Then a frond began to flicker red and there came a hiss and a crackle.

He took up station near the door, holding his breath as the room filled with smoke. The last thing he saw as he fled the room, closing the door securely behind him, was Presley lying in the same position, as inert as a sack of potatoes.

He waited on the corner of the road, in the shadow of a high hedge. There was no movement from inside the house, just the faint glow of the front room lights from behind the curtains. Then came a shifting of intensity in the light, wavering

119

and flickering and he thought he saw a lick of scarlet flame at the window. Once those curtains went up it would be no easy job to halt the blaze.

Time to go.

The things I do for you, Alan, he thought as he unlocked his car.

CHAPTER SIX

Alice had to force herself to get up. It had taken an age for her to get to sleep. The evening with Luke had gone well—up to a point. He'd seemed a bit shy in the pub, as if he'd made all the effort to get her there but didn't have the nerve to capitalise on it. She'd felt sorry for him when she'd pooh-poohed his dinner plans but she'd had visions of a long stiff evening with him thinking that paying the bill was good enough to impress her. Well, it wouldn't have been. And it was true she wasn't dressed for a fancy place like the Cloisters.

But the evening had been fun. They'd forgotten their awkwardness with one another and had a good time. There was mystery about Luke and she wanted to know more of what lay beneath his hesitant manner. His shyness hid a dry sense of humour and when his face broke into a smile she couldn't help responding. She'd enjoyed getting to know him.

However, she wondered if the learning process would continue. He'd upped sticks and run off in a way that suggested they wouldn't be repeating the experience in a hurry. It would be her luck to be left hanging in the wind just when a man had finally aroused her interest.

She'd almost picked up the phone to Luke several times before midnight. But some kind of basic dating sense had held her back. It wasn't her place to call. It was his—and he hadn't.

Now, as she got ready to go to work, she remembered that there was no reason to congratulate herself for her restraint. She might not have chased after Luke but she had rung someone else. When she'd woken for the third or fourth time, she'd called Robin. It had to be some kind of emotional reflex, calling him when she was at her lowest ebb.

The only saving grace had been that Robin had not picked up the phone. Maybe he reckoned that two in the morning was too inhospitable an hour to speak to anyone. But, as a vet, he was used to being rung up in the middle of the night. Maybe he was out.

Out where? With Gloria probably, though if she'd read the signs right, the Gloria days were coming to an end. In any case, it was hardly her business.

She closed the door behind her and set off down the drive for the surgery with a spring in her step.

She sincerely hoped Luke would phone her today but if he didn't she'd forget about him in a blink. It would be his loss.

*　　　　*　　　　*

Sarah had heard the siren in the night but after she'd registered that it wasn't anywhere near her street she'd turned over and gone back to sleep. The night hours seemed so short and precious that

121

she resented anything that kept her awake. She'd not got in from Neil's mum's till midnight and Neil would be up for his shift at five. Then the kids had to be roused and despatched to school and she would have to be bouncy and capable for their sake, like she'd been before poor Jeannette's accident. They were upset enough at losing their favourite aunt; it was important their lives got back on an even keel—and that was down to her.

A lot was down to her at the moment. For all their natural good cheer and church-going habits, the accident had knocked the in-laws for six. Jeannette had been the youngest child and the favourite. Neil had resented this preference; he frequently used to bad-mouth his sister and the memory was now eating him up, as Sarah was well aware. She'd done her best to tell him his guilt was perfectly understandable and he shouldn't add to his grief by beating himself up over it. He'd hugged her silently when she'd said that and then wept with huge wracking sobs. He was a big tough man who never cried—it had been an unnerving experience.

There'd been a lot of weeping since Jeannette had gone. Sarah spent most days with Bridget, her mother-in-law, who'd turned from a bustling, capable woman into a zombie who had to be told where the tea bags were kept in her own kitchen. And the rest of them weren't much better. Sarah had had plenty to do but being bouncy and capable for the whole world's benefit was exhausting.

She walked the kids to the end of the lane and watched as they cut along the footpath by the football pitch to the school.

A middle-aged dog-walker she knew by sight

was heading along the path towards her. He slowed as he reached her. 'Nasty fire last night,' he said.

So that explained the siren.

'Up Peacock Lane.' The man dropped his voice as he added, 'They've found a body. Charred to a cinder, that's what I heard.'

Sarah barely acknowledged what he said. She just turned and rushed home, her heart pounding—and not from the exertion. She couldn't say she'd ever been close to Mark Presley but she'd not been as judgemental as Bridget and the rest. Like her, Mark was a newcomer to the family and she'd been able to let off steam with him sometimes without feeling disloyal. And whatever Mark's shortcomings, like being an ex-boozer, he clearly adored Jeannette and made her happy. In Sarah's book, the marriage had been a success, which should have been crowned by the arrival of their baby in the spring. Poor Mark.

There was no policeman waiting at her door— she was half expecting one. Should she call them? Or ring the fire brigade?

It might take a while to get the information she wanted. It was much quicker just to get round to Mark's and make sure he was OK. Just because he lived in Peacock Lane didn't mean he was the victim of the fire; it was a long winding street with several cottages along its length.

She grabbed the car keys to her Mini and forced herself to drive carefully. It was a direct walk to his place but an indirect journey by road. All the same, it was faster to drive.

It couldn't be Mark. Two tragic accidents in the same family in ten days—surely that wasn't possible.

But suppose it wasn't an accident. Mark had been shattered by what had happened to Jeannette, almost impossible to talk to. Unreachable. She didn't believe he would have eaten last week if she hadn't made him. And there'd been that bottle of vodka in the house. It had been opened too—she'd noticed the last time she'd been inside. Which had been three days ago—no, more than that, four. She'd meant to go over yesterday but Bridget had called. Oh God. She'd never forgive herself if anything had happened.

How can you make a grown man throw away a bottle of vodka? She didn't know but she'd wished she'd tried.

The turning to the bottom end of Peacock Lane was taped off so she parked across someone's driveway and hurried off on foot.

As she turned the corner, the smoky smell thick in her throat, her eyes picked out the roof of Mark's cottage. A fire engine was parked on the verge outside. She'd hoped against hope but hope died and she broke into a run. She should have come yesterday—she'd meant to.

Too bloody late.

*　　　*　　　*

Breakfast in Seb's kitchen was a poor thing without Martine to warm the croissants and make the coffee. He missed her. She should be here with him. He'd suggested she move in but she'd turned him down.

'I couldn't possibly come to live with you,

Sebastian. My father would not approve.'

'I respect your father, Martine, but it's your life.'

'Absolutely. And I am not the kind of girl who lives with a man until he is tired of her and throws her out. That is not the way we do it in France.'

Sebastian could take a hint. The way they did it in France was to precede the cohabiting with a wedding ceremony, which was hardly what he envisaged at this stage of his life. He had plotted his future a long time ago, after he'd ridden his first big winner and realised that, if he devoted himself entirely to his job, he could go right to the top. And now he was on the summit he fully intended to stay there without the distractions of family ties. A steady girlfriend was one thing, but a wife with a legal option on his body and soul, that was another matter entirely.

But this was Martine, who was different to every other girl he'd been out with. She was as pretty as any of them but with more style and more balls—if you could say that about a woman. At first he'd thought he wasn't going to put up with a lippy female by his side but he'd grown to admire the way she stood up for herself and their rows always ended in red-hot fashion. Maybe it was a French thing, but she made up with a passion that obliterated everything that had gone before. 'My ambition is to spoil you for English women,' she'd once told him. He was beginning to think she had achieved it.

So maybe he would marry her—if she'd have him. Her father would have to approve. Jean-Luc's word was law with Martine; he was the only person she deferred to. But, considering how friendly Jean-Luc had been at dinner, parental permission might not prove an obstacle after all.

The real problem was Mark bloody Presley. If Mark spread the poison then neither of the Moreaus would ever give him the time of day again.

Seb had burnt the toast and he scraped it carelessly over the sink. He couldn't be bothered to make any more. He ate it dry, together with a black instant coffee. Despite last night's modest intake at the restaurant, there were two glasses of champagne to be accounted for.

Marsha's prophecy of time in the sauna was likely to be accurate.

The *Racing Beacon* was spread over the table and the television was on. A baby-faced newsreader in serious spectacles announced the latest Home Office cock-up but Seb wasn't listening. His attention was briefly caught by the banner scrolling across the bottom of the picture: 'House blaze in Yorkshire claims one victim.'

He chewed his toast and turned back to the runners at Chester.

*   *   *

Luke was driving on autopilot. Fortunately, the drive to Chester was one he could accomplish without thinking too hard.

He had three rides; one of them, for Peter Lloyd—Killer Punch—had a good chance. This was his fourth for Peter since Don't Touch and they seemed to be getting on. But he'd not won for him yet and he needed this one to cement the relationship—that's what Ivan, his agent, had said when he'd called this morning.

'You feeling OK?' Ivan had added. 'You sound a bit off to me.'

Luke had reassured him he was fine. That was the truth if you overlooked the fact that he was about to be exposed for covering up a fatal hit-and-run accident and that the girl he'd just fallen for would soon hate his guts. Apart from that, things were tickety-boo.

He shook his head as if that would somehow clear his thoughts. He'd spent the whole night mulling it over and he could see no way out. Better to put the Claire Scott business out of his mind and concentrate on the day ahead. He could do that. That's what he'd been doing for five years.

He turned on the radio and tuned to a talk station. He needed distraction.

'Police have confirmed that the body discovered in a house fire in Yorkshire in the early hours has been identified as that of Mark Presley. Mr Presley is the husband of stable girl Jeannette Presley whose death in a road accident was widely reported earlier this month. Police are still looking for two youths in connection with the incident.'

Luke pulled into the side of the road, causing a flurry of complaints from the drivers around him.

Mark was dead. He could barely take it in. He felt sorrow and fear and physical revulsion. But he felt something else as well—relief. The kind of relief that rolled over him like a wave.

How terrible for Mark. But, for himself, it was the miracle he'd never thought possible.

*   *   *

'And where were you last night?'

Robin knew it might be a mistake to finally return Gloria's calls but the storm had to be faced some time.

'You've got another woman, haven't you? If you're cheating on me I swear I'll cut your bloody balls off.'

'I was out last night, Gloria.'

'I know you sodding were. I sat in my car outside your place for two ruddy hours waiting for you.'

Robin didn't like the sound of that. The woman was becoming obsessive.

'Why on earth did you do that? We didn't have a date, did we?'

'We could have done if you ever answered your bloody phone. Clive had a last-minute to Majorca. So what's the name of your latest little tart?'

Robin would have laughed if the woman hadn't sounded so frantic. Gloria was a voluptuous armful with wild red hair and a temperament to match, which made for many excitements in her company. On the other hand, threats of castration from such a party were to be taken more seriously than from your average mouse.

Keeping all levity out of his voice, he said, 'If you really want to know, I was having dinner with my brother.'

'At two o'clock in the morning?'

She'd been sitting outside his place at two o'clock? That could have been awkward. At that time he was setting light to Mark Presley's front room. If she'd hung on another hour, she'd have caught him returning, stinking of smoke.

'I got a bit pissed at Alan's place so I stayed over.'

'Huh.' She wasn't entirely convinced, that was

128

plain, but at least he'd stopped the juggernaut. Now to turn it round.

'Is your lord and master still on his jolly?'

'Not back till tomorrow.' Her voice had softened.

'So why don't you pop round this evening? I'll demonstrate to you just how much pent-up energy a man can expend when he's been starved of female company.'

'You randy sod.'

'I thought that's what you liked about me.'

She didn't take issue with that.

*   *   *

When Seb returned from walking the course he found a familiar figure waiting for him outside the weighing room. He hadn't realised Eddie was coming to Chester—he'd not mentioned it yesterday. But they had had a few other things on their minds.

'Come over here,' was the first thing Eddie said and steered him away from a group of race-goers.

Seb's gut clenched. There could be only one reason why Eddie had turned up out of the blue. The Mark business must be about to blow up.

When they were far enough away from anyone to be overheard, Seb said, 'What's going on?'

'You tell me.' Eddie's face was pale and serious, with no trace of humour in his features. 'What have you been up to?'

Seb was perplexed. He'd have thought Eddie was playing some kind of joke except, from the cold glare in his eyes and the steely grip of his fingers on his arm, Seb knew his friend was in earnest.

'What are you talking about?'

'You really don't know?' The glare softened and the steel grip relaxed. 'You don't know about Mark?'

'What's he done now?'

'He's dead, Seb.'

Seb struggled to take it in.

His reckless mate from way back, who could have died in any number of daredevil stunts and stupidities in the past but who'd turned his life round and gone down the straight and narrow— dead all the same now.

'How?'

'The house caught fire. It's been on the news. The place went up like a bonfire apparently.'

'If he was in the kind of state we found him in that's no surprise.'

Eddie nodded. Having delivered the news he seemed to have run out of things to say. Seb reckoned he was thinking plenty though—just as he was.

'When you asked what I'd been up to, what did you mean?'

Eddie hesitated. 'Well, it is kind of convenient, isn't it?'

He could say that again.

But Seb couldn't let the remark go. Had Eddie seriously thought that he had a hand in Mark's death?

There was no one nearby. Seb made sure before he said, 'Are you implying that I had something to do with it?'

Eddie's gaze was steady. 'I just wondered.'

'Jesus Christ.'

'Because if you did, mate, you've got bigger balls than I ever thought.'

'Eddie!' Seb couldn't believe what he was hearing. It was like some weird dream—but then the events of yesterday fell into that category too. The things Eddie had said in the car, for example. 'There's more chance you killed him than me.'

Eddie snorted with amusement—fake amusement.

'Don't make me laugh,' he said.

'You said as much last night, you said if we got lucky he'd take all those pills.'

'It was just something I said. Anyway, you were thinking it, weren't you? That's why you brought it up about the pills.'

This was mad. Surely they weren't going to have an argument.

'Well,' Seb said, 'it wasn't pills and it wasn't anything to do with us. How on earth did the stupid sod manage to set his house on fire? He must have got pissed again.'

'Yeah.' Eddie nodded, started to say something then stopped.

'Go on.' It was important to Seb to know exactly what was in the other's mind. 'What are you thinking?'

'I'm thinking that we aren't the only ones who wanted our little problem to go away. Maybe someone else paid him a visit and torched the place.'

Seb was lost. 'Like who?'

'After we split up last night I went to see Luke.'

Seb was surprised. 'I thought we were going to leave him out of it.'

'I reckoned it was about time he knew what was

131

going on. He's a bright lad, after all. I thought he might have some idea we hadn't come up with to keep Mark quiet.

'And?'

'Maybe he did.'

If it wasn't such a desperate business, Seb would have laughed out loud. 'You're not suggesting Luke burnt Mark's house down?'

Eddie said nothing, just looked at him with a straight face. Good God, the man was serious.

'No chance,' Seb said. 'Luke's not capable. Anyway, he was always the one who wanted to own up.'

'Not last night, he didn't. He's got plenty to lose if certain stuff comes out.'

'Not as much as you or me.'

Eddie smiled. 'You think so? There's his rides for Alan Scott, for a start. And last night he'd just come in from a date with a bird who works for him. Luke's a bit keen on her.'

'So?'

'She only happens to be Scott's sister-in-law. Claire's sister. He had his knickers in a twist about how he'd never see her again if the truth about the accident came out. Think about it.'

Seb was thinking. He knew what it was like to fall for a woman. You did stupid things. If Mark stood between Luke and this girl, was it possible he had the guts to go out and silence him for ever?

He couldn't say. It was impossible to know people. A year ago he'd have said it was impossible for Mark to be seized by the urge to confess and land them all in this situation. And he'd have said it was impossible that he would be happy to hear that his old friend was dead. But leaving aside the whole business of how Mark had met his Maker, it was the best news he'd heard in a very long time.

*　　　　*　　　　*

Alice had forgotten about Luke by eleven thirty. She congratulated herself on the fact. If he was going to call then he would have done so by now, she reasoned, and since he hadn't—well, the message was obvious. Not that she cared.

By twelve she'd stopped listening out for the phone, wondering if every call might still be him, and by twelve forty-five she'd genuinely given up hope. She was surprised to find how much it mattered. He was just a skinny awkward boy, like plenty of others. Most of them she dumped after a couple of nights out though sometimes things ran on longer, out of companionship more than anything else. A girl had to get out and have a bit of fun, after all, and there were plenty of lads offering to squire her around. At least, there used to be. Eager suitors seemed to have dried up of late. 'You're a bit of an ice maiden,' Liz told her, which had affronted Alice at the time. But she'd come to terms with it now. If it meant she was fussy about who she invited in for coffee late at night that was OK by her. Some things were worth being fussy about.

Maybe that's what was upsetting her about Luke. She'd invited him in to her flat for cheese on toast and coffee would undoubtedly have followed had he not run for the door.

Was there something about her these days that was putting men off?

'You're looking a bit down in the mouth,' said

133

Liz on her way out for lunch. 'You must have heard the news.'

Alice wasn't interested in any news. She just wanted to bask in the sensation of being unlovable. Destined for a life of frustration and loneliness.

Liz was not about to leave her in peace, it wasn't her style. Normally her chatter was full of trivia but for once she had something important to say. 'You remember that stable girl who was run over? Her husband has just died in a house fire.'

'What?'

That was dreadful—weird. She'd been trying to speak to the man just yesterday afternon and now he was dead. How stupid of her to indulge in self-pity when there was real tragedy in the world.

As Liz told her the details of the news report, Alice's thoughts turned to Alan. How was he going to take it? When she'd told him first thing she'd failed to get hold of Presley, he'd said, 'Never mind, leave it to me.' But if the fire had happened overnight, then he wouldn't have got a reply.

She should have tried Presley yesterday evening, out of office hours. Instead, she had been wrapped up in her date with Luke.

Now they would never know what the dead man had wanted to say about Claire's accident.

How was Alan going to handle that?

*　　　*　　　*

Luke didn't pay much attention to the conversation around him in the changing room. His mind was elsewhere. Seb was in his usual place on the other side of the room, his face dark. He'd nodded to Luke. The pair of them needed to talk

134

about Mark.

Luke went through the motions of getting ready for the first race. Habit was useful at times like this. Shameful though it was to admit it, inside he was bubbling, his spirits as high now as they'd been low on the drive to the course. Before he'd heard the news of Mark's death.

Was he some kind of freak, being able to rejoice at the death of a friend? No, he knew he wasn't a freak. He'd never wanted anything bad to happen to Mark but it would be hypocritical not to admit that this tragic event hadn't suddenly made life much better. Like storm clouds lifting or the sun rising. Or the pistol pointed at your head only firing a blank.

He'd suffered enough over that horrible accident all those years ago and he hadn't even been there. He'd agreed to cover for his mates without knowing what he was letting himself in for.

It didn't excuse some things, he knew that. Like he should have insisted to the others that they come clean. He guessed he'd just been too weak at the time—and things hadn't exactly changed.

Seb was still looking at him from across the room. Shooting quick little glances in his direction as he pulled on his boots.

Luke took a deep breath and banished the dark thoughts. No time for them now. The condemned man had just been granted a reprieve and it felt fantastic.

It was now safe to think of good things. As he walked through to the weighing room he summoned into his head a picture of Alice. With Mark gone, there was no reason why she should ever discover his part in her sister's death. Maybe, even, one day he could tell her himself and she would understand how it had come about. But that day was a long way off. Perhaps the sympathy that had grown up between them last night was an illusion but at least now he was in a position to find out.

He'd call her when the meeting was over.

*   *   *

Seb couldn't believe he'd been beaten. He knew the tight turns of Chester like the back of his hand. He could have ridden the course with a blindfold on and still known where he was from the feel of his mount as it adjusted its balance to the turns and camber. In his book he had timed his run off the final bend to perfection, he had passed Luke's horse in the final furlong, but then Luke had come back at him. There were many attributes that went into making a champion jockey but, as in most sports, it nearly always came down to strength. And Seb knew he was the stronger. When he got a horse in front with a hundred yards to go, it stayed there. But not today. Luke had done him.

As they crossed the line, Seb heard the commentator call for a photo but he had no doubt.

'It's yours,' he said to Luke as they began to pull up.

Luke stared back at him, his face contorted in glee and triumph, his teeth unnaturally white in his pale face.

It gave Seb the creeps and he thought of the way Luke had behaved in the changing room earlier. He'd seemed remote, deliberately not joining in with the conversation. Could Eddie's suspicions have been right?

He had to say something.

'Bad business about Mark,' he said, as they pulled up and began to turn back to the winner's enclosure.

'Bloody awful,' Luke replied.

Their eyes met and Seb saw no sadness there— any more than Luke would have seen in his own gaze.

What hypocrites they were.

If Luke had done it, then he took his hat off to him.

*   *   *

Luke kept his own counsel as the talk in the changing room turned to Mark. A couple of guys remembered him from his racing days, to the rest he was known simply as the husband of the girl who'd been run over.

'I was best man at his wedding,' Seb said. 'He was a great fellow.'

'How was he holding up since his wife's death?' asked one of the others, Kevin Foley from Dundalk.

'How do you think?' Luke thought Seb would rather not have been asked. 'He was shattered. He worshipped Jeannette.'

'A bit of a boozer though, wasn't he?' Kevin continued.

'He packed it in when he got married.'

'I heard he was back on the sauce.'

'Bollocks.' Seb was angry. 'I saw him yesterday and he was fine. Didn't touch a drop. What exactly are you getting at?'

137

Luke admired Seb's defence of his dead friend, though he knew from Eddie's account of their visit that it was the opposite of the truth. They'd had to wake Mark from an alcoholic stupor and pour coffee down his neck to sober him up. But what good would it do to broadcast things like that?

'Sorry.' Kevin looked abashed. 'I was just wondering about this fire. It's a bit of a coincidence him having an accident so soon after his wife. Suppose he was back drinking and torched the place? I mean, in his situation, I might want to end it all too.'

Seb shook his head. 'No. I don't believe Mark would commit suicide. He wouldn't do that.'

Luke wasn't so sure. What was going back on the drink if not a self-destructive act? Mark might well have believed he had nothing left to live for.

But he did have something. He had the urge to spill the beans about Claire Scott's accident. Eddie had been quite adamant about Mark's determination to go ahead with a confession at whatever cost.

A sudden thought blew away all of Luke's newfound sense of being reprieved. If Mark had killed himself—and he agreed with Kevin that it was a distinct possibility—had he posted a suicide note?

Suppose even now a confession was on its way to Alan Scott. Or the police.

If that's what Mark had done then he would be back in the mire. Up the creek without a paddle and all hope of Alice lost forever.

He wouldn't be making that call after all.

*   *   *

138

Robin found Alan in one of the stables, inspecting a horse's surgery. Despite his recent operation, the horse looked in better shape than Alan who wore what Robin thought of as his 'blank wall' face. His eyes were without light and there were hollows in his cheeks. He felt the urge to put his arms around his brother and breathe some joy into him. Was it any wonder he had to protect Alan from a world that caused him so much pain?

He was gratified to see Alan's face break into a small smile as he stepped into the stall.

'You've done a good job here,' Alan said, rubbing the gleaming chestnut coat. 'He looks tip top.'

As if aware he was being discussed, the horse turned a wet pebble of an eye on Robin and challenged him to disagree.

'He's a handsome beast,' Robin said, a sentiment which ought to keep the animal happy. 'Alan, can I ask you a favour?'

His brother's expression soured. 'How much this time?'

Robin was affronted. A request for money had not been on his mind. Though, God knows, he could do with some.

'It's not money, Al. It's just that, if Gloria asks, would you mind saying I had dinner at your place last night and slept over?'

Alan considered the request. 'And what were you really doing? No, don't tell me, I'd rather not know.'

Robin kept a straight face. Alan could draw his own conclusions about his activities last night— they'd be as wide of the mark as Gloria's.

'I'll do it but you know I don't like lying to your girlfriends, Robin. Can't you just find one good woman and settle down with her?'

'I've tried that on a couple of occasions, mate, and it's cost me a fortune.'

'So you would like some money?'

'I didn't come in here for that reason, but if you're offering, I am a bit short.'

Alan reached into his jacket and pulled out a chequebook and a pen. He wrote quickly and handed the slip of paper to Robin.

It was for a thousand pounds, more than twice his usual offering. Robin's thank you was effusive.

'It's OK,' Alan said. 'You deserve it. I've not been pulling my weight recently and you've been doing my job for me.'

In more ways than one, thought Robin as he pocketed the cheque.

'Have you heard about Mark Presley?' said Alan.

It wasn't a surprising thing to ask but, coming so hard on his own train of thought, Robin was startled.

'Yes.' There was no point in pretending otherwise. 'It's a bit too much of a coincidence, don't you think?'

'What do you mean?'

'I think the news bulletins are already speculating that it might be suicide.' Robin had no idea whether they were or not, but it was surely only a matter of time. The notion that Presley was responsible for his own death was worth spreading around. Not that it was so far from the truth.

Alan looked Robin squarely in the eye. 'If that's what they're saying they are wrong.'

'It's a reasonable supposition, surely? He was apparently distraught over his wife.'

'I don't think he would have killed himself, intentionally or otherwise.' Alan reached for his jacket pocket again and held out a folded sheet of paper. 'Take a look at that. Tell me if you think it's written by a man who's intending to commit suicide.'

Robin realised what it must be before he'd read a word. The letter Presley had written to Alan. So it had arrived after all. Robin had searched the office and he'd kept an eye on the incoming post. He'd hoped it had got lost but here it was. He opened it with some trepidation, praying that it did not contain a full confession. If so, he might just as well have left Presley to continue the task of drinking himself to death and not accelerated the process.

Thank God, it was vague enough.

'It was marked personal and Liz held it back till I got into the office,' Alan said, 'so I only got it yesterday. I tried to ring him and so did Alice when I was off at the conference but there was no reply. I even tried this morning but I couldn't get a ringing tone on the line. Now I know why.'

Robin nodded, keeping a sombre face, but inside he was breathing a big sigh of relief. If he'd left his meeting with Presley until today then maybe Alan would have got through and the drunken fool would have spilled his guts down the phone. He could guess what would have happened then. Alan would have turned the police on Mark Presley and the whole affair would have been dragged back into the open, causing heartache all round.

He put his hand on his brother's arm. 'Alan, you've got to let this go.'

'What do you mean?'

'I mean Claire, I mean the accident, I mean you sinking into a pit of despair every time someone gets hit by a car. Honour Claire's memory of course, celebrate her with the memorial race, but get yourself a life again. She wouldn't have wanted this constant harping on about the past. She's dead, man. Learn to get over it—please.'

He'd never spoken this frankly to Alan before about Claire. And as the words were spilling out, Robin was aware that maybe it wasn't wise. But he couldn't help himself. He was a cool customer, he knew, to be able to do what he had done last night but the strain and pent-up passion had to come out somehow.

Alan stared at him, absorbing the words and the intensity with which they were spoken. A scarlet flush had flared across his cheeks and Robin recognised that his brother was on the brink of shouting at him, but he held himself in check and the silence in the small space grew thick and oppressive.

Finally, Alan covered Robin's hand with his own. 'You're a good brother and you may be right. But I can't let this lie. Presley said in that letter that he could tell me what happened to Claire and who was responsible.'

'But he's dead!'

'I don't care. He knew something. This is the first lead we've ever had and we must follow it up.'

'How on earth are you going to do that?'

'I don't know.' He took the letter from Robin's hand. 'Don't you see, until I find out the truth behind Claire's death, I can't possibly get over it.'

Robin had feared as much.

He'd thought that putting an end to Mark Presley had drawn a line under this terrible business for ever but he'd been wrong. His job wasn't done yet.

CHAPTER SEVEN

In the course of his duties Harry Giles had the opportunity to attend many funerals—not that he often did so—but he could not remember two occasions so close together as the departing ceremonies of Jeannette and Mark Presley. Here he was in the same church, surrounded by many of the same people as he'd been only ten days ago. It felt unreal and he could see the shock of déjà vu on many of the faces in the congregation.

In general, people thought Giles was a hard-hearted bastard. He didn't mind the description— in all honesty, he thought it was pretty accurate. But he was here on his own time, not to impress the bereaved family or his colleagues or even out of respect for the dead. Mark Presley had not inspired much respect. The intense pale young man had not seemed worthy of a wife who had evidently been loved by all. But Harry Giles was here all the same. Because Mark Presley had put his faith in him and he'd failed.

Presley might have thought that Harry didn't care whether he caught the two idiots who had caused his wife's death but that was far from the truth. To Harry, it was deeply frustrating that, for all the resources the police had thrown into the manhunt, they'd come up with nothing.

They hadn't given up, of course, but the search had been scaled down as other dramas had claimed their attention—and the headlines. And privately Harry conceded that the two joyriders had got away with their crime. But he also knew it would be only a temporary reprieve. Two irresponsible individuals like that were bound to step out of line in the near future and the chances were that their past misdeeds would come to light. He just prayed that he would be on hand to savour the moment.

But that day was in the future and any eventual conviction for Jeannette's death would be of no comfort to her dead husband. Harry had spoken to the fire brigade and the medics who had attended the house blaze. In the front room downstairs they had found candles, alcohol, and poor-quality furnishings with little or no fire resistance. In all likelihood Presley had been drunk and careless. Though the inquest was some weeks off, all the indications were that the coroner would declare the death to be accidental.

Harry wasn't convinced. Technically, such a verdict might be accurate but it didn't get to the underlying cause of Mark Presley's negligence. In his book, Presley had killed himself, either deliberately or out of wilful carelessness. Harry had seen the desperation in the man's eyes when he'd spoken to him after his wife's funeral. The only thing that had been keeping him going was the thought of catching the kids who'd run over his wife. And when the police had failed to do that— when Harry had failed to do that—Presley had done away with himself.

144

Jesus, he might have waited a bit. He didn't give us much of a chance.

Face it, he was an unstable character. An accident waiting to happen.

It's not my fault we haven't caught those boys. I've done everything I possibly could.

Standing in the church, mouthing tunelessly to the hymn, these thoughts did not make Harry feel any better.

There'd been some repercussions. The fire had put the hit-and-run back on the front pages and questions had been asked about the kind of care bereaved relatives could expect. Harry had spent some time with Gary, the family liaison officer assigned to Jeannette's folks, going over his dealings with Mark. The husband, it transpired, had been a prickly character, pushing away most friendly overtures. After they'd had a couple of sessions on the practical implications of his wife's death, Gary had left him to Sarah, Mark's very capable sister-in-law who, sad to say, had taken his death badly. Harry felt sorry for her. Nobody could blame her if Mark had decided to self-destruct, but it seemed the poor woman blamed herself.

There were fewer people in the congregation. For Jeannette's service, there'd been more mourners than seats. Now a quarter of the pews were empty. Naturally Jeannette's family were out in force, feeling no doubt that the occasion was as much for their beloved Jeannette as for her husband. Although some of them, the men of working age, looked as if they couldn't wait to get the business over with so they could return to their gainful employment. Harry could sympathise. Only the most indulgent bosses would be happy with two

145

days off for funerals in a bare fortnight.

Those missing, Harry reckoned, were Jeannette's friends and co-workers—and anyone who counted as Mark's family. He didn't appear to have any relatives. However, there were some new faces, the dead man's colleagues and acquaintances, most from the racing business.

There was a good turn-out of jockeys and Harry recognised a few of them. He placed Sebastian Stone straightaway, standing beside a dark-haired young woman who wore her mourning suit like a *Vogue* model. They were next to a sombre-looking Luke Eliot and a round-faced fellow who had the height of a rider. These had to be pals of Mark Presley's from his racing days.

He'd catch them on the way out.

*   *   *

Luke had been alarmed by the tall policeman with the sympathetic face who'd made a bee-line for him in the church hall. Mark, it appeared, did not merit a full-scale wake back at Uncle Peter's but he doubted if many felt short-changed. Most people, he suspected, just wanted to pay their respects and get home.

The policeman, however, seemed keen to make small talk over the teacups, which made Luke suspicious. How come he'd picked on him?

'Delighted to meet you, Mr Eliot,' he said, holding out a hand which seemed to engulf Luke's fingers. 'DI Giles. I've been involved in the sad case of Mrs Presley. This is a terible business.'

Luke agreed. It was the truth.

'And what was your connection with Mr

146

Presley?'

'We met when Mark was still in racing. He started out as a jockey.'

'Oh yes?' The policeman's soft brown eyes invited confidences—just what you might expect from an inquisitive copper. The invitation for Luke to continue was plain.

'About five years ago. Mark was a good rider but he got injured and never got well enough to make a go of it. He was as good as Seb.'

Luke waved Seb over. He'd prefer not to be the sole object of scrutiny. 'This is the policeman who's been searching for the lads in the van who killed Jeannette.'

Seb didn't bother with any small talk. 'When are you going to catch the little toerags then?' he demanded.

Giles seemed unperturbed. 'I couldn't tell you. Only that we will get them in the end. Lads like that fall into our lap sooner or later, you can bank on it.'

Seb didn't look convinced. Luke hoped he wasn't going to say something stupid. *What about Claire Scott? It's been five years and you've not got anybody for her death, have you?*

Instead, Seb said, 'But it's gone off the boil, hasn't it? Poor Jeannette will soon be forgotten.'

'Not by me, she won't.' The policeman's benevolent manner had slipped. 'And not by my team either. Don't think we don't care as much as you do, Mr Stone. We've got loved ones too.'

'Sure, but what happens if months go by? Years even?'

Luke noticed the set of the policeman's jaw, as if he resented the turn the conversation had taken.

147

Luke wasn't happy with it either—why couldn't Seb just leave it alone?

'We never close the book on serious crime,' said Giles. 'Our Cold Case Unit regularly reviews past crimes and gets results.' He broke into a surprising grin. 'We can't have the guilty enjoying a good night's sleep, can we?'

Luke smiled along with him. It was an effort. He couldn't wait to get out of the hall and away from this man.

But as he glanced at his watch and framed an excuse in his mind, Giles laid a hand on his shoulder.

'Did either of you gentlemen see Mr Presley recently?'

'I saw him at Jeannette's funeral,' Luke said.

'But not since?'

Seb spoke up. 'I visited Mark on the day he died.'

'And how did you find him?' The policeman's penetrating gaze was fixed on Seb's face.

'I found him sleeping off a bender, if you want to know. It was hard work sobering him up.'

Giles absorbed the information. 'I heard he was a recovering alcoholic.'

'He was drinking again, Inspector. Back on the booze big-time. I wasn't surprised, considering Jeannette and everything.'

'I see.' The policeman nodded. 'You're aware that you must make a statement. The coroner may require your presence at the inquest.'

'I shall be very happy to assist in any way I can,' Seb said, with the air of a righteous citizen.

Emboldened, Luke seized his chance. 'Do you think there's a possibility Mark took his own life?'

Giles turned back to him. 'That's for the coroner to decide.'

'Because I'd find that very hard to believe. I mean, if he was going to commit suicide, he'd have left a note or something, wouldn't he?'

That was the question. If Luke had had more time to consider he would never have dared to ask it. Surely the police would know if Mark had left a suicide note with somebody. He studied the policeman intently, hoping he wasn't being too transparent but unable to help himself.

Giles appeared to take him at face value. 'That's not necessarily the case. Suicides don't always leave notes, though it's a compelling piece of evidence.'

'But the absence of a note would surely point to it being an accident, wouldn't you say? And since he didn't leave one . . .' Luke left the sentence unfinished. He'd probably overstepped the mark. Fortunately the policeman misunderstood his concern.

'For what it's worth, Mr Eliot, the coroner is most unlikely to bring in a verdict of suicide without a powerful reason. He'll be well aware of the concerns of family and friends. I wouldn't worry too much if I were you.'

Luke felt a surge of relief. Unless the detective was a brilliant actor, Mark had not left any incriminating messages and the secret of Claire Scott's death was safe.

Giles had turned to Seb and was now quizzing him on the likely going tomorrow at Redcar. Maybe that's what he'd been after all along—to talk racing. Luke stifled the smile that rose to his lips and pretended to be absorbed in their

149

conversation.

They were off the hook—they must be.

*   *   *

Billy Chesil had seen plenty of the insides of nightclubs, not to mention the outsides, working the door, warning off the scags, keeping an eye open for trouble. His native city of Liverpool was famous for late-night malarkey. But the funny thing was, the most trouble he'd ever come across in terms of consistent bad behaviour from the punters was here in York on under-eighteen nights at Splash. On Mondays and Wednesdays the venue was open from five thirty to nine, selling soft drinks to teenies who posed and cavorted to the resident DJs, MistAH Fix and Lubella. It was a nightmare.

When Mr Sheriton, who'd hired him—to Billy's surprise—had warned him that the kids were a handful, he'd barely suppressed a laugh. But Mr Sheriton was right. The under-eighteens might not be able to buy booze but that didn't stop them bringing it in by all kinds of means. And the drugs were even harder to keep out. By seven thirty the place was clogged up with pissed-up adolescents, some a hair trigger flare-up away from reaching for a knife, others simply full of puke. But the ones who freaked Billy out the most were the pubescent girls who cursed like dockers in their cups and shed their clothes like trees in autumn. 'Touch one of them,' Mr Sheriton said, 'and you're liable to have your liberty curtailed as well as your employment.' Billy believed him.

Mr Sheriton was a tough man in a smart suit

150

with an extensive vocabulary and a weary eye. There wasn't much he hadn't seen. Who he fronted for, Billy didn't know or much care, he was that grateful to get the job. But he suspected there was a Liverpool connection because, unlike everybody else, he hadn't been fazed by Billy's unfortunate involvement in the Jeannette Presley hit-and-run.

'I hear you're OK,' was what he'd said when Billy had presented himself for interview.

'Who from?' Billy had asked.

But Mr Shertion had simply balled up his tatty CV and lobbed it into the bin in the corner of his office. 'Why should you care? You're in.'

And Billy hadn't argued. The job was all right, apart from the kids' nights, and Annie was pleased with him. He'd moved out of her flat, of course, and he was able to get Annie and the yuppie, Terence, into Splash on Saturdays which kept him in their good books. Whenever he rang his mam, she said how well Annie thought he was getting on and did he think he would settle down in Yorkshire now?

The answer to that was that he didn't yet know. He had some pals here but no real friends and he missed the 'Pool. He loved his sister but he could see where things were heading with her and the yuppie. Terence had a managerial job at a national supermarket and it wouldn't be long before he was posted off somewhere else. Billy had no doubt Annie would go too. She wanted a family and the clock was ticking. Terence, for all his irritating ways, was her future and good luck to her.

So he wasn't exactly putting down roots here in Yorkie land. But he couldn't go back yet. Not with those two scallies who'd nicked his van on the loose.

He'd been shocked to read about Mark Presley dying like that. He'd met the guy for less than an hour but he was as cut up as if he'd lost a mate he'd known all his life. He supposed it was because he felt responsible. He'd known that something else bad was going to happen to Presley. He'd seen it in his eyes. The paper hadn't said the bloke had killed himself and he probably hadn't done it deliberately but, all the same, he'd come over like a dead man walking. He would have handed Billy fifty thousand pounds if he'd had it, not five hundred. He just didn't care any more. Except about catching the boys who'd killed his wife.

Billy swore to himself he'd stick it out at Splash for the moment. It was the place to go for under-eighteens. Every Monday and Wednesday the place was heaving. Sooner or later, surely, the two dirtbags would show up at the door. What he'd do then he didn't know but those kids weren't going to get away with the destruction they'd caused. If not for himself, Billy owed it to a dead man.

*   *   *

Alice bit down on her lower lip as she often did when she was engaged in something difficult—like trying to capture on paper Henry's air of nonchalant grace. Even when he picked at the grass in the paddock, the horse exuded superiority. He'd been a Group winner who'd graced the turf at Newmarket, Epsom and Ascot and he expected the deference which came with such a distinguished past. Once a thoroughbred, always a

152

thoroughbred—that's what his haughty stare appeared to say. Though it was one thing to observe it and another to manage more than a superficial similarity. Hence the bitten lip. The pressure of her teeth was a calculated distraction, keeping her mind occupied so her pencil could lasso a likeness directly from her eye to her hand.

'Bravo, Alice, that's really very good.'

Alan's voice came from behind her, halting the movement of the lead across her sketchpad and destroying her cocoon of concentration. Damn.

She squashed the complaint at once. It felt like disloyalty. Alan had been a distant figure these last few days, since the news of Mark Presley's death, and she was delighted to see him out in the yard again, looking like his old self.

'It's a while since I've seen you drawing,' he said.

That was true. She'd not picked up a pencil or a brush in months. She'd only started again after Luke had taken an interest in them. By looking at her horse drawings again through his eyes she'd remembered the pleasure they'd given her. Not that Luke's presence had been anything more than coincidence.

'You've got talent,' he continued. 'You shouldn't let it go to waste. Claire was convinced you were going to follow in your father's footsteps.'

'No, she wasn't,' Alice protested. 'She thought my work was feeble and all Dad's stuff since the sixties complete crap!'

Alan's craggy face creased into a broad smile and she realised she'd been had. It was a standing joke that Claire had loathed their father's messy abstracts and had been barely polite about Alice's little efforts. Claire had had higher standards.

It was good to see a grin on Alan's face.

'I've come to ask a favour,' he said.

'Ask away.' Anything she could do to help her brother-in-law through his sticky patch she would do willingly. He only had to say.

'You're friendly with Luke Eliot, aren't you?'

She would have preferred it if he hadn't said that.

'No.'

The smile was replaced by puzzlement. 'But I thought you went out with him the other evening.'

How did he know about that?

'We went for a drink, Alan, but I haven't spoken to him since.'

'Oh dear. I'm sorry to mention it then.'

'We didn't fall out or anything. We just—well, we haven't been in touch.'

'It's OK. Forget I said anything.'

Alice knew she ought to let it go but how could she? Why was he asking her about Luke? She wormed it out of him eventually.

'It's that letter.'

He didn't have to explain which letter.

'What has it got to do with Luke?'

Alan pulled a newspaper from his jacket pocket. It was folded open to a photograph of mourners at Mark Presley's funeral. The camera was focused on a man Alice recognised as the jockey Seb Stone, next to an elegant girl in black. In the background, Alice spotted a familiar face—Luke.

'As you can imagine,' Alan said, 'I've been turning the whole thing over in my mind, trying to work out a connection between Claire and this man, Mark Presley. I know nothing about him but if Luke was at the funeral, maybe he could give us

154

some background. Then it occurred to me that you might be in the best position to ask him. I mean, that's when I thought that you and he were . . .'

She laughed. Alan was positively squirming with embarrassment.

'Leave it to me, Alan.'

She would probably regret it but that was too bad. She owed Alan.

'About the letter,' he went on. 'I've been thinking I might show it to the police. Robin disagrees. He thinks I'm obsessing too much about Claire and this whole business with the Presley couple. He says it would be best to let the matter lie and get on with life. What do you think?'

Alice laughed. 'I think that you're going to carry on being obsessed. You've just asked me to go digging into Mark's past with Luke. And you're going to show the letter to the police whatever Robin or I might say.'

'Oh.' He looked taken aback by her candour. 'But do you approve? You're Claire's sister and it matters very much to me what you feel. Honestly, Alice, if you tell me to stop, I will.'

He was sincere, she could tell. She could put an end to the whole morbid affair right here. Robin was right, in so many ways. But she hated to think how Alan would cope. Claire's fate was in his blood and, who knows, he might yet stumble onto the truth through Mark Presley's mysterious letter.

'I'm going to get in touch with Luke,' she told him. 'We can't stop now. Anyway,' she added, her resolution firming as she spoke the words, 'I don't want to.'

*   *   *

155

Harry Giles liked racing people. He didn't run into them often but he always took time out to chat whenever he did. Basically, he admired their guts. They were up before dawn, dealing with dangerously large animals of limited intelligence, many of them paid very little and, in the case of jockeys, they put their bodies on the line every day in the cause. And, for all that effort, results were by no means guaranteed. Pretty much like police work, you could say.

But the racing connection was not the primary reason he'd made a point of attending Mark Presley's funeral. There was something about the whole business that got beneath his layers of cynicism and self-preservation. And that something was an old case with many similarities to the death of Jeannette Presley.

Five years ago he'd been a humble detective constable and up to his ears in a dozen urgent things when he'd been hauled in to assist in the hunt for a joyrider who had been involved in a hit-and-run. The dead woman in that case had been another driver, thrown clear by the impact of the crash.

Harry had always wondered whether Claire Scott might have survived if help could have reached her quicker. If the driver of the other car had stopped and called for assistance, might she not have lived? That's what the woman's husband had asked him, over and over, in the days after the accident. Why didn't he stop?

Because he was a scared and selfish little shit who was concerned only with saving his own neck—that was the answer. Not that he'd said it so

156

bluntly to Alan Scott at the time.

The Mondeo had been nicked on the outskirts of Doncaster. CCTV evidence had turned out to be useless. The cameras had picked out various groups of youngsters in the centre of town that night and they'd all been identified and questioned, without a result. In the end the camera evidence had proved a distraction and the stolen vehicle itself—a partially burnt-out carcass by the time they'd retrieved it five miles out of town—had yielded nothing at the time.

Then as now, Harry had expected the thief or thieves to trip themselves up. He'd be bound to get into trouble and, if there was more than one, grass the others up in some deal or other. But it hadn't worked out like that. The little sod had disappeared so completely into thin air that Harry had concluded he couldn't have been local.

He'd said as much to Alan Scott when it had all cooled down. Not that things had ever seemed to cool with Alan, poor fellow. Harry had taken to the vet, but in the circumstances Alan Scott could only look at him in one way. And that was as one of the men who'd failed to find his wife's killer.

The same went for the dead woman's sister. A studenty type with big green eyes which, for a lot of the time Harry had spent with her, had been swollen and red, filled with held-back tears. He'd not seen her at the races when he'd bumped into Alan, which was a pity as he'd have liked to have had sight of her with a smile on her pretty face. That was a regret, one of many where women were concerned.

One day he ought to take another look at the Claire Scott file.

But as he entered the CID room with its ringing phones and overloaded desks and a voice that called out, 'Hey, boss,' all such thoughts vanished from his mind.

*   *   *

Martine Moreau was accustomed to sudden demands from her father and she knew better than to disobey them. So, even though she had been intending to ride out for Marsha Hutton, she drove to York and caught the first train to London. By a quarter to one she was pulling into King's Cross and by a quarter after, a cab was depositing her outside JLM's flagship office in Princes Street just across the road from the Bank of England.

She was hardly dressed for the city—she had swapped jodhpurs for a crumpled navy skirt and jacket. Had she not been in such a rush she could have looked so much better. She'd have put on a decent pair of shoes for a start. She even caught Eileen, her father's frumpy English assistant, casting a disparaging glance at her feet as she ushered Martine into the lift. Martine gave the woman one of her best frosty glares in return. *Tant pis.*

Fortunately she was in time for lunch. At the very least her father owed her a decent meal after all this rushing around.

'I'm famished, Papa,' she announced as she strode into his office. 'There was nothing edible on that beastly train.'

He looked at her without warmth. She knew that look and feared it of old, his battle mask. But she was not an enemy and she knew how to melt

158

her old papa.

She kissed him on both cheeks, as smooth and cold as marble. He did not bend or smile, just pointed to the chair in front of his desk.

'Ah, so we are not eating,' she said as she sat. She smiled winningly. She'd melt him shortly, just as soon as he'd got whatever it was off his chest.

The room was not tycoon huge but it was comfortable and stylish. The desk was a rich and solid mahogany, the chairs leather-padded, the bookshelves looming. Here in the City of London the French businessman had assumed the mantle of a clubbable Englishman and his designers had arranged the effects. Images of horses were everywhere, from a traditional oil painting of an old champion with his groom to photographs. Jean-Luc was pictured by the side of magnificent thoroughbreds in parade rings and winner's enclosures, accepting trophies at Newmarket and Longchamps and Churchill Downs. On top of a brown folder on his desk was a photo of Tartuffe, a two-year-old chestnut colt with white legs, currently in training at Marsha Hutton's yard where Martine regularly rode him out.

Tartuffe was the reason, Martine soon discovered, for her father's foul mood.

He pushed the folder towards her.

'Open it.'

She did as she was told out of habit and because she had decided that was the way it had to be until she was married and in a position to tell darling Papa to stuff it, if she felt so inclined. She hoped she would have the courage to act on her inclinations.

Inside the folder was a photograph of a man, a

159

scruffy elderly lump with two days' worth of grey fuzz on his spade of a chin. He was pictured hunched inside a battered anorak with his baggy stained cords tucked into a pair of mud-streaked wellington boots.

'Do you recognise him?'

'No, Papa. Should I?'

He didn't reply, just reached across the desk and flipped the photo to one side. Beneath it was another. A man in a blazer and tie, clean-shaven and smiling, with a trilby at a jaunty angle on his head. Around his neck hung a pair of powerful binoculars trailing a string of small cards that Martine immediately recognised as racecourse badges. It took a moment for her to register that the men in both photographs were the same. The British had a phrase for it—'he scrubs up well'. This man certainly did that.

'You recognise him now?'

'No.' But as she denied it, doubt set in. 'At least not like this.' She stabbed at the first photo. She lifted the second from the folder and studied it. 'But about this I am not so sure.'

Her father leaned back in his chair, considering her. His grey eyes did not waver and she knew he was judging her, deciding whether or not she was putting on an act.

'There is something familiar about him,' she said. 'Maybe I have seen him but I don't know where.'

He tapped the file and she saw there was a third photo, an interior scene of a horse being paraded before spectators sitting in banked rows. She recognised the auction ring in question because she had visited it a year ago.

160

'Is this Tattersalls at Newmarket?'

He nodded. She knew his infuriating silence was calculated to intimidate. It was a tactic she was familiar with, but that did not lessen its impact.

She looked again at the image. At the end of a row in the top left, one head had been circled. Though the face was partly obscured she recognised a square jutting chin. It was the same man. But so what?

Her father was staring at her steadily. He was waiting for her. She was about to protest when she made the connection. She *had* seen this man before, just once. He had not been dressed as a farm layabout but had been a smartly turned out bidder at Tattersalls the previous autumn—the occasion when her father had spent close to a million pounds on the chestnut with white legs in the photograph.

Unfortunately the horse's ability had not so far matched his price tag. He'd scrambled home in his maiden race at Rippon in the spring but had not won since then. As a seasoned racehorse owner, Jean-Luc had been philosophical in the face of this disappointment.

However, he did not look philosophical at the present moment and his full attention was on her.

She concentrated on the photo in front of her. This man, the slobby peasant type who dressed up for the horse sales, had been the underbidder in the sale for Tartuffe.

She'd attended the auction with Eddie, who was bidding for the horse on behalf of her father. She'd gone along to keep an eye on events for Jean-Luc who'd been halfway round the world chasing some deal, and also because she and Eddie, at the time,

161

were a little more than friends. It had been a fallow period for her, between serious boyfriends, and Eddie had been fun company. She wasn't naive. She knew his friendship with her had helped him gain her father's confidence but she'd used him pretty shamelessly herself, to squire her around English racing circles while she looked for a better long-term prospect—like his friend, the champion jockey Sebastian Stone. And everybody had been happy. Up to this point anyway.

'I remember now,' she said. 'This man was bidding against us for Tartuffe. I agree that here,' she pointed to the first photograph, 'he looks like a tramp, but so what? He is probably some eccentric millionaire. English horse people can be very peculiar, Papa. Some dress like beggars and still have a Rolls-Royce in the garage.'

Jean-Luc shook his head. 'Not him. His name is Joseph Clegg. He drives something called a Vauxhall Astra which is fifteen years old and he lives in an old farmhouse with a leaking roof and dry rot. He works part-time as a menial at Black Croft Equine Supplies. Does that mean anything to you?'

'Absolutely not. But why was he bidding?'

He nodded, as if acknowledging her point, then pulled out a final photograph. In a yard in front of a large barn the man—the shabby old one—stood in conversation with an all too familiar figure.

'Inside that building is a paper-shredding plant owned by our friend Eddie Naylor. Clegg runs the place for him. He has done so for the past four years.'

Martine pondered the information as she gazed in disbelief at the photograph. So, when Eddie was

162

fighting to win an auction on her father's behalf, he was bidding against his own employee.

The auction had turned into a stubborn head-to-head battle. Just as she'd thought the horse was secured the other bidder had sent the price spiralling again. She remembered it well because her father had trusted her to authorise the final price. Eddie had ended up getting the animal for 950,000 guineas, just under her father's ceiling of a million pounds. Of course, Eddie had been well aware of Jean-Luc's limit because she'd told him.

She felt the blood drain from her face. Opened her mouth to speak but no words came out. What could she say?

Jean-Luc got up and came round to her side of the desk, put his arms around her from behind and held her in a familiar fatherly embrace.

'It's OK, *ma petite*. Let's go and have lunch now.'

She burst into tears and shook her head. She no longer had an appetite.

CHAPTER EIGHT

Despite the chill of autumn, Luke took his drink into the front garden of the Black Sheep where he had a clear view of the driveway into the car park. He was wondering if he'd been stood up. But it wasn't him who had initiated the rendezvous. He'd been surprised to get a text from Alice. He'd not been in touch with her since their evening together and imagined that she would have taken his silence as lack of interest. At least, that was how he hoped she'd interpret it, far from the truth though it was. He had plenty of interest in Alice—for all sorts of reasons.

A scruffy black Golf turned down the drive and he glimpsed a shock of blonde hair. So, she'd not taken revenge on him by leaving him twiddling his thumbs. She spotted him and waved as she locked the car and walked towards him across the lawn. She looked even better than he remembered.

'Hi, Luke.' She kissed him on the cheek. 'Thanks for letting me drag you out.'

'It's no drag. I'm on holiday today.' This wasn't strictly true. He had no rides this afternoon but he'd been riding out all morning and had some homework to put in on the form book for tomorrow. But that wasn't on his mind right now.

There was a tussle over who was getting who a drink, which he lost. Alice insisted since she had asked him over. He also got the firm impression that she was laying down the rules. This was a meeting she intended to control, a friendly get-together and certainly not a date. She made it clear that she was expected back at the clinic by half past two.

All of which suited Luke fine. Attractive though she was, he couldn't allow himself to get too involved. He wasn't scared of half a ton of charging horse or of being kicked like a football across a racecourse or of facing down a pack of angry punters when he failed to meet their expectations. But he was scared of intimacy with a green-eyed girl who could turn around and ask him what he knew of the death of her sister.

So he almost choked on his drink when she said, 'How did you come to be friends with Mark

Presley?'

'Mark?' He played for time, took another sip of Diet Coke to cover his confusion. 'Oh, you know. I bumped into him on the circuit.'

'You must have been quite close. I read you cancelled your rides to go to his funeral.'

He wasn't the only one. Seb had done the same and the *Racing Beacon* had reported it—that must have been where she read it.

'Why do you want to know?'

'It was terrible what happened to him. I mean . . .' she hesitated. 'I hope it's not insensitive to ask but I feel a kind of personal connection with him because of Claire.' He must have looked at her blankly because she began to explain. 'My sister Claire who was killed in a road accident like Mark's wife.'

'I remember. You told me.'

'Alan was very upset about Jeannette Presley. He takes these things so much to heart. He's been upset about Mark too.'

Luke took a sip of his drink. The glass was empty.

Why was she talking like this?

It was just the kind of thing he'd been afraid of when he'd discovered Alice's conncetion to Claire. That she'd start to unburden herself about her dead sister and look to him for sympathy. But this was worse, she was also looking for information.

A wild thought floated to the surface. Now would be the time to make a clean breast of everything. And the next thing he knew he'd be sitting in a police interview room.

He didn't have the courage. He was still a coward.

165

'Mark was a great guy,' he said. 'A good jockey too until his ankle got smashed up. Then, when he found he couldn't carry on riding, he went a bit haywire. He got into drinking and went through a few jobs till Jeannette made him clean up. She saved him. So it was doubly cruel what happened to her. He went straight back on the booze after her funeral.'

'Is that why the house caught fire?'

He shrugged. He could do this better than he'd thought. It was just gossip about a dead pal. Not respectful maybe but the kind of chatter that makes the world go round.

'I don't think he committed suicide, if that's what you're asking, but I'm sure that him being pissed had something to do with it.'

'But when you first met him he wasn't drinking, was he?'

Luke shook his head and got to his feet. 'Can I get you another?' Her glass was half full and she declined. He vanished to the bar for a breather and ordered another soft drink, thinking that he could do with something stronger for once. When he returned she picked up where she had left off.

'When was it you first met Mark?'

'Years ago. When I was an apprentice.'

'You must have been very young.'

'Sure. I was sixteen when I started out. I left school straight after my GCSEs and went to a yard in Lancashire, near Preston.' This was better—give her the edited biography and steer away from Mark. 'That was a shock to the system, getting up at the crack of dawn every day. Living with a load of tough lads who thought it was a laugh to piss in your riding boots. My mum was on at me to go

166

back to school and I nearly did.'

He took a sip of his drink. She was looking suitably interested in his account so he carried on.

'I'm a townie, brought up in Manchester, but I always wanted to be a jockey so I stuck it out. I went off to the HHA—the Hands and Heels Academy. My aunt used to work there. It's just down the road from the Northern Racing College.'

'Do all jockeys go to a riding school?'

'Yeah, most of them.'

'What about Mark? Did he go?'

'I don't know. He could have done. Like I said, most jockeys do.' (Jesus. Why was she so curious about Mark?) He looked at his watch. 'What time did you say you had to be back?'

*　　　*　　　*

Alice found Alan in his office when she returned from the pub.

'Any luck?' he said.

'Yes and no.' She dropped into the chair across the desk. 'He was very vague about some things. I couldn't get him to talk much about how he'd met Mark but he was quite happy to tell me about Mark's drinking. Apparently he was an alcoholic till his wife straightened him out then he went back on it. Luke thinks the fire was down to an accident when Mark was drunk.'

'But did he know what Presley was up to five years ago?'

'That's what he was vague about.'

Alice blamed herself. She'd gone charging in with both feet. Too many direct questions—she should have been subtler. She'd been too honest,

167

in fact. Same old story with her and boyfriends. Except that Luke was not a boyfriend and it was plain from his manner—he'd virtually called time on their meeting halfway through—he was never going to be. Which didn't explain why he had appeared so keen in the first place. Why was getting a decent relationship together so damn difficult? What was wrong with her?

She pushed her confused feelings to one side and tried to concentrate on what Alan was saying.

'Do you remember that copper who was around when Claire was killed? Giles.'

Yes, she did remember. He was tall and loose-limbed, with twinkly eyes. Not that they were twinkling at the time, which had been the worst of her life. She'd cried a lot, trying to express herself through her tears, and the policeman had been endlessly patient. Harry, that was his name. He had a sister, too, and he'd talked about what she meant to him. He'd promised he was going to catch whoever had stolen the Mondeo and fled from the accident and he hadn't.

She ought not to feel he had let her down. She was sure he'd done his job to the best of his ability.

'What about him?' she said.

'I've made an appointment to see him. I'm going to show him Mark Presley's letter.'

'Do you think he'll care after all this time?'

'I'm sure he will. Anyway, it's not down to his personal whim, is it? This letter sheds new light on an unsolved crime. He has to take it seriously.'

Alice wasn't so convinced but she kept her doubts to herself.

*　　　*　　　*

168

Martine picked half-heartedly at her sandwich. She was still sitting in her father's office—he had sent out for coffee and a snack. Even though she'd got her emotions under control, she could scarcely eat.

She hadn't been in love with Eddie—at least she'd not felt about him the way she now did about Seb—but she'd been close to him. They'd enjoyed an intimate friendship based on trust. Or at any rate she'd thought that was the case. Now, from talking to Jean-Luc, it was plain that Eddie had conned her father out of a lot of money—and he'd used her as a smokescreen to do it.

Jean-Luc had uncovered the swindle when he'd obtained a copy of the preliminary tax return of Malcolm Pearce, the breeder who had sold him Tartuffe.

'Pearce is claiming that he paid Eddie two hundred and thirty thousand pounds in commission for the sale of Tartuffe.'

'But that's too much!'

'Of course it is. I've been robbed. But here is what I think took place. Eddie approached Pearce before the auction and asked what he wanted for the horse. Pearce probably told him half a million pounds and Eddie promised him more than that on the understanding they split the difference. Then, with the help of his employee Clegg, they bid the price up to nine hundred and fifty thousand guineas. I transferred the money into Tattersalls' account, who paid Pearce and he paid Eddie half of the money in excess of five hundred thousand. And Pearce declared it as a commission fee in his accounts because he didn't want to pay tax on it.'

Martine could understand that, even though she

169

wasn't overfamiliar with the British tax system. What it didn't explain was how her father had access to Malcolm Pearce's accounts.

'Who told you?' she asked. She knew that her father wasn't averse to employing private detectives. He'd even put a *flic* on her tail when she first came to England and lived on her own—'for your own protection', he'd said when she'd remonstrated with him. So she could imagine him setting a watcher with a camera on Eddie and Clegg once he'd had suspicions. But until a few days ago Tartuffe's value for money had never been questioned. Someone had put it in his head.

'I can't tell you,' he said.

'You don't trust me!'

That was what she feared most out of all this. That he suspected her of being involved. It had obviously crossed his mind. That was why she'd been summoned so peremptorily and quizzed with such coldness. Her father had had doubts about her and had studied her every response for artifice. She'd thought she'd convinced him of her innocence but there was always room for doubt.

He shook his head. 'Of course I trust you, Martine.'

'Then tell me how you found out.'

He considered the request, looking past her at the painting above the fireplace, weighing the matter in his mind. 'OK, but you keep it to yourself. It would not be fair to Marsha if it got out. She has always been a very good friend to me.'

So he'd uncovered the plot through Marsha Hutton. That wasn't a big surprise, the trainer had always been loyal. 'But how did Marsha find out?'

He shrugged. 'She shares a bookkeeper with

170

Malcolm Pearce. The bookkeeper is maybe not as discreet as he should be, especially with someone as sympathetic as Marsha.'

'That was lucky,' she said but she knew in some ways luck had nothing to do with it. When a man was as wealthy and influential as Jean-Luc, everyone wanted to be his friend. No doubt the bookkeeper would have been well rewarded for his indiscretion.

'What are you going to do about it, Papa?'

'I shall get my money back.'

'Are you going to sue them? You have the evidence.'

He smiled. It was a nasty, less than charming expression which she knew of old.

'The courts take too long. There are other ways.'

Martine did not ask what those were. She didn't want to know.

*   *   *

Harry considered the visitor across the desk. It was Durnside's most salubrious interview room, reserved for non-threatening meetings, but that still didn't say much for it. There was no natural light and the blue glare of the strip lighting overhead did nobody any favours.

Alan Scott looked appreciably older than when he'd last seen him, some four years earlier. His jawline had a baggy look and his hair, though still thick, was greying. All the same, there was something pleasurable about coming face to face with him once again. They ought to be meeting up on the Champagne Terrace at York or the Lawn

Bar at Beverley, where Scott could mark his card and spice the conversation with racing gossip. But the vet had insisted on coming in to the station—it was a police matter, he'd said.

Harry had recognised Alan's voice on the phone before he announced his name. He'd just been thinking about Alan Scott, so for him to turn up on the same day was spooky.

Now he reread the letter Alan had passed him across the table. It had been written by Mark Presley a few days before his death. What were the odds of he himself being involved in both Claire Scott's case and the deaths of the Presleys? Likely enough in the great scheme of things, Harry thought. He was an optimistic gambler—optimistic enough to believe in long odds coming up once in a while.

Eventually he spoke. 'What are you asking me to do, Alan?'

'Suppose this man knew who was driving the car that hit Claire?' Alan was getting agitated now, leaning across the desk, his cheeks reddening. 'He could have been sitting on the secret all these years, then his own wife was killed in a similar fashion and he realised the pain it causes—look, that's what he says in the letter: "I now know exactly what you have gone through."'

Harry nodded. 'You've got a point, but I'm not sure exactly what we can do now Mark Presley's dead.'

'You can find out where he was living and what he was doing at the time of my wife's accident, can't you? Then we might have some idea whether he could have any direct knowledge of Claire's death. That would be a start.'

Harry considered the request. He had more than enough on his plate without one of his past failures coming back to haunt him. But he knew he wasn't going to send his old acquaintance away empty-handed. For one thing, the letter might have some bearing on the inquest into Mark Presley's death. For another, he remembered saying to Alan all those years ago that it was only a matter of time before they got a break. The idiot in the Mondeo wouldn't be able to hide for long, someone would open his mouth. Well, it looked like they finally had. It was a pity that somebody was now a corpse.

'Give me a couple of days,' he said to Alan, getting to his feet and offering his hand. 'I promise I won't forget.'

The vet's grip was firm and warm. 'Thanks. My sister-in-law would be very grateful.'

'That's young Alice, right?'

'That's correct. Only she's a proper grown-up woman these days. She runs the clinic for my brother and me—we couldn't manage without her.'

Harry wondered whether the speech was deliberate. He wouldn't put it past an experienced campaigner like Alan Scott to bring all guns to bear on his request.

He'd always felt he'd let the pair of them down in the past. Maybe this was his chance to put things right.

*   *   *

Alice would have preferred not to be on first-name terms with Gloria. After all, it was easier to fob the woman off when there was no suggestion of friendship. 'I'm sorry, Mrs Harper, but Dr Scott is still in the operating theatre' had a satisfying hands-off ring to it, as if she were merely the messenger. But Gloria had somehow got herself on terms that implied an intimacy between them, as if Alice were a willing accomplice in her tortured affair with Robin. It was embarrassing to be forever making excuses on his behalf. If he was going off the damn woman why didn't he make a clean break with her?

'He can't still be operating, can he?' Gloria protested.

'It *is* a long list today,' Alice replied, which wasn't far off the truth. 'I'll make sure he gets your message as soon as he comes out of theatre.'

'He's found someone else, hasn't he? You see him every day, you must know what's going on. Who is she?'

Oh, for God's sake. This was precisely the reason why Alice wanted Gloria to be Mrs Harper. She'd been sucked into too many of Robin's emotional messes over the years and she'd had enough of them.

'Gloria, I have no idea. I make a point of not getting involved. Now, I'm sorry, there's someone on the other line.'

She put the phone down and marched into Robin's office. He was sitting at his desk, a familiar sheepish look on his face.

'I'm so pissed off with you,' she began. 'Why don't you put the bloody woman out of her misery?'

He shrugged. 'I like Gloria. In small doses.'

'But it's not fair, Robin. If you've found a new girlfriend, the least you can do is tell her.'

He looked surprised. 'Who says anything about

174

a new girlfriend?'

'She does, for one. And Alan. He told me you asked him to cover for you the other night if Gloria got on to him. He had to pretend you got sloshed and slept over at his place.'

He stared at her. The sheepish look had gone, to be replaced by an expression she couldn't read. Then his face broke into a boyish grin. 'OK, you got me. But it was a one-off. I doubt I'll see that one again.'

She glared at him, trying to force all her disapproval into a look of venom.

'Jesus, Robin, don't men like you ever grow up?'

'Sorry, but you did ask. I'll phone Gloria in a moment.'

It was on Alice's mind to rebuke him for cheating on the woman but she stopped herself in time. Gloria was betraying her own husband, after all. The whole thing made her sick. When it came to sex, why couldn't people be decent and honourable? The way she felt right now she was better off being single.

'Don't go.'

She had been heading for the door.

'I don't want to talk about your sordid love life, Robin. I'm sorry I asked in the first place.'

'It's not that. Sit down.'

She did so reluctantly.

'I'm really worried about Alan. I think he's getting carried away with Mark Presley's letter. He's never going to get his life back on track if he doesn't simply remember Claire as she was and stop obsessing about the way she died.'

'But this letter is the first hope we've ever had of finding the men who caused the accident.'

175

'So you're in favour of him running off to the police?'

'I'm in favour of justice for my sister. If showing the letter to the police is going to help get it then, yes, all in favour.' She hadn't realised she felt so strongly but now she'd said so out loud, she realised it was the truth.

Robin considered her words. 'Fair enough. It's not just Alan, is it? I get so worried about him that sometimes I overlook how you must feel. I'm sorry.'

She reached across the desk and took both his hands in hers. For all his faults, she did love Robin. He'd been her best friend over the past five years.

'Look, I'm worried about Alan too. Living alone in that place, surrounded by all of Claire's things still. No wonder he gets depressed.'

'To be fair, he's asked me to move in but I don't fancy it.'

They both laughed. Alice could imagine how living with his big brother might cramp Robin's style. For all the luxury of the Hall, randy Robin was better off suffering the freedom of his poky hideaway above the newsagents.

'Look, why don't we get him to reorganise the place?' It was an idea that Alice had been mulling over. 'Redecorate, chuck out Claire's old things, freshen the rooms up. He's not thrown out even a hairpin of hers. Did you know that when he gets really down he locks himself up in their old bedroom and surrounds himself with all her clothes?'

He nodded. 'You'll have to sell it to him. Only you can get him to get rid of Claire's stuff but I'll back you up. I'll help, for God's sake. I think it's a

176

great idea.'

Impulsively, she leaned across the desk and hugged him. It was a warm brother/sister sort of embrace. He smelt of aftershave and surgical scrub and somewhere in the mix, in the weave of his jacket maybe, was the scent of fire and smoke— perhaps he'd been burning autumn leaves.

'We've got a deal,' she said.

*   *   *

Seb wasn't much of a cook—he certainly wasn't the kind of cordon bleu master who could impress a young Frenchwoman who had been dining at Michelin-starred restaurants since she'd been weaned. On the other hand, he knew how to stroll into an extortionately expensive delicatessen and hand over his credit card. The result was a pretty selection of cheeses and meats and salads spread across his dining-room table. The champagne was on ice, of course, and he'd loaded the CD player with music by Ludovico Einaudi, Martine's current favourite; personally he was unimpressed by this kind of Continental weirdo stuff but tonight was going to be a special occasion and sacrifices had to be made.

He'd spent time making sure everything was just so: clean sheets on the bed, for one thing. After they'd lingered over supper he envisaged carrying Mademoiselle off to the boudoir—that's if she didn't drag him there first. After what he had to say to her, he thought that the second option was quite likely.

When she finally turned up—he knew she was going to be late because she'd called to say she was stuck on a train from London—she looked predictably travel worn.

'Champagne, *chérie?*' were his opening words, a phrase he was rather proud of. It couldn't fail to please, in his opinion.

She scowled at him as if he were an idiot. 'No. I have a headache and I feel horrible from sitting on that shitty train. I don't know why I agreed to come. Tell me what's so urgent and then I'm going home.'

Not being an idiot, Sebastian immediately recognised that the surprise he had planned for the evening might best be postponed. He was wondering how to backtrack on the conversation they'd had earlier, during which he'd begged her to come round as he had something particular to tell her, when she spotted the food. She also registered the ice bucket by the table and the gentle pulsating of a piano in the air.

She shot him a suspicious glance. 'You seem to have gone to a lot of trouble.'

'You deserve it.'

'Why?'

That was an odd thing to say. 'Because you're always cooking, making a fuss of me. I thought it was my turn. Just to show you I'm not a self-centred eejit a hundred percent of the time.'

She looked as if she might debate the point but thought better of it. Instead she stepped up to the table and snaffled a piece of smoked salmon.

'I'm starving,' she announced and broke off a hunk of baguette that he'd just crisped up in the oven.

'Sit down and take a plate. How about that champagne?'

'OK. One glass because I'm driving.'

He didn't argue. He'd get one glass down her and see how she felt then. Maybe he hadn't wasted his time changing the sheets after all.

For a slender girl she could certainly eat, he reflected. But then, she was French. She had no shame about indulging any of her appetites. And that was one of the many reasons why he loved her.

He told her so, though what he said was, 'God, I adore the way you eat when you're hungry.'

She was gobbling a drooling wodge of Camembert, shoving the dangling laces of cheese between her lips with her fingers. 'You think I am a greedy cow?'

'No. I like the way you take what you want. You just grab it and shove it in. It's so earthy. So French.'

'Ha.' She attacked a salad of couscous and pine nuts, forking it straight out of the tub and into her mouth. 'At least I am honest. You British, you say one thing and then you stitch a person up behind their back.'

He was puzzled, and not just by her mangled metaphor. Though it was true he wasn't really coming straight out with what he wanted to say.

He would have preferred to wait until she'd finished eating before he proposed but she'd just challenged him and he wasn't the kind of man to back away from that.

'Martine, I love you.'

She spat an olive pit into her hand and reached for another, as black and shiny as the eyes which regarded him with scorn. 'So you say,' she said.

'No, I'm being serious. I love you, Martine. I want to live with you for the rest of my life.'

179

She said nothing, just looked at him and spat again.

He pushed back his chair and knelt down. Might as well do this properly. 'Martine, will you be my wife?'

*   *   *

Alice sat at the dressing table in the bedroom at the Hall which her sister had shared with Alan. Nowadays he slept downstairs in a boxroom just big enough to hold a single bed and a desk, a statement of monkish intent in her opinion. For Alan, there never would be another Mrs Scott.

As ever, she found it a trifle eerie to be in a room she associated so strongly with her dead sister. She could remember spending half the morning in here as a student when she visited during vacations. Alan would be out at work and the sisters would have the place to themselves. In summer, when the weather was good, they'd open the windows and listen to the wind in the leaves of the trees outside. Claire would bring up a lavish late breakfast on a tray and the two of them would sprawl across the big bed in their nightclothes swapping news and gossip. They'd discuss Alice's progress at art school and her boyfriends of the time—though those topics were soon exhausted. Of more interest was their mother's love life, which was always lively, and their father's failures as an artist, husband and father, which was a downer. Then there was Robin's divorce, a hot topic at that time, and Claire's hopes for a baby—soon, pray God.

In a way, Alice had got to know her sister in this

room. With an eight-year difference in their ages, growing up had not been a mutual experience. But in here they'd met as adults, near enough, and become friends. It was because of that friendship and her fear of drifting rudderless after art school that she'd taken a temporary job at the clinic. And she was still here, though Claire and her dreams of a family were not.

Come on, jump to it, she urged herself. She mustn't mope, she had a job to do.

She'd imagined that Alan would resist all attempts to reclaim the Hall from Claire's memory but he'd not put up much resistance when she'd confronted him.

'Oh dear,' he'd said when she'd caught him in his office at the end of the day. 'You're coming to speak to me about something serious, aren't you? I can tell from the expression on your face.'

She nodded. 'You trust me, don't you, Alan? You know that I only want what's good for you. And that now that Claire's not here, you are my responsibility.'

He laughed. 'If you say so.'

Then she'd explained that he couldn't keep half the Hall as a mausoleum to a dead woman and that she must have a free hand to reorganise, discard and liberate all of Claire's belongings.

'Liberate?'

'In a way. There's stuff of Claire's that I'd like— jewellery, clothes, books. You told me to take what I'd like years ago but I've never wanted to. Now I think it's necessary.'

He'd nodded thoughtfully. 'Don't ask me to help, please.'

'It's OK. If I need muscle, I'll ask Robin. You

won't need to do a thing.'

So here she was, embarking on her task. It had sounded so easy when she'd first outlined the idea to Robin. Now as she slid open the top drawer of the chest in which Claire used to keep her sweaters, the fragrance of her dead sister rose up into her face and caught in her throat.

This was going to be harder than she had thought.

$$*\qquad *\qquad *$$

As Seb picked himself off the floor, he watched Martine stalk across the large open-plan sitting room towards the door. The back of his head tingled from the thump it had taken when she'd shoved him over and his anger at the assault fizzed in his veins, but still a part of him could not help admire the swing of her hips and arrogance in her stride.

'For God's sake, Martine,' he cried. 'I thought you understood English—I just asked you to marry me!'

She turned at the doorway and glared at him. Even at this distance her black eyes scorched.

'You want a big wedding, I suppose. With all my family and my father's business friends.'

'Yes, sure. I mean, if that's what you want.' He scrambled to his feet. 'But if you'd prefer a small do, that would be fine too. Just our immediate family and a few friends.' He was halfway across the room towards her. It must have been the shock that had sent her into crazy mode. French women certainly had a funny way of taking good news. But he was feeling more confident now. 'Look,

182

Martine, we'll organise it however you would like. Big or small, a wedding still counts. The important thing is that we commit to each other.'

He was close to her now, reaching out to draw her into his arms. She'd say yes and they'd kiss in a fever and he'd carry her off to the bedroom like he'd planned.

She stepped back, anticipating his move. 'Just tell me who will be your best man,' she said.

Best man? What a funny thing to ask.

'Eddie, of course. He brought us together, didn't he? Without him we wouldn't have met. Plus, of course, he's my best mate.'

'Don't you talk to me about that pig. I bet you're in it with him, aren't you? You pretend to be in love with me while he swindles my father. I hate the pair of you. I hope I never, ever see you again, you bastard.'

She hit him across the mouth, a vicious full-blooded swipe that he didn't see coming.

As he reeled back in pain, the taste of blood in his mouth, the sound of a slamming door echoing in his ears, he resolved never to try and give a woman her heart's desire ever again.

Crazy French bitch.

*　　　*　　　*

Harry Giles wasn't on nights but he was still in the CID room gone ten. It wasn't unusual for him to work late, being single and without domestic demands on his time. As a rule, though, he worked on reducing the sludge of paper admin that slowed down the river of real police work. Tonight—he could hardly believe it, but he'd promised—he'd taken on an extra burden and was thumbing through the file on the death of Claire Scott.

Things weren't exactly as he had remembered them. The bones of the incident, yes. Mrs Scott had been travelling north-west on a country lane in her silver BMW coupé when she'd been involved in a collision with a stolen Mondeo travelling in the opposite direction. Her car had come off the road and she had been thrown out. She had sustained a serious injury to her head and, by the time the emergency services were summoned to the scene over an hour later, she had died.

The Mondeo had not remained at the scene but had turned off the road before Bawtry and had been discovered in a field, destroyed by fire, south of the River Idle. The car had been stolen in Doncaster and all attempts to trace the thief had proved unsuccessful.

Looking at the file now, Harry was surprised to find that the stolen vehicle had not been as badly damaged as he had thought. A section of the interior of the car, the front passenger door, had survived the fire sufficiently to yield samples of DNA. Maybe, on reflection, this discovery and the lab report that accompanied it had not been made until some time after the accident—which would explain his failure of memory. Further notes indicated that this DNA did not belong to the Mondeo's owner.

Now, wasn't that interesting? The chances were, in that case, that the sample belonged to the thief. Unfortunately, no match had been found on the national database though the search had been carried out over four years ago. Harry resolved to instigate a new one. It was unlikely it would bear fruit but, all the same, it gave a new impetus to this once-dead case. That and the letter from Mark Presley, of course.

There was other material here that he'd forgotten too, such as the statement from Liz Pendry, the secretary who worked at the Silston horse clinic. Harry was amazed that she still worked there, given the amount of bile she threw over her employers. He remembered that he'd been tempted at the time to tip Alan off but had reckoned the vet had enough to cope with. Maybe she had learned to keep the lid on her more lurid speculations.

Earlier, Harry had been cursing Alan Scott for dumping a time-wasting case back in his lap. Now he wondered if there was a chance he might possibly be able to give Alan some good news after all. And his sister-in-law, too.

He'd not forgotten Alice.

CHAPTER NINE

Harry spotted Sarah well before she noticed him. He'd stopped by on the way to Durnside and was waiting by her garden gate as she returned from seeing her kids off to school. She walked heavily along the road, a thin energetic woman now worn down by her current burdens which, he was aware, would not be made easier by his presence. Harry had been impressed by Sarah and he felt bloody sorry for her. All the same, he had some questions.

'Good morning, Mrs Duncan.'

It took her a moment to register who he was.

'Sorry, I was miles away. What are you doing here? Have you caught those boys in the van?'

Regrettably he hadn't, they'd vanished like specks of dust on the wind. He made reassuring noises about the hunt continuing but the light that had lit up in her eyes at the anticipation of good news had gone out.

He didn't explain that he had come in search of another murderous joyrider but she anticipated his need to steal some of her time.

'Come in, Mr Giles. I'll get the kettle on,' she said as she ushered him into the house.

'Don't go to any trouble for me. I've just got a couple of quick questions.'

'Well, I need tea even if you don't. It's been a long morning already.'

He knew that these days she was the lynchpin of the family. He sat down at the kitchen table as directed.

'How are you all coping?' he asked as he considered the builder's brew she had placed in front of him.

'They'll never get over it,' she said, placing a biscuit barrel on the table.

'And the fire?' It seemed a bit too crude to ask how Jeannette's family felt about Mark's death. Did that count in the same way?

She knew what he meant.

'I don't know that I'll get over that. Mark and I had things in common, both outsiders in the family, you see. And I was meant to be keeping an eye on him. I did a great job, didn't I?'

'As a matter of fact, you did. I saw the way you held Mark up at Jeannette's funeral, not to mention everybody else. You mustn't take any of

186

this on yourself.'

'I saw he had alcohol in the house. The last time I went round, there was a bottle of vodka. I should have made him get rid of it.'

'It wouldn't have made any difference. If he was determined to drink he'd have soon got more.'

She put her mug down on the table with a thump and glared at him. 'It would have made a difference to me,' she said with emphasis and stood abruptly.

He heard her make a low sobbing noise as she rushed from the room and went up the stairs. Damn. The last thing he'd intended to do was to upset her. But upset went hand in hand with his job.

He'd finished his tea by the time she returned. Her face was pale and her eyes red-rimmed.

He got to his feet. 'I'm sorry to upset you. Perhaps we should do this another time.'

She waved him back into his seat. 'For God's sake, no. Whatever it is you want, let's get it over with.'

He sat down again and fished out his notebook. 'I've just got a few questions about Mark. Do you know, for example, where he was living five years ago?'

She looked surprised. 'I've no idea. I only met him when he started going out with Jeannette and that wasn't more than eighteen months back.'

'What do you know about his life before then?'

'Only that he used to be a jockey and got injured. Then he had a business that went under— so, not a great deal. That was one of the things Bridget and everyone had against him. He came from Belfast but there wasn't any family to speak

187

of. He was brought up by his mother, who died a couple of years ago. I think he had an elder brother but he emigrated. According to Jeannette they didn't get on.'

'Do you know when Mark came to England?'

'Not exactly. Why does this matter?'

He didn't want to tell her. She had enough to cope with without thinking her family might unwittingly be dragged into the business of Claire Scott's death. On the other hand, if anyone deserved a straight answer, this woman did.

'It's to eliminate him from another inquiry. Just a technicality, really.'

'Some crime that was committed five years ago?'

'Yes.'

'So, what's he supposed to have done five years ago?' she asked. 'Rape? Murder?'

'Don't worry, Mrs Duncan. It's nothing like that.' He got to his feet, aware that his welcome had run out. 'I've just got to check. You know, routine.'

He hated lying to her, especially when he could tell she didn't believe him.

At the door she faced him. 'Jeannette only had two proper rides in races but she was very proud of the fact that she would always be part of racing history. That's what she said anyway.'

Despite the fatigue in her face, her eyes were bright. She was a very bright woman, he thought.

'Mark was riding five years ago,' she continued. 'Won't those rides be part of history too?'

Of course they would. Why hadn't he thought of that? Raceform, the official form book of the industry, would have a record of all Mark Presley's races, with details of race order and weather

188

conditions and weight carried—more information than he could possibly need, including which trainers had given him rides. If Mark Presley had been riding at the time of Claire Scott's death, then Harry would be able to find out precisely when and where. With that information he'd be well on the way to answering the question of the dead man's past.

'Has anyone ever told you, Mrs Duncan, what an invaluable woman you are?'

At least he left her with a smile on her face.

*   *   *

Alice took Henry on a long hack up the bridle path that bordered the Hall. There was a chill in the air and a stiff breeze from the east but the fresh air was just what she needed. Clearing the bedroom had taken most of the day, what with sorting and packing and cleaning. She'd got her friend Ellen, who worked part-time in a charity shop in Rotherham, to come by in her brother's van to take away Claire's clothes, including dozens of pairs of shoes.

'These are so gorgeous,' Ellen had exclaimed as she'd examined the booty.

'Help yourself,' Alice replied as Ellen tried on a pair of black patent dress shoes that she remembered her sister bringing back from a trip to Milan. 'I can't get into them, worse luck.'

It was a pity her sister had been built on such a small scale because she'd had taste to go with her spending power and an appetite for shopping that Alice had never shared. Nevertheless, she'd hung on to a couple of summer dresses, some

189

sumptuous cashmere sweaters and, at Alan's insistence, a midnight-blue evening gown that fitted like a second skin.

'You must keep that,' Alan had commanded. 'Claire always said it was your colour and not hers. And I'll take you to the banquet after Don't Touch wins at Doncaster.'

She told him she'd look forward to it, though she didn't imagine much banqueting would be on the cards in such a dress.

As she pushed Henry up the rise through the woods to the top of the hill, she planned her next move. Having cleared the bedroom, she had an appetite for making over Alan's living quarters. And then there was the garage. He had a couple of expensive cars under wraps that he and Claire used to cruise around in. He'd never been near them since her death, sticking to an old Volvo estate that had seen better days—many of them.

In an ideal world, however, it would not be her ringing the changes in Alan's life but some other woman. Yet it would be hard for such a person to make any alterations, given the way Claire's presence still permeated every inch of the Hall.

Alan was a desirable man in the prime of his life, professionally successful and with plenty of money behind him—a middle-aged babe magnet was how Alice put it when she was out to tease. And there were plenty of babes, middle-aged and otherwise, ready to be attracted. Alice noticed them as they tripped in and out of the surgery, from the recently divorced Mrs Price, Jemma's mother, to girls who worked in the yard who were younger than Alice herself. But Alan never noticed any of them. And even if he did, the chances of him whisking them up to the Hall for a night of passion would be doomed from the start. The ghost of Claire would see to that.

Alice's plan was to turn the bedroom into a study. Such a room already existed, downstairs, overlooking the back garden. It housed a marvellous antique roll-top desk, a chaise longue, glass-fronted book cabinets and some of the best paintings in the place. Claire had spent much of her time in there, working on her various pet projects, planning fund-raising events and carrying out lengthy correspondences. It contained a computer, state-of-the-art at the time of Claire's death but now doubtless a museum piece, and an elaborate sound system. It used to be a much-loved and well-used room built for every kind of office comfort.

Alan never used the study. He carried out any paperwork on the small table in his boxroom or in the kitchen and he stuck to the computer in his office at work. Once a week, the cleaner would vacuum and dust, but otherwise the room and its possessions—Claire's possessions—were abandoned to her memory.

Suppose, thought Alice, as Henry reached the top of the path, we simply swap the rooms over. Upstairs, overlooking the front of the house, would make a fabulous room to work and read. And Alan could sleep downstairs in the peaceful room at the back, in a proper-sized bedroom for once, and the boxroom could be used for storage again.

They were out in the clear now, where the wind was sharpest but the view the finest in the area. Looking back down into the valley she could see the corner of the Hall and the grounds surrounding it. She filled her lungs with fresh air and considered that she'd made real progress with her ideas to revamp Alan's life. Maybe she was more like her elder sister than she'd thought.

*   *   *

It didn't take Harry long to find out Mark Presley's whereabouts five years earlier. That was the advantage of tracking down an ex-jockey. A call to Raceform and a few minutes on the telephone to a friendly compiler had yielded the information he sought. Mark Presley, claiming 10 lbs, had had his first ride in public at Catterick in May 2002 on a horse trained by Freddy Simpson. Subsequent outings, some half a dozen over the next three months, were for the same yard.

Harry wasn't familiar with Simpson's operation but he found a contact number on Google and was straight on the phone. The secretary at the Lancashire yard had no personal knowledge of Mark but she was keen to be helpful. She only kept him waiting a couple of minutes before she turned up the answer he was looking for.

'I've had a word with Freddy and he says Mark went off to the Hands and Heels Academy shortly after he started here.'

'Does he remember what year?'

'He says that would be five years ago, in two thousand and two.'

'Thank you, my dear, that's just what I was after.'

*   *   *

Alice was taking another journey into the past. Like the morning she'd spent in her sister's bedroom, the exercise of going through the study in Silston Hall was a trip down memory lane—and not entirely comfortable travelling. She'd not thought it would be as difficult. She did not have to battle with the physical nostalgia of her sister's clothes whose texture and smell called Claire so vividly to mind. But the study held other traps.

There were her sister's CDs, a highly personal selection of titles which reminded Alice of sitting in this room or riding in her car. Claire had liked gloomy but muscular songwriters, the kind of stuff that had never appealed to Alice—or Alan, who was strictly a Radio 3 man. She put on David Gray but as the drum and piano rhythm filled the room, even before the voice kicked in, she jabbed the Off button. She couldn't listen or she'd cry. The sense of a woman five years dead was overpowering. No wonder Alan never came into this room.

But the music wasn't an end to it. There were books, though they were easier to deal with— mostly. The paperback thrillers and old holiday reads were no problem, nor the fancy literary offerings. Many of them were presents or collected for their shelf appeal. Alice knew her sister well— she'd never seen her curled up on the sofa with a Booker Prize-winner. The reference books were tougher to deal with, volumes on furniture and painting, the many art books, some of which Alice remembered from their mother's home; some were even hers which she could now reclaim. Then there were dictionaries and encyclopedias, dog-eared volumes that had accompanied Claire since her schooldays. She couldn't possibly get rid of those.

Alice separated out the titles it was necessary to keep. All the others could go—she'd ring Ellen later.

Then she turned her attention to the desk. In fact, there were two, one simply a surface for writing and computer work, the other the handsome old roll-top that she remembered Claire buying with excitement from an antiques shop in Shropshire.

She rolled back the top, unsure what to expect. It was like lifting a lid on 25 October 2002. That was the date on the pull-off desk calendar that faced her. The pigeonholes were stuffed with envelopes and postcards, there was a mug holding pencils and ballpoints and a ceramic ashtray held a crumpled hair scrunchy, assorted hairclips and a small bar of Cadbury's fruit and nut.

A list had been scrawled in Claire's neat round hand down one side of a lined A4 pad. It started with 'dry cleaning' which had been scratched through and was followed by a selection of mundane aides-memoire—Claire's to-do list for the day she had died. Oh God. She'd only got through half of it.

Under the pad was a folder with 'Gallery Project' scrawled across it, containing a jumble of papers: scribbled drawings of room plans, city centre maps of York and Leeds, estate agents' flyers, and several pages of financial calculations. Claire's plans to open an art gallery had followed her around for years.

Next to this pile was a glossy magazine illustrated with the painting of a horse. Above the picture it read 'Cadogan Craig Auctioneers', and below, 'Paintings, Drawings and Prints, October

2002'. An auction catalogue.

A yellow Post-It note protruded from the pages.

Alice was puzzled at first. Why had Claire flagged up this page in the catalogue? Had she been thinking of buying the painting that was shown there? A horse picking at the grass in a hedgerow and eyeing a spaniel while the horse's rider smiled at the dog's owner, a pink-cheeked maid. It was a pretty scene. It was also familiar.

Alice kicked herself for being a fool. Of course it was familiar. It was strikingly similar to the painting hanging on the wall to the right of the desk. It had been Claire's favourite of Alan's pictures, which was why it hung here in her study. Alice had not seen it for five years—that was the only excuse she could offer herself for not recognising it instantly.

It couldn't actually be the same painting surely. Maybe the artist had made another one that was similar.

She turned her attention to the picture on the wall and then back to the image in the catalogue. She could see no difference in subject or tone or detail—except that one was three foot by two and hung on the wall, whereas the other was just a couple of square inches in a glossy brochure.

The catalogue entry identified the artist as 'Rawdon, Peter 1875–1914'. Of the painting it said, 'Great Minds, oil on canvas 1914.'

It was the same painting, she was sure of it. It looked exactly the same and was signed P. Rawdon in the bottom right-hand corner. And she remembered the title because Claire had explained it to her on her first viewing—'The horse has got his eye on the dog and the rider has got his eye on the girl. Great minds think alike, see.'

'Of course I see, Claire. I'm not thick.' She'd been at an age that bristled at any suggestion she might be being patronised.

'OK, if you're so clever, and since you're studying art,' Claire had said, 'tell me something about the artist.'

That, of course, had been an impossibility since, at that stage, representational art had been anathema to her, and to her teachers. More to the point, as Claire had admitted, Peter Rawdon was hardly a household name. 'But he might have gone on to be as famous as Munnings if he hadn't got himself killed in the First World War. Machine-gunned in a cavalry charge apparently, before they realised tactics had changed since the Crimea.'

That conversation came back to Alice now as she contemplated the catalogue she had found in Claire's desk. How could it be that it advertised the very picture that was hanging in this room?

She lifted the painting off the wall and took it into the glare of daylight by the window.

For a picture that was almost a hundred years old, the surface was remarkably fresh and new. Surely there would be some patina of age after all this time? But the figures gleamed and the landscape danced. Was this a testimony to the skill of the artist? Or was it an indication that what she held in her hands was not the original at all?

She resisted her first impulse to dash down to the clinic and lay her fears before Alan. Maybe there was an explanation.

She turned to the catalogue. Cadogan Craig's head office was in London. She dialled the number and was put through to someone who plainly had

196

little interest in discussing a sale that had taken place in the dim and distant past. Could she put a request in writing?

Alice supposed she could. By the time she'd finished it, using Claire's paper and pen, sitting there at her dead sister's desk surrounded by her things, she couldn't wait to get out of the room. There must be a simple explanation to the puzzle of the picture but right now she'd had enough of raking over the coals of poor Claire's life.

*   *   *

It was a good four years since Harry had last turned down the drive to Silston Hall but it felt as if he had been here much more recently. Nothing appeared to have changed, except maybe for a coat of paint on the stables. The clinic looked closed but if he didn't find Alan here he'd go up to the Hall.

As he pressed the bell for the second time, he heard footsteps behind him. He turned to see a woman walking towards him. She wore riding boots over her jeans and they sounded sharp and clear on the paving stones. A riding helmet dangled from one hand and her cheeks were flushed pink. Up close, her eyes were sea green, just as he remembered.

'Hello, Miss Young. DI Harry Giles. We've met before.'

Her smile seemed huge. There was a rash of tiny freckles across the bridge of her nose and her eyelashes were impossibly long—how could he have forgotten those details?

'It's good to see you, Harry.' Her hand had

197

found its way into his, it was hot and moist.

'Good to see you too. You're looking . . .' What? Good enough to eat? Even more gorgeous than you used to be? A million dollars? 'Very well,' he finished lamely.

'Actually, I'm a bit grubby.' She removed her hand. 'I've been for a long ride. Have you come to see Alan?'

'Yes, but I'm not getting any reply.'

'Typical,' she said. 'He'll be in here somewhere. He doesn't believe in answering the bell.'

She was correct. They found the vet in his office. He jumped to his feet at the sight of them.

'Have you had any luck, Inspector?' he said.

Harry flicked a glance at Alice who'd entered the room as well. He could vividly recall how fragile she'd been at the time of her sister's accident. Was she as keen to pore over the old entrails as Alan?

The vet caught his hesitation. 'It's OK. Alice knows about the letter.'

She nodded. 'I promise I won't burst into tears, Harry, whatever you say.'

Fair enough, he thought, and described his calls to Raceform and the Lancashire yard where Mark had been apprenticed.

'I've also spoken to the Academy. They confirm that Mark Presley started a nine-week course on the fourteenth of October 2002.'

For a few seconds no one spoke. Claire had met her death on the twenty-fifth.

Alan pulled a map from his desk drawer and opened it. 'There are only three racing schools in England. The British Racing School in Newmarket, the Northern Racing College and the

Hands and Heels Academy, both of which,' he stabbed with his finger, 'are just outside Doncaster. That's interesting, wouldn't you say?'

He would. The school was within five miles of the site of Claire's accident.

*   *   *

Alice didn't ride out at Peter Lloyd's yard every morning and, after a long hack on Henry the previous day, she would have probably given it a miss today. But she had a good reason for attending.

She hung around in the yard after first lot and waited for an opportunity to get Luke on his own.

'You know you told me you went to the HHA?'

'That's right.'

'What year was it?'

'What year? I can't remember.'

'Oh come on, Luke. How old are you now?'

'Twenty-one.'

'And you went to riding school when you were sixteen—that's what you said. Five years ago.'

He laughed. It sounded forced to Alice. She pushed on. 'And you went in the autumn after you left school, so that would make it around October two thousand and two. Is that right?'

'Are you making notes for my biography or something?'

'Don't flatter yourself, Luke.'

He turned an angry face towards her. 'I don't see that it's any of your business.'

She regretted forcing the matter but his attitude was irritating her. Why couldn't he just give her a straight answer?

'Was Mark Presley at the HHA with you in October that year? Just tell me, yes or no.'

He seemed to gaze through her, transfixed by the urgency of her demand. His brow furrowed.

'Why do you want to know?'

'Answer me, Luke.' *Or I'll choke it out of you.*

'He might have been, I suppose.'

'Is that a yes or a no?'

'Yes, he was.'

Was that so hard?

'Why didn't you say so before?' Her hands were shaking. She consciously forced herself to relax. She was frightened by the passion that had gripped her.

He shrugged. 'Honestly, I couldn't remember. Mark and I worked together at Freddy Simpson's yard and that was my first job after school. So it was like I'd always known him. Why does it matter to you so much?'

That was a good question from his point of view. She must have seemed very odd a moment ago. She didn't know him well enough to lose her rag over something like this.

'I'm sorry, Luke. It's all tied up with my sister's death so I guess that's why I get so worked up.'

'What has Mark being at the Academy got to do with your sister's death?' he asked.

She supposed she owed him an explanation. She'd been on the verge of physically assaulting him, though luckily he was unaware of it.

'It's complicated. Alan got a letter from Mark before he died.'

'Oh God.' The words seemed to burst from Luke involuntarily.

She looked at him curiously. 'Are you all right?'

200

'Yes. Go on, what did it say?'

'Mark claimed to have information about Claire's accident. He said he knew who was responsible for it and asked Alan to get in touch with him. But then Mark's house burnt down and he died before they could meet.'

'But the letter didn't give any details?'

'No. He said he now understood how Alan must have felt when Claire died and that's why he was prepared to talk about it. But he didn't actually say what had happened.'

'I see.'

'So we've been trying to work out whether Mark really could have known anything about Claire. There's a detective, Harry Giles, who's helping us out.'

'I've met Giles. He was at Mark's funeral.'

'He was also involved in the investigation into Claire's death. He's nice, isn't he?'

'He's all right, I suppose. He's racing mad.'

She laughed. 'That's Harry. Anyhow, he's found out that Mark went to racing school in October five years ago and you've just confirmed he was at the HHA with you at that time.'

'Yes?' He looked puzzled.

'Don't you see? Claire was killed just five miles away from the Academy five years ago in October. So it looks like Mark really did know something about Claire's death.'

'But now he's dead, how are you going to find out what it was?'

'I don't know. But whoever left Claire to die by the side of the road has never been identified. Five years might have gone by but there's still a chance we could find him. This is the only clue we've ever

201

had. We've got to follow it up. I'm sorry I was so pushy but this is really important to me, don't you see?'

'Yes.'

'So you'll forgive me being rude?'

'Of course, Alice. I understand perfectly.'

'And you'll help, won't you?'

He looked alarmed despite the smile that had sprung to his lips. 'What can I do?'

'Well, you were at the Academy at the same time. And you said your aunt used to work there.'

'She was one of the wardens who ran the student accommodation.'

'She won't mind talking to us, will she?'

'I don't know.'

'What's her name?'

'Lily Dougherty. She's my mother's sister.'

'Thanks, Luke. See, it wasn't that difficult.'

*   *   *

Harry meant to get back to the Claire Scott file first thing but there was a flap on and he didn't return to Durnside till gone one. He grabbed a sandwich from the canteen and took it straight to his desk.

Something was nagging at him—irritating him, if the truth were told. He'd seen the letters 'HHA' when he'd gone through the Scott papers the first time but he'd been rushing, trying to refresh his memory, and he'd not translated HHA into the Hands and Heels Academy.

Now he found the reference he was looking for. Officers had visited the racing school in the days following the accident and conducted interviews

202

with a couple of staff members. According to the notes, students were required to be in their quarters and in bed by ten thirty. On the night in question, the staff verified that all students had been present and correct, observing the curfew.

But he now suspected that Mark Presley had been one of those students and he had claimed to have knowledge of the accident to Claire Scott. That didn't mean, of course, that he was not tucked up in bed at the time—the information he wanted to pass on to Alan could have been gained secondhand—but at the very least it begged the question that perhaps Mark was not where he was supposed to be.

From Harry's experience of institutions, educational, penal and otherwise, the rules might exist but it didn't mean that everybody stuck to them.

*   *   *

Luke caught up with Seb as the riders walked back to the changing room after the third race at Leicester. He had to talk to someone about the conversation he'd had that morning with Alice but there were precious few he could confide in—only Seb and Eddie.

Seb glanced at him as he fell in step at his side but said nothing. He'd been looking pretty morose in the changing room and the others had been giving him a wide berth.

'We've got to talk,' Luke muttered.

Seb looked round. There was no one within earshot, provided they kept their voices down, but he replied, 'I don't want to talk.'

Luke ignored him. 'Mark wrote to Alan Scott. Said he was going to tell him all about the accident.'

That got Seb's attention. 'And did he?'

'No. He died in the fire before they could meet.'

'There's a stroke of luck.' Seb's voice was heavy with irony, as if luck was a stranger to his existence. 'So why are we bothering to have this conversation?'

'Because Scott has Mark's letter. He's shown it to the police. The whole thing's going to come apart.'

Seb sighed heavily, his exasperation manifest. 'Look, don't wet yourself. Nothing will come apart provided we keep our mouths shut. And I suggest you get into the habit.'

'What do you mean?'

They were approaching the door to the weighing room. Seb stopped and turned to Luke. 'I mean, silence is golden, pal. I told you I didn't want to talk and you went ahead anyway. Why don't you just eff off and keep your trap shut?'

And he pushed his way into the changing room, leaving Luke standing open-mouthed.

Kevin Foley was just behind him.

'You didn't make the mistake of talking to the champion jockey, did you?'

'What's up with him?'

'The girlfriend chucked him last night. Smacked him in the kisser, too. So he's feeling a bit sore.' Kevin's ruddy face broke into a broad grin.

Luke forced himself to laugh along, but it was an effort.

CHAPTER TEN

Luke picked up the phone and then put it down again. It was not the first time he'd steeled himself to ring his Aunt Lily and backed away at the last minute. Perhaps it would be better if he went to see her. But he couldn't pitch up out of the blue, she'd smell a bigger rat than if he just rang. He couldn't remember when he'd last visited her unannounced, whereas he did call her three or four times a year.

At least he had a reason to talk to her. Though she was a busy woman, breeding Labradors, working as a local councillor and a school governor, she retained a nostalgic memory of her time at the Hands and Heels Academy and for the lads who passed through her care. After his conversation with Alice, Luke just had to reassure himself that Lily's memories were the correct ones.

This time he completed the dialling process and after a couple of rings he heard his aunt's familiar voice, flat and nasal, but filled with warmth when she realised who was calling.

'Good Lord, it's Luke. Let me get a chair, I'm weak with shock.' There was a cacophony of barking in the background. 'Shut up, Sheba. I don't want to miss a word from my nephew's lips. I might have died of old age by the time he next picks up the phone.'

Luke put up with the familiar banter, aware that it was merited. He'd seen a lot of his Aunt Lily when he was growing up, after his dad had left home and his mum was working. He'd spent all of his school holidays with Lily in Yorkshire, where she'd opened his eyes to the joys of country life and encouraged his ambitions to be a jockey. A few years ago, she'd been the most important person in his life, next to his mother. Now, he saw her at Christmas and phoned her rarely. He deserved all the sarcasm she wanted to throw his way.

He let her get her jibes off her chest before he said, 'I was wondering if you'd heard about Mark Presley.'

Her tone changed in an instant. 'Of course I have.' There was more barking. 'Let me just put the dog out. She's almost at the end of her term and won't leave me alone—she can't bear to share my attention.'

Luke pictured Lily shepherding the big yellow creature out of the room. His memories of staying with Lily were full of dogs and puppies. He remembered carrying the little creatures around buttoned inside his shirt. He'd not thought there were any better animals in the world than horses but Lily's yellow Labs pushed them close.

'I read about it in the paper,' Lily said. She sighed heavily, 'I always thought he was an unlucky lad.'

Unlucky—that was certainly one way of putting it.

'I just wanted to warn you that the police might need to speak to you about Mark.'

'Why would they want to do that? I haven't seen him since he left the Academy. I couldn't claim even to know him these days though I'm very sad to hear what happened to him.'

'The thing is, before he died he wrote a letter

206

claiming that he knew something about a road accident that took place while he was at riding school. A woman was killed. Claire Scott.'

'That's right. A tragic business. The police interviewed us at the time to see if any of our students were involved and I was delighted to tell them that they couldn't have been because they were all in bed. You were the one who told me, don't you remember?'

Yes, he remembered it all too well.

*   *   *

Alice's stomach was in turmoil as she changed into her racing silks. It was always like this before a race. She didn't know why she made herself go through it, except that to come out on the other side of the experience, alive and kicking, was the kind of buzz nothing else gave her, no matter how she fared in the contest itself. She only managed half a dozen or so rides a year, mostly for Alan, though sometimes Peter Lloyd put in a word for her with another owner. So far this season she'd had one win and two places—she'd had worse years. But even if she came dead last in every run, she'd still ride, provided the owners let her. And every amateur she knew felt just the same way.

Today she was partnering No Account, a five-year-old stalwart owned by Alan, over a mile at Doncaster. It was a charity race in aid of the Injured Jockeys Fund and the last on the afternoon card. As such it was similar to many other events she'd taken part in and she knew most of her female competitors well. But the girl with the short, styled black hair and model's features on the far side of the room was a stranger to her.

All the same, the woman was familiar. She'd spotted those striking cheekbones and that haughty stare before. 'Martine Moreau,' another rider replied when Alice enquired. 'She's on one of her daddy's horses.'

It fell into place. She was the girlfriend of Sebastian Stone and the daughter of a wealthy French owner. It wasn't unusual for amateurs to ride their father's animals but, in this case, the horse was liable to have cost a small fortune. Indeed, Pollux, Martine's mount, was quoted as the short price favourite.

Something about that superior French stare and the notion that the girl would be sitting on a few hundred thousand pounds worth of horseflesh irritated Alice. Naturally, she always wanted to win her races, but she never felt an urge to beat a particular opponent. It was irrational, but she realised she'd get a lot of satisfaction out of finishing in front of a woman who turned up at a funeral looking like a fashion plate.

Maybe it was the extra competitive edge that had ratcheted up her nerves. She looked for an explanation as she walked to weigh out. It certainly couldn't be that Alan had told her he was expecting Harry to turn up this afternoon.

'When I told him you were riding he said he'd make a point of it. He likes a bit of a flutter, as I remember, so I expect he'll lump on you.'

Thanks, Harry, she thought. No pressure then.

*　　　*　　　*

Martine was oblivious to the other girls in the

208

changing room, even those she'd ridden against before. She believed that to ride a successful race a rider had to give it her full attention from the moment she arrived at the course. Tunnel vision was required and complete attention to detail. She was not so experienced that she could afford to relax and, in any case, it was not in her nature.

Today her focus was particularly intense because of the drama of her personal life.

Sebastian had proposed to her. She'd had suitors before but not serious ones. The son of one of her father's business cronies had made a play for her a couple of years ago in Paris. Alain had been handsome, rich and amusing but, when she looked into his eyes, she saw style not substance. And her other suitor, though undoubtedly a man of backbone, had been twice her age and a widower with two teenage daughters; she'd have had to be crazily in love to take on the role of stepmother to those two sulky bitches.

Sebastian was different. He was a brave man, making his own way in the world; a top sportsman in a game where he could become a legend. He could have had his pick of many lovely and resourceful women but he had chosen her—which proved that, *au fond*, he had good judgement, in some areas of his life at any rate. Naturally, being a British man from poor origins, he needed shaping. In their time together she had put in a lot of work and it hadn't been easy. But at least with him it was building for a purpose, she'd felt she was sculpting from marble, creating something that would last.

Until that afternoon in her father's office she would have said that a proposal of marriage from Seb was exactly what she was looking for.

But, when it had come, she had hurled it back in his face.

Now she wondered if she had done the right thing to turn him down. The timing had been so dreadful that she had just exploded like a bomb and he had taken the full force of the blast.

Thinking about it—and she had done nothing else—she remembered that she'd met Seb through Eddie and not the other way round. Eddie had undoubtedly used her to get to her father and Seb was his friend but it was hard to see why Seb would be implicated in the swindle of Tartuffe. And if he had been, if his romantic friendship with her was meant to lead her on and distract her, why would he continue to pursue her once the horse sale was done? Why, if he was involved in his friend's dodgy dealing, would he ask her to marry him?

After all, she was the one who had been befriended by Eddie. She used to sleep with him and it had been fun, part of a light-hearted friendship while they kept their eyes open for something better. She'd found Seb and Eddie had found what he'd really wanted all along—her father's money.

She'd slapped the wrong man in the mouth, it was plain; she'd wanted to take her anger and guilt out on someone and Seb had been the innocent in the firing line.

And now she didn't know what to do about it. She could crawl back to Seb and apologise. Lay the whole thing before him and ask him to take her back. And say, yes please, I would like to be your wife.

She couldn't see herself doing that.

Anyway, what would her father say? 'Your first

210

British boyfriend robs me and you want to rush off and marry the second? Are you mad?'

Something told her that, right now, her father would not approve.

Now was not the time, if ever, to crawl.

Marsha Hutton legged her up into the saddle. 'You OK?' she asked.

Marsha knew about Seb. Martine had blurted out her troubles the night she'd left Seb clutching his swollen lip in his glass-and-chrome living room. It helped that Marsha knew about Eddie's crimes, and that she was the kind of cool head in a crisis that Martine herself was not. Marsha's advice was to do nothing for a few days and to let the waters subside. In the meantime there was a horserace to ride. And though it was only a minor charity race, she was riding in her father's colours on a horse that he loved.

But he hadn't come to watch her. Martine knew she was being punished.

It made it even more important that she rode Pollux to victory.

*　　　*　　　*

Alice never regretted the time she spent riding out in the early morning and hacking around with Henry of an evening though she knew it cut into her time for her other interests, like her art. She sometimes wondered whether she could have made more of that if she spent more time drawing and painting. But, when it came to race days, she really appreciated the effort she put in.

She knew that friends like Ellen, who enjoyed a day out at the races but who'd never sat on a horse,

211

appreciated that riding a race required skill and nerve but had no idea how much physical energy was needed. To power a fully grown thoroughbred like No Account for a mile along the straight course at Doncaster a jockey had to have the kind of strength and stamina only acquired by working bloody hard. Apart from her regular rides, she tried to get to the gym two or three times a week and she also used an Equiciser, an artificial horse that Alan kept in the yard—specifically for her benefit, she suspected.

Was it any wonder there wasn't a man in her life? She didn't have time.

Already, only two furlongs into the race, she was feeling exhausted. No Account had been struggling to go the pace from the moment the stalls opened. Because he was going almost faster than his legs could carry him he was becoming unbalanced and tired, and when horses get tired the first thing that happens is that their heads go down. Alice was feeling the strain of simultaneously trying to keep his head up, squeezing with her legs to keep him laterally balanced and moving her body backwards and forwards. But she didn't dare let up for a second, not if she wanted to have a chance.

The French horse, Pollux, was leading the group of three just ahead of her and pulling away. It was quite probable, given the animal's superior form, that he would lead from start to finish, leaving the rest of them wallowing in his wake like a crew of second-raters.

Alice couldn't allow that. Even if she hadn't already conceived a dislike of the Moreau girl on Pollux, she would still have wanted to bust a gut to haul her back. Alice smacked No Account on the flank with her whip as a signal there was plenty more work to be done. *Come on, we can't let her get out of sight.*

No Account plugged on as the others around her began to tire and they overtook two of the group ahead on the stand side. Thank God there was plenty of room and no bends to worry about.

There was just one horse between them and Pollux and that animal was also labouring. No Account inched by and Alice pushed him on to make up the ground on the French girl.

Were they gaining? She thought so. At the one-furlong marker Pollux was only two lengths ahead and Alice was feeling wrung out. There seemed to be no strength left in her arms or her thighs but she knew if she slackened her effort one jot the horse beneath her would read it as a signal to ease off the gas. After all, he was knackered too.

Maybe she would have allowed things to slip if, just then, Moreau hadn't flicked a glance over her shoulder. *Yes, I'm breathing right down your neck,* thought Alice. *And I'm coming to get you!*

She gritted her teeth and smacked the horse once more for a final effort. He'd have been within his rights to ignore her but, like the game fellow he was, he lengthened his stride.

Inside the final furlong they overtook Pollux and the French girl, bulling past them with a lung-busting effort.

Gotcha! Alice shouted to herself as the winning post flashed towards her.

But her view of it was obscured by a shadow of black, Pollux and Moreau interposing their bodies to squeeze past her on the line.

She couldn't believe it. Triumph had been there

in her hand, her fingers closing on the victory, when it had been snatched from her grip—by the one person in the contest she resented losing to.

She'd never felt such a sensation of loss and frustration and rage at the end of a race before. How could she have let it slip?

They rode on past the finishing line, the horse slowing and Alice moving up from her riding crouch. Maybe it was the exhaustion that now turned her bones to jelly or the frustration of losing so narrowly, but her concentration was elsewhere. No Account stumbled and, the next second, Alice was pitched onto the ground, the breath shooting from her body as she rolled face down on the turf.

As she lay there winded, gasping for air and thinking she was about to die, hands gripped her shoulders. 'Are you all right?'

She turned her head to find the Moreau girl's sweat-covered face, eyes glittering with concern, inches from her own.

'I'm fine,' she wheezed, pulling herself up into a sitting position. Figures were rushing towards them, ground staff and handlers. One of the other jockeys had caught No Account.

Alice knew she should congratulate her opponent but it was difficult to formulate the words and the French girl got them in first. 'You were fantastic,' she said. 'That was the best race of my life.'

Alice wondered why she had taken such a dislike to the other girl. 'Mine, too,' she said.

*   *   *

Harry couldn't remember a more enjoyable afternoon—well, he could, but the final afternoon he'd spent in bed with his last girlfriend was already two years in the past. He could think of it now without that lurch in the guts that had, ever since, accompanied his memories of the long-limbed American who'd planted herself in his life for three months before announcing she was going home for good. She'd said she couldn't stick the lousy climate any longer but, since she came from Chicago, Harry reckoned that was just an excuse.

Anyhow, an afternoon at the races on his day off could not be weighed in the balance with the pleasures and pains of the heart. At Alan Scott's invitation, he'd accompanied him to Doncaster racecourse, had a look round the new grandstand, spurned the restaurants in favour of bacon sandwiches in the open air and blown his cash indiscriminately, winning on Alan's tips and losing on his own fancies. He'd thought that he was about to recoup all his losses when Alice appeared to have scored in the last but ended up clean out of pocket when Pollux stole the race.

But what had really made the day was to find himself sitting in Alice's car, driving her back to Silston Hall. Since he'd parked at Silston and travelled as Alan's passenger, it made sense for him to chauffeur Alice back after her fall. She'd claimed she was OK to drive but the Red Cross medics who'd given her a once-over had told Alan they'd prefer it if she didn't. And when Harry had volunteered, she'd turned her big green eyes on him in gratitude and said, 'OK then, since it's you.'

Now, sitting next to Alice in the confines of her little Golf, the silence was enjoyable. For all her attractions, Chicago girl had not been one to spurn the opportunity to talk.

'That was some race,' he said, a repetition of earlier remarks but the image of the two horses neck and neck on the line was vivid. 'You could watch the whole of Royal Ascot and the Cheltenham Festival without seeing such a great finish.'

'Really? I wish I'd seen it.'

'You should be proud.'

'I'd be prouder if I'd won. I really wanted to beat Martine Moreau.'

'Who?'

'The French girl on Pollux. The one with the rich owner for a father, who looks like a film star.'

'Oh, her. She's quite pretty, I suppose.'

Alice laughed. 'I thought you policemen were meant to be observant.'

Harry suppressed the reply that sprang to mind: *next to you, she didn't look that special.* It was too obvious. Instead he said, as a sudden cloudburst slowed the traffic, 'What's your opinion of the climate here in South Yorkshire?'

The green eyes narrowed, assessing the nature of his question. Then she replied, 'Actually, I think it's the finest in the world.'

It was a good reply.

*　　　*　　　*

Billy was on the door outside Splash when he saw the spotty kid. He stuck out like a sore thumb amongst the gaggle of chattering teens, done up in their finery, uncaring as the sharp evening wind ruffled the boys' silk shirts and turned the girls'

216

thighs blue with cold. Where were their coats? wondered Billy, but kids didn't believe in coats, he remembered, not from his observation of his nephews and nieces back in Liverpool.

The spotty kid had a coat of sorts, it looked like a blazer with the collar turned up. Beneath it he wore a sludgy brown T-shirt with sword and sorcery stencilling over grey trousers. Besically, it looked like he'd tried to trend up his school uniform and failed.

Billy looked for the other kid, the skinny one who'd been driving, but there was no sign of him, which was a pity.

As the boy approached the front of the queue, Lucas, who was on the door with Billy, keeping an eye open for undesirables, said, 'Sorry, son.'

'Oh, come on,' moaned the boy. 'I got my mates inside.'

Billy stepped in. He'd shaved his head and wore a skull cap and an earring. In a double-breasted suit and dark shirt and tie he bore little resemblance to the delivery driver who'd had his van nicked.

'Let me have a word,' he said to Lucas, who gave him the kind of look that said, 'Why are you interested in this tosser?'

Billy pulled the kid off to one side. He was close enough to grab him—grab him by the throat and smack his stupid head against the brick wall behind him. Only he couldn't do that. He wasn't sure exactly what to do, except he mustn't let him get away.

'You say you got friends inside?'

'Yeah.' The kid perked up. 'Go on, let me in.'

He stared into the boy's muddy eyes. His pupils

were tiny and he was swaying slightly. The little scrote was stoned. Whatever, he didn't recognise Billy.

'OK, then. In you go.'

The kid mumbled something that could have been a thank you and stared insolently at Lucas as he marched into the club.

Lucas, who suffered from bouncer personality disorder, muttered, 'Twat,' loud enough to be heard. Whether the insult was aimed at the spotty kid or him, Billy didn't know.

All he cared about was that one of the scallies he'd been hunting was inside the club.

'Give me a moment,' he said to Lucas and pulled his phone from his pocket.

The police had not been all that sympathetic to him when the van was nicked. Considering the circumstances, he supposed that wasn't surprising. DC Compton had treated him best and invited him to make a note of his number in case he should come across the two thieves.

He got Compton's number up on screen and pressed the call button.

*   *   *

Robin watched the two cars arrive and park in the forecourt of the surgery—the team were returning from their afternoon at the races. He'd looked up the result of Alice's race on the internet and hung on late to congratulate her on her second place. At least, that was the impression he wanted to give. The truth was somewhat more underhand.

He'd never taken to Giles. For all his reassuring words and heart-of-oak persona, he'd not found the driver of the car that had hit Claire any more than he'd tracked down the joyriders who'd run over Jeannette Presley.

The irony was that Giles's deficiencies were a bit of a relief. Robin didn't want the policeman getting too suspicious about the manner in which Mark Presley had met his end.

As for the inquiries Giles was supposed to be making based on Presley's letter, Robin had no great expectations. Personally he'd have tried to bury the matter, consign the whole horrible business to the past and forget it. All in all, Claire's accident had eaten up too much of their lives. He'd made this point, first to Alan and then to Alice, and they'd both ignored his advice which, he supposed, was understandable.

It went without saying that he would rather the police were no longer involved in the death of his sister-in-law. In a sense, they were no longer needed. Vengeance had already been meted out.

It was a pity that Alan wanted to push it further. Without his brother's determination, Robin was sure he could have talked Alice into letting the whole affair drop. But he'd tried to dissuade both of them from taking the letter to the police and he'd failed.

Robin wasn't big on regrets—except where some women were concerned. Since he couldn't derail the investigation, it was important he kept up with developments, followed it from the inside, if that was possible. Maybe the policeman would spill a few beans if he was handled correctly.

He could tell from the way the fellow looked at Alice as the pair of them walked into reception that Giles was stuck on her. Most unprofessional of him, though Robin didn't blame him. He'd be stuck on Alice himself if he hadn't learned a long time ago that it was not wise to mess on your own doorstep. He also knew that some women were far more useful as friends than lovers, though it had taken him a lot longer to learn that.

He shook hands with Giles and looked him in the eye. 'Good to see you again, Inspector. I wish I could have been there to see Alice's triumph.'

'It wasn't a triumph at all,' she protested. 'I got beaten on the line and then I fell off.'

'She gave him a great ride,' said Alan. 'She was beaten by a quality horse who was too damn good for that race.'

'She was bloody fantastic,' said Giles. 'Nearly pulled off a miracle.'

An unbiased view, obviously. Robin caught Alice's eye and winked. He found she was blushing.

*   *   *

Harry saw Robin's glance at Alice and realised he'd gone a bit overboard but, frankly, he didn't care. He did think Alice was fantastic and, though he'd shied away from saying so in private, in the confines of her little car, he wasn't ashamed to say so publicly.

Alan put an arm round Alice and steered her towards an open office door which, Harry knew, led to his office.

'Time for a drink,' the vet said. 'That should ease your aches and pains, my dear. We could all go up to the Hall but personally I can't wait that long. Robin, why don't you drag in another chair.'

Harry noted the way the elder brother took command and the younger followed orders. He did it with good grace, however. It was good to see brothers getting on.

Robin arranged chairs while Alan dispensed alcohol. Harry watered his Scotch to the brim and resolved to stick at one.

'So, Harry, any news?'

Alan's question was not unexpected. Harry had admired the way Alan had kept away from the subject of the investigation during his afternoon off, treating him instead like an old friend keen to get an inside glimpse of the racing world. But now he was expected to sing for his supper. Not that he minded, it was only fair.

'I've been back through the original file,' he said. 'There's a statement from someone at the racing school which says that all students were in their sleeping quarters by ten thirty on the night of Mrs Scott's death. Since the accident took place around eleven fifteen, it means that the lads at the Academy were in the clear. As you know, at the time we were optimistic of finding the culprit by other means. CCTV and so on.'

'A fat lot of use that was,' said Alan unnecessarily.

'But now we know Mark was at the school,' said Alice eagerly, 'surely that proves that students could have been involved. I mean, there's bound to be a way they could have got out at night.'

'Have you got a list of the lads who were staying there at the time?' asked Robin.

'I've asked the Academy to dig one out for me,' said Harry.

In fact, he had the list already. The school

secretary had faxed it over to him at Durnside the previous evening. It made for interesting reading. There were a few names he recognised besides that of Mark Presley, including Luke Eliot and Sebastian Stone. But Harry was reluctant to share his knowledge at this stage. He could see in which direction their thoughts were heading: Mark had claimed to have knowledge of the accident, therefore, since he was at the Academy at the time, it must have been him in the car that collided with Claire Scott.

That might prove to be the case but there were a few hoops to be jumped through before it could be stated with any authority. And connecting the name of the champion jockey, or any other former student, with such an allegation was fraught with danger. Not that Harry didn't trust his present companions, but if any of this should turn up in a newspaper it could be costly in all sorts of ways.

He would be happier when he got the results of the DNA test comparing a sample taken from Mark Presley's Toyota with that taken from the Mondeo involved in Claire Scott's accident. He'd prioritised the request.

He said as much to his expectant audience to whom it was news that DNA had been taken from the crash vehicle. They were eager for more but there wasn't anything else he could say at present.

Alice seemed to understand his predicament. She put down her glass and stood up slowly. 'Alan, I've got to go home or else I'll fall asleep right here.'

Harry seized his chance to make his own escape. He remembered that Alice lived at the Hall, ten minutes' walk up the drive—which she might not feel like undertaking in her present condition.

'I'll drive you to your door and get on my way,' he said.

She walked slowly by his side to the car. 'I'm going to ache all over tomorrow,' she said and he didn't doubt it.

He was as good as his word, seeing her to her door. 'I'd ask you in,' she began but he stopped her.

'You should get to bed,' he said.

'OK. But what are you going to do about Mark?'

He couldn't help grinning. She didn't know when to stop pushing.

'I told you. I'm going to wait for the DNA result, see if it matches Mr Presley and take it from there. You have to be patient. A few more days isn't going to make much difference.'

She pulled a face, plainly tempted to argue the point. 'I've got a suggestion,' she said. 'I've found the name of the woman who worked at the HHA five years ago. Lily Dougherty. She used to look after the student accommodation.'

He wondered why her name wasn't in the file. 'How did you come across her?'

'She's Luke's aunt. You know, Luke Eliot the jockey.'

Harry did know. The engaging lad he'd chatted to at Mark Presley's funeral. Was he close to Alice?

He shut the thought away, it really wasn't any business of his. The woman could have half a dozen boyfriends and it wouldn't be his business.

As he drove home he wished it was.

*   *   *

223

Alice eased herself into a steaming bath liberally anointed with Wild Fig and Vanilla bath fragrance, her current favourite. The name smacked of dessert in a pretentious restaurant.

Would Harry Giles appreciate her served up on clean sheets smelling of Wild Figs?

She laughed. The thought was ridiculous—and appealing.

She couldn't imagine what it would be like to have a job like his, dealing with tragedy and disaster and the worst side of human nature on a daily basis. Having the task of clearing up society's messes and getting precious little thanks when the stains couldn't be washed away. She didn't blame Harry or any of the other officers who'd failed to discover the other driver involved in Claire's death—unlike Robin who, she knew, had a low opinion of the police effort. Some jobs were just hard, she thought.

She could understand that Harry was unlikely to dash around questioning people on a case five years old in which many of the players were dead. She got the impression he was handling this on the side, in addition to his current workload, mainly as a favour to Alan and herself. And, quite reasonably, there must be things he wasn't telling them and other leads he wouldn't follow up until he was sure of his footing.

He'd made a note of the name of Luke's aunt, though she appreciated he wouldn't talk to her until the DNA result was through and he knew for certain that Mark Presley was in the Mondeo. Without that, there was no definite link between the racing school and the accident, especially since the school had given all the students an alibi. Suppose Mark had simply wanted to pass on some local gossip which he felt he should have reported to the police at the time?

That would be disappointing. Though she'd not been fully behind the idea of taking the letter to the police in the first place, now that they had done so and information had begun to emerge, she was keen to push the business along as quickly as possible.

Luke's aunt, for example. Harry might be reluctant to speak to her at the moment but she didn't see why she should be similarly constrained. She could go to see her off her own bat.

The bath water was cooling rapidly and she hauled herself into a sitting position to pull out the plug. It was an effort. As she stood and reached for the towel, every sinew in her body seemed to scream. It took an age for her to towel her body dry and make it as far as the bedroom. As she collapsed onto the bed, her phone jingled—she had a text.

Harry, checking how she was?

Robin, maybe, bored on a woman-less night.

But it was neither of them. It was Martine. She'd talked to the French girl as she'd changed after the race and they'd ended up swapping numbers.

Funny how wrong you could be about someone. She had just about enough strength to text Martine back.

*　　　*　　　*

Mr Sheriton was pissed off with Billy. He didn't shout or throw things around the office like some bosses Billy had had to endure, but he ground his jaw as he spoke, as if he was chewing the words before he spat them out.

'I don't know exactly how they do things in Liverpool, Chesil, but we have procedures here. Systems of operating that are time-honoured and well-tested and all of them go through me.'

Billy let it wash over him. He was pissed off too. After he'd called his police contact he'd tried to keep an eye on the spotty kid but that hadn't been easy. There'd been a lot going on—a fight, a drug dealer operating out of the boys' toilet, a girl having hysterics, not to mention five hundred adolescents milling around in three darkened rooms, letting off steam to deafening so-called music.

'It's not that I'm against employees taking initiative within agreed parameters,' continued Mr Sheriton, 'but those parameters do not include calling in the law when I know bugger all about it.'

That's what had really got to the boss, the fact that he'd been in the dark when a lurid red Astra with blue and yellow side panels and the legend CRIMESTOPPERS across the rear end had appeared outside. The two uniforms who'd got out had enjoyed throwing their weight about. Mr Sheriton had made it clear that this kind of conspicuous police activity was not good for the club or its customers.

But, from Billy's point of view, what hurt most was that the spotty youth had been nowhere to be found. He'd felt a right prat all the way round.

'I'm very sorry,' he said, words which did not simply refer to his communication balls-up.

Mr Sheriton sighed heavily and reached for the

door of the fridge behind his desk. He lobbed a can of Carlsberg at Billy and opened one himself.

'Cheers,' he said.

There was a moment's silence as both men drank. Billy could have repeated his tale about the spotty boy and the theft of the van but Sheriton was not the kind of man who appreciated being told the same thing twice.

'You haven't fitted in all that well here, have you?' he said.

'Are you complaining about my work?'

'Not as such, but you go about the place with a face like a wet weekend. We're in the entertainment business, my son. Lighten up.'

Billy took a long pull on his beer. He couldn't argue with the boss's analysis.

'And some people say you think you're a bit above this kind of job.'

Billy knew who those people were. 'Lucas and I don't get on,' he said. Lucas was a meathead in Billy's opinion.

Mr Sheriton appeared to read his mind. 'I admit Lucas is not the most stimulating of colleagues. However, he has worked for me for three years solid and you've not done three weeks.'

'Are you giving me the sack, Mr Sheriton?'

'No, son. I'm just telling you what I think. There are people I rate who rate you. That means you get another chance. But, next time you've got a situation, allow me to help you sort it. Understand?'

'Yes, boss.'

He understood but he didn't see what good it would do.

He'd really screwed up—again.

227

CHAPTER ELEVEN

Martine was fast asleep when the phone woke her. In her exhausted state she was tempted to ignore it. She'd exchanged texts with Alice earlier and made a date to get together—to make a friend of an English girl her own age, that was pleasing—so surely this call would not be from her.

It might be Sebastian. Very likely. It had been a few days—and nights—since their row and an acrimonious phone conversation in which she'd spelled out the reason for her displeasure. Since then she'd not heard from him. Time for his bruises to have healed and for him to be missing her very badly. Maybe she wouldn't have to do the crawling after all.

She might let him stew a little longer. While she had the upper hand, why not use it like a fist? It might put her in a stronger position for the future.

But suppose it was her father? They'd had one curt conversation since her trip to London and it was plain she was still in his bad books. Perhaps Papa wanted to congratulate her on her victory this afternoon. He'd know all about the race, that was certain, because Marsha would have reported to him by now. She was sure the call must be from him.

She reached for the phone on the bedside table. 'Hello, Martine?'

It wasn't Papa. It was a familiar voice she had no wish to ever hear again.

'It's me, Eddie. Thank God you're there.'

She was still half asleep and not thinking

quickly, or else maybe she would have killed the call right then.

'Martine, you've got to help me, there's been a terrible misunderstanding.'

She knew immediately he was talking about Tartuffe, the horse he'd acquired for her father at such enormous cost. It would be interesting to hear how Eddie was going to explain the little matter of ramping up the price at Tattersalls by bidding against his own man.

'Look, I'm sorry to call you late. I hope I'm not interrupting anything but we're old mates, aren't we?'

That was debatable but Martine had no intention of discussing their past relationship. 'Just tell me why you are calling, please.'

'God, you sound frosty. There's no need, Martine, honestly. I think you and your father have got the wrong end of the stick.'

'What about my father?'

There was a pause. Now Eddie was sure he had her attention he seemed to be composing himself. Or maybe just getting straight the lies he was going to tell her.

'He came to see me this evening. There was another man with him. A big bruiser with a bent nose.'

Gaston, Papa's chauffeur—or Uncle Gaston as Martine knew him. He had a chest the size of a domestic boiler and legs like tree trunks. She used to scramble up him when she was little as if he really was a tree.

'That's Gaston,' she said. 'He's lovely.'

'Are you mad? Your father said he'd get him to snap me in half and feed me through the paper shredder.'

'Well,' Martine was beginning to enjoy this, 'you did swindle Papa out of half a million pounds, didn't you? It's not surprising he's angry.'

'That's not true. That is the price the horse went for at auction. You were there, you know it was all perfectly legitimate. I only bought the horse on your authority.'

Mon Dieu, did he really think he could blame her?

'I can assure you, Eddie, that I wouldn't have given you that authority had I known the man you were bidding against was employed by you in your paper factory.'

There was a short pause. 'But that's where you're wrong, the man just happened to look like Joe. It's a case of mistaken identity.'

So that was his defence. She wasn't convinced. Joe Clegg's chin was pretty distinctive.

'I have seen the photographs, Eddie, and it looked like the same man to me. Anyway, how do you explain the cheque that the horse breeder wrote you for nearly a quarter of a million pounds?'

'Commission.'

'That's ridiculous. That's a quarter of what the horse is worth—more, since you artificially raised the price.'

'Look, Mr Pearce was just feeling generous. He'd had a bit of a windfall because of the other bidder and he decided to share it with me.'

'I don't believe you.'

'Please yourself but that's what happened. It's not illegal or anything. Though I bet sneaking a look at someone else's tax return is. I've a good

230

mind to instruct my solicitors to take action.'

Martine was fully awake now. Angry though she was with Eddie, he had some nerve.

'Why don't you? I would imagine my father would have a much stronger case than you.'

'Not if I told the court how he turned up uninvited at my place of business with a hired thug and behaved like some gangster. He just barged into my offices and accused me of fraud. Then, like I said, he told me that Gaston ape was going to throw me in the shredder.'

'But obviously he didn't.'

'Not yet he bloody hasn't. He's given me two days to raise half a million quid. That's mad, Martine. I don't have that kind of money.'

She laughed. His discomfort was most enjoyable. 'Don't tell me you've spent it all. The least you can do is repay your share of what you took.'

'Martine, I don't have it. It was months ago and it's gone.'

'Raise money on that business of yours then. I'm sure if you set something in motion my father would be reasonable. I would be prepared to talk to him on your behalf provided I had proof that you were honestly trying to repay him.'

There was a long pause this time. Eventually, Eddie said, 'OK. I might be able to come up with something but I can't do anything like a quarter of a mil. Will you speak to him for me? Tell him I can get him fifty grand by the end of the week.'

'And the rest?'

'Bloody hell, fifty grand is a lot of money. Like I said, it was a legitimate business deal though I admit I got a bit lucky. Tell him I'm prepared to refund fifty thousand by way of a goodwill gesture, and that's it.'

She had half a mind to tell him to get lost and she was tempted to express it more forcefully than that considering the way he had treated her. On the other hand, she needed to build a bridge with her father and maybe coming up with some cash from Eddie would show Papa she was working on his behalf. Though fifty thousand pounds was significantly short of the amount he had lost, it was serious money and it was a start.

'OK,' she said. 'I will see what I can do.'

'Thank you.' There was relief in his voice. 'You're a sweetheart, Martine, a real pal.'

That annoyed her. 'I am no friend of yours. You betrayed me. You used me to get to my father so you could defraud him. I tell you honestly that I would enjoy very much to see you beaten to a pulp by Uncle Gaston. I am only agreeing to speak on your behalf because I do not want it said that my father is a gangster. Do you understand?'

He sighed. 'Yes, Martine.'

'And one more thing. I am sure Sebastian has told you that he has proposed marriage and I have refused him. If I should ever entertain the remote possibility that our relationship might still have a future it will be on the understanding that he severs all connection with you.'

On reflection, as she put the phone down, she was pleased with that parting shot. Eddie was bound to relay some version of it to Seb and so he would know that there was still a distant possibility that he had a chance with her. Then it would be up to him to make the first move and she could negotiate from a position of strength.

She wasn't her father's daughter for nothing.

*   *   *

Alice had found out a few details from Luke about his aunt. She'd discovered that since Lily had retired from the HHA she'd turned a hobby into an occupation and was now breeding Labrador puppies professionally. So it was easy to look her up on the internet and find her contact numbers. She could have asked Luke to take her to visit Lily, no doubt, but he'd been so cagey about her interest in the riding school that she wasn't sure of his goodwill.

There was another reason she didn't necessarily want to turn up at his aunt's being squired by Luke. If she were to accompany him, the aunt would be unusual if she did not draw the conclusion that Alice and Luke were an item. And that was definitely no longer on the cards.

Taking advantage of Alan's offer to take some time off after her exploits of the day before, Alice drove to Lily Dougherty's address on the outskirts of Bawtry. She parked on the gravel drive beside a bungalow of faded russet brick overgrown by clematis and ivy. She stepped into the porch and rang the bell, feeling a bit of a fraud, having posed as a buyer in search of a puppy when she'd rung earlier that morning.

'I don't have any to show you just yet,' said the brisk voice on the other end of the phone. 'But one of my dogs is expecting a litter shortly. It's possible there may be one available—it depends on how many she has.'

'Ooh, can I come and see her?' Alice didn't have

to force the enthusiasm. She'd have had a dog like a shot if it wasn't for Henry and riding races and weekly visits to her Father and all the other demands on her time. It wouldn't be fair to take on a dog and not give him the attention he was due.

So here she was, looking forward to inspecting a very pregnant yellow Labrador and wondering exactly how to get Luke's aunt chatting about events at the Hands and Heels Academy five years ago. If it came to it, she'd simply lay her cards on the table and tell her about Claire.

Alice had been waiting for a while so she rang the bell again. She was expected and bang on time so what was keeping Luke's aunt? It would be galling to have to go home without accomplishing her mission.

Just as she was contemplating pressing the bell yet again, the door swung open to reveal a small woman in a flower-patterned blouse and jeans that fitted snugly on the hip. At first glance she looked about thirty—not what Alice was expecting at all. Had she come to the right place? But when she looked closer she noticed the fine wrinkles round the eyes and the loose skin of the neck beneath the glossy brunette bob. These days, some women appeared to defy age.

The woman was not exactly in a flap—she didn't seem the sort—but there were plainly other things on her mind than entertaining prospective dog-owners.

'I'm sorry, Alice, but can you come back another day? The moment I put down the phone from you Sheba began giving birth and I don't have time for you right now. I should have called you back but I got caught up.'

'She's having her puppies right now?'

'She's had six so far and I don't think she's finished. So I'm sure you'll understand if—'

But Alice already had her foot in the door and she had no intention of retreating, not when there was something as exciting as this going on.

'Please can I see her? I'd love to watch.'

The woman gave her a searching look; she seemed reluctant.

'I work for a vet,' Alice added quickly. 'I'm used to being around animals. It would be fantastic. Please.' She was aware she sounded about ten years old but she didn't care.

For a moment Lily looked as if she might debate the point, then she said, 'Follow me,' and pushed the door shut behind Alice. She was in.

She followed the trim, energetic figure down a long corridor, past doors to rooms which seemed cluttered with plants and books and chintz. She'd expected the place to smell of dog but there was an aroma of coffee and fresh baking. At the end of the corridor Lily opened a door into a big, sunny room whose far end had been turned into a conservatory.

'It's a bit stuffy in here, I'm afraid,' Lily said, 'but I've got to keep the puppies warm.'

Alice stared at a sizeable square, open-topped wooden box shielded by an ancient orange three-piece suite. Inside, on a bed of newspaper lay a large golden dog—Sheba, plainly—and nuzzling and squirming into her flank were several tiny light caramel shapes. Alice caught her breath.

'Oh, they're wonderful.' She sat cautiously on the old sofa. 'Am I OK here? I don't want to upset her.'

'I doubt you could upset her.' Lily took a seat beside Alice. 'She's a sweet-tempered dog. She likes me to be here though, don't you, darling?'

Sheba shifted her big soft head at the inflection in Lily's voice. She knew when she was being discussed.

Time passed in a hot, heady blur as Alice savoured the thrill of the moment and plied Lily with questions that would be suitable for a would-be owner. The breeder had relaxed now she was by her dog's side and supplied more information than Alice could possibly take in.

The upshot, of course, was that she badly wanted one of those puppies.

Sheba began to shiver.

'Have you ever seen a puppy being born?' Lily asked.

'I've seen horses and sheep giving birth. But not dogs.'

'You're in luck then. It looks like there's another on the way.'

It took about a quarter of an hour but Alice was scarcely aware of the passage of time. Lily explained that it was necessary to remove the other pups from the whelping box so the mother wouldn't hurt them in the spasms of birth.

She put them in a basket lined with towels placed in Sheba's eyeline.

'Here we go,' said Lily and Alice watched as a glistening bubble appeared between the dog's legs. 'That's the amniotic sac,' Lily explained. 'Look, you can see the puppy's head.'

So she could; beneath the filmy membrane there was a definite miniature doggy snout. Sheba pushed and heaved and the bubble grew bigger,

236

emerging in a steady movement.

'There's a clever girl,' said Lily as Sheba turned her attention to the new arrival. 'She'll clean the pup and cut the cord without any intervention from me. I like to be here though, just in case anything goes wrong.'

Alice was hardly listening. She was watching the little newborn who was already blindly rooting at her mother's breast. It was love.

'That's the one I want,' she said without thinking.

Lily gave her a sharp look. 'I don't think you should get carried away.'

'But I've just seen her being born. She has to be mine.'

'Not necessarily. I already have a list of candidates I've talked to about these puppies. You and I have only just met.'

Alice was taken aback. Candidates? It made it sound as if she was applying for a job rather than offering to buy a dog.

Lily was replacing the other pups in the box. 'I have a feeling that she might be finished now. I suggest we leave her to get some rest.'

Alice peered closely at the little family and in particular at the tiny scrap of fur she'd just seen emerge into the world.

'Don't worry,' said Lily, 'I know which one you've got your eye on. And, by the way, it's a boy.'

*   *   *

Seb left the Stewards Room at Nottingham racecourse spitting blood, having been slapped with a three-day ban for misuse of the whip. Three days for simply doing his job! It was scandalous. He'd told the old fools that Mental Oyster, the stubborn two-year-old he'd been accused of mistreating, needed a good slap on the backside to get him up off the floor in the morning let alone gallop seven furlongs. In his opinion, the animal was as stupid as his name and he was only trying to get some honest effort out of him. He was aware that the bluntness of his manner had not helped his cause.

Neither did it help his mood that Mental Oyster, if he'd felt so inclined, could have won by half a dozen lengths. As it was, the stubborn yak had refused to get down to work in the last furlong and had finished a disappointing third—which meant that Seb was still searching for a winner since the catastrophe of his evening with Martine. He'd been looking to the rigorous pursuit of his profession to lift his spirits and see him through this grim period in his life. So far he'd looked in vain.

What's more, that morning Ivan had rung to warn him that the offer of riding Jean-Luc Moreau's highly regarded Par Excellence at Newmarket next week had been withdrawn without any reason. The trainer, Marsha Hutton of course, had simply said the owner had changed his mind. And now he couldn't ride at Newmarket anyway because of this damn ban.

So this was not the best-timed moment for Eddie to appear out of the crowd and grab his arm as he was about to enter the weighing room.

'Champ,' Eddie said as chirpily as ever. 'Great to see you.'

'It's not great, actually. I don't have time to

238

talk.'

'Why not? You're not in the next. I just need a couple of minutes.'

The hand on his arm irritated Seb and he shook it off.

'Look, I haven't got a couple of minutes to waste on you. Martine's walked out on me, I'm losing rides her father promised me and I've just picked up a three-day ban—and you're the reason why.'

Eddie's grin might have wobbled but it refused to go away. 'Come off it, mate, you can't blame me if you try and flog some horse to death in full view of the beaks.'

'You know what I'm saying.'

Sebastian had made it crystal clear in previous phone conversations that he considered Eddie to blame for Martine's defection. Eddie had refuted her allegations, of course.

'But I told you, Martine and her old man have got it wrong. He's only gone sour because the horse is no good and I got a sweet deal for once. It's the truth.'

'I don't care about the truth, Eddie. I only care what they think. And they think I'm involved in your monkey business. It's called guilt by association. So I no longer wish to associate with you. Got it?'

'Wait, wait.' Eddie had his hand on him again, preventing him from going through the weighing-room doors. 'I came to tell you I've got Martine back onside.'

'I don't believe you.'

'God's truth.' The dodgy grin was gone and Seb could tell by the intensity of Eddie's grip that this was more than just a line. 'I rang her last night and

239

she's promised to help me with her dad. She's going to negotiate a repayment—sort of a kill fee so we can put all this unpleasantness to bed.'

'You're going to pay him back the money you owe him?'

'Hang on, I never said I owed him anything. It's more of a goodwill gesture.'

'The other day you said he could whistle for any money. What's made you change your mind?'

They'd moved to the side, away from the door, but nevertheless Eddie dropped his voice. 'Moreau came to see me. Just turned up at the factory. He accused me of taking him to the cleaners at Tattersalls over Tartuffe and, basically, demanded his money back. I told him what I've told you—that, you know, it wasn't what it seemed and it was unfortunate that the horse has turned out to be only average.'

'The horse is crap, Eddie.'

'But you can't pin that on me. Nobody knew that. I mean, it's racing, isn't it? Sometimes the best bred horses would come last in a snail contest and the grottiest mongrel runs like the wind. It's a gambling business, isn't it?'

'I should imagine that went down well.'

'I didn't put it like that, though I did point out that if Tartuffe was in the running for the Racing Post Trophy he'd be slapping me on the back and not threatening to break my neck.'

Sebastian found himself laughing. For some perverse reason—maybe it was finding Eddie in worse shit than himself—this conversation was cheering him up.

Eddie did not join in. 'I'm serious. He threatened me with physical violence—there was

240

some great gorilla with him. Moreau said it would take too long to drag the business through the courts and he'd chuck me in the shredder if I didn't cough. Then the pair of them went down the road and threatened my manager, Joe. Now he's got the hump with me and packed in the job. It's a right balls-up.'

'So you're asking Martine to get you off the hook?'

'She promised she would and he'll listen to her. She's a good kid.'

Gloom descended on Seb once more. He was well aware of it.

'Did she say anything about her and me? I mean, what happened the other night.'

Eddie looked Seb in the eye. 'She said you had proposed to her.'

'Yes?'

'And that the possibility of you getting married was remote.'

'Remote?'

'Yeah, sorry, mate. That's what she said.'

'OK. Thanks.' Why was he thanking this rat— this swindling, conniving, so-called friend?

Because Eddie hadn't said the possibility of marriage was non-existent.

Seb could live with remote—he still had a chance.

*   *   *

The sofa in Lily's sitting room was much more comfortable than the one in the conservatory. The room was smarter altogether with well-lined bookshelves, a vase of wine-red tea roses on a table in the window and framed photographs everywhere, mostly of dogs and young men in riding gear. Alice had already spotted a couple of Luke.

They sipped tea and ate freshly baked seed cake which, Lily explained, had nearly been ruined by the unexpected arrival of the puppies. 'You can blame Sheba if it's a little dry,' Lily said as she proffered a slice. Alice had no complaints.

She'd quickly volunteered that she was a keen rider and a bit of an amateur jockey, hoping that this would send Lily into reminiscences of her connection with the nearby jockey school. Instead she'd begun to calculate how much time Alice would have available to spend with a puppy.

'You live on your own, do you?'

Alice admitted that she did and that she had no regular partner. Also that she worked full-time—and rode her horse, of course.

Maybe she was being optimistic about becoming a dog owner. Time to change tack.

'I got your name from your nephew,' she said. 'That's him over there, isn't it?' She pointed at one of the pictures on the mantelpiece.

'You know Luke? Why didn't you say so before?'

'We've only just met really. He rides for my boss sometimes. And he spotted a breathing problem in one of the horses and we operated on it at the surgery.'

'Well, fancy that.' Lily was looking at her in a fashion that Alice had anticipated, sizing her up in a different light to puppy owner. 'I spoke to him the other day and he never mentioned you.'

'I didn't tell him I was coming to see you

242

today—it was a bit of a spur of the moment thing.'

'I see. You might mention to him, when you next see him, that it's not a difficult journey to my house. I think he's forgotten the way.'

Alice let that pass and stood up to examine the photo on the mantelpiece. It looked fairly recent. 'I'd love to see pictures of him when he was younger. Do you have any?'

That was a silly question, of course. Lily opened a cupboard door and the floodgates with it. There were two large carrier bags of loose photographs. Among them, somewhere, must be photographs of Luke at the HHA and the students who were with him. Surely that might spark Lily's reminiscences.

First, though, Alice had to be shown Luke's boyhood photos. Fresh tea was made and more cake offered, refused with regret.

Alice could have been bored, but the primary subject matter of Lily's camera, apart from her young nephew who was plainly a surrogate son, was dogs and horses. Alice loved both. But where were the jockey-school pictures?

In the other carrier bag, it turned out. When Lily nipped next door to see how Sheba and her new family were doing, Alice burrowed fast into the hoard, looking for later pictures.

'Where's this?' she asked as Lily returned. She held out a photo of a group of lads in riding clothes.

'Those are some of my boys from the Academy. I used to work as a warden up the road.'

'The HHA? Luke told me. He went on a course there too, didn't he?'

Lily agreed that he had.

'Have you got any photos of when he was

243

there?'

It took a while but Lily located them in the end. Luke in a yard mucking out. Luke on an enormous chestnut looking scared but determined.

Luke in the middle of a bunch of other lads. She picked out a dark, handsome young man staring at the camera with disdain—Seb Stone hadn't changed a bit. A cheery, grinning fellow was next to him, holding up two fingers in a bunny-ears gesture behind the boy on his other side, who was another familiar face.

'Ooh, there's Seb Stone,' said Alice. 'Who are these two next to him?'

Lily looked and her face lost some of its cheer. 'That's Mark Presley, poor lad. He died in a house fire last week. A very sad story.'

'I think I heard about it.' *Go on, Lily, tell me more.*

'He injured his foot at the beginning of the course. He stayed on hoping it would get better but it never did. He had to give up riding in the end. Look, you can see he's got his foot in plaster.'

So she could. Mark was leaning on single crutch and an unmistakable blob of white was visible beneath the right leg of his jeans.

'And who's the joker sticking his fingers up?'

Lily rolled her eyes. 'Eddie Naylor.' She said it without hesitation. It was a name she plainly remembered. 'He came from London. A Cockney charmer, slippery as they come. I wonder what he's doing now. He didn't go on to be a jockey, I know that much.'

'Was he friendly with Luke and Mark?'

'He was friendly with everybody—that kind of boy always is. Always looking for a favour, if you

244

know what I mean. But I'll say this for him, he was a great help to Mark after his injury. There were two to a room and Eddie shared with Mark. He looked after him really well, which is to his credit.'

So Eddie Naylor had roomed with Mark.

'And who did Luke share with?'

'Sebastian Stone.' Lily pointed him out unnecessarily. 'Our current champion jockey, though Luke's going to catch him in a season or two, I hope. If you ask me, it's no accident that the two students who have had most success shared a room together on that course. A lot of knowledge must have changed hands.' She shot Alice a look full of meaning. 'You seem very interested in my nephew, my dear.'

'He's just a friend.' Honestly. But she could see that Luke's aunt was sceptical.

Time to go. She scribbled down her contact details and stood up. 'Could I just have one more peep next door?'

Sheba was fast asleep and her new family were attached to her chest in a complex jumble of miniature limbs. The air was filled with a faint murmur like a buzzing of bees.

'That's a good sign,' said Lily. 'It's gone so well I think you must have brought us luck.'

Alice picked out her puppy, the little scrap of life rooting energetically on the end. Come to think of it, Scrap would make a good name for a dog.

She hadn't given up on the idea yet.

*   *   *

'Papa, do you have a few minutes?'

245

'For you, *chérie,* of course.'

So far the conversation had gone well. Martine had been afraid that her father might refuse to speak to her or Eileen would ask her to leave a message. But she'd been put through straightaway and Jean-Luc had apologised for not being at Doncaster to see her ride Pollux. 'Marsha says you were tremendous. A real fight to the finish and you came out on top. Bravo!'

He'd sounded sincere and Martine basked in the compliment. Then she remembered that he'd not been at Doncaster because he was on his way to harass Eddie.

'Papa, I had phone call from Eddie. He said you threatened him.'

There was no immediate reply and when her father spoke again there was ice in his tone.

'We had a meeting.'

'He says you turned up at his offices and threatened him with Uncle Gaston. It is not civilised, Papa.'

Jean-Luc sighed. 'Martine, he has no offices—it is a barn full of old newspaper. Gaston, as you know, is a gentle man at heart. And for one man to swindle another, that is the behaviour that is not civilised.'

'But he was very frightened. I could tell by his voice.'

'I am delighted to hear it.'

'He said you had given him two days to raise half a million pounds.'

'Half a million pounds which he stole from me.' Jean-Luc's voice was now raised in pitch. 'He has had the use of it for some considerable time. It is not unreasonable to ask for its immediate return.'

246

'But he thinks you're going to harm him if he can't pay. He believes you're a gangster!'

'Don't be alarmed, *chérie*. In business you have to talk tough sometimes. That's all it is, just talk.'

Martine was relieved to hear it. She knew there was a mean side to her father but she could not believe he would stoop to behaving like a thug. It was good to hear it from his own lips, however.

'But, Martine,' he continued, 'I don't want you to be involved with Eddie Naylor any more. I thought you understood how much he had taken advantage of you already. Leave this to me. He cannot be allowed to take my money.'

'OK, Papa, but suppose I tell you he is prepared to pay some of it back. He says he will pay you fifty thousand pounds right now.'

The silence this time was prolonged. Eventually Martine was forced to break it. 'Did you hear? I said he would pay fifty thousand pounds immediately.'

'You realise how much he owes me, don't you?'

'Of course. But why don't you take the fifty and if he doesn't pay the rest soon then take him to court for it. Fifty thousand pounds is better than nothing. Or I could say to him you must have a hundred thousand now—we could negotiate.'

This time there was no denying the anger in her father's voice as he brought an end to the discussion.

'I don't negotiate with thieves, Martine. I'll handle this matter my own way.'

And he put the phone down on her.

CHAPTER TWELVE

Alice could hardly remember the drive back to the office; she was on such a high, it passed in a blur. Thank God the roads were quiet.

'They told me you were exhausted,' said Liz as Alice bounced in. 'You're supposed to be taking the day off to recover.'

'Rubbish, I'm fine. Better than fine, in fact,' she said as she dumped her bag on her desk and switched on her computer. She was tempted to tell Liz about her encounter with Sheba and her pups but there were more urgent things to do.

As the computer booted she called Durnside police station to be told that DI Giles was not available. She left a message. Ten minutes later as she busied herself on Google, her phone chirped.

She had a text from Harry. 'Tied up now. Have news. Drink at seven? You choose place. Harry.'

She replied, naming the Black Sheep, and turned back to the screen, pleased with herself. Things were moving at last.

She was so absorbed with what she was doing that she wasn't aware of Robin coming into the room until he took the seat opposite her.

'Feeling better?' he said.

'Not you too. I only rode in one race.'

'And fell off. You could hardly walk straight last night. I thought you were going to collapse into the arms of Inspector Giles.' He was grinning. 'Did he offer to tuck you safely into bed?'

It was fortunate for Robin that there was nothing more damaging than a pencil to throw at him. He caught it neatly.

'So,' Robin said, 'did Harry tell you any more than he told us?'

'No.'

'Surprise.'

His cynicism infuriated her. 'I know you don't have a great regard for how the police have handled things, Robin, but Harry is doing us a favour.'

'Sorry.'

She knew he was only saying that to appease her. 'It's true. And it's up to us to do everything to help.'

She clicked Print and waited for the printer to whirr into action.

His eyes narrowed with suspicion. 'What exactly have you been up to?'

She couldn't keep the grin off her face. 'I've just spent a couple of hours talking to a lady called Lily Dougherty. She ran the accommodation at that riding school where Mark Presley went.'

'Did she remember him?'

'Oh yes. She was quite nostalgic. She showed me photographs and I discovered something very interesting. Mark Presley could not have been driving that car.'

'Why not?'

'Because he had his foot in plaster and was walking with a crutch. It was in the photo, plain as day. And there was a date on the back—it was definitely taken before Claire's accident.'

'Really?' Robin thought for a moment. 'So if this DNA test comes back positive on Presley, it means he was just a passenger.'

'That's right.'

'I suppose it was always possible there was more than one person in the car.'

'Yes.' She took the paper from the printer tray. 'And I've a good idea who might have been with him.' She placed the sheet on the desk in front of Robin. 'This man here.'

He looked at the photo and caption. 'Eddie Naylor?'

'He was sharing a room with Mark. He looked after him when he hurt his leg.'

'That's what this Lily lady told you?'

'Yes. She said he was a bit of a Cockney charmer who she didn't entirely trust. But she said that she was impressed by the way he had taken care of Mark. I bet he's the driver.'

Robin chewed over the information. 'I've never heard of this Naylor fellow. Is he a jockey?'

'I've just been looking him up on the net. He's now a dealer in horses and bedding for stables. He's got a company called Black Croft Equine Supplies.' She took another sheet from the printer tray. 'Look.'

Robin took the page printed from the Black Croft website.

'It's a bit of a long shot, isn't it?'

'You think so?' She was taken aback. Robin was always supportive of her hunches—unless they were way off beam.

'You've got no real proof. Just because he was friendly with Mark doesn't put him in the car, does it? How many other students were there at the time? Besides, I hate to pour cold water on your theory, but I've driven a car with my foot in plaster. It's still possible Presley acted on his own.'

Oh. Suddenly Alice wasn't feeling quite so

pleased with herself.

*   *   *

Harry arrived at the pub ten minutes late and in a mess, he'd not had time to go home and change his shirt. Yesterday's fun at the races had been wiped out by the grim reality of a pensioner now lying in intensive care having interrupted a burglar in his house in the early hours of the morning. Mr Boothroyd had been game enough to arm himself with a hammer in case of just such an eventuality. In the event it had just provided a handy weapon for his aggressor who had left him lying in his own blood to be discovered by his daughter in the morning. Harry had spent his day at the old man's gloomy terraced house, a dwelling that had seen the passage of a century without modernisation. Then he'd progressed to the hospital where Mr Boothroyd's daughter waited in a fever of anxiety and guilt. It had been a deeply depressing day.

The sight of Alice improved Harry's spirits no end. She looked spectacular in a sweater that matched the leafy green of her eyes.

'Nice jumper,' he said awkwardly.

'It's cashmere. It used to belong to my sister and I found it when I was clearing out her clothes the other day.'

'The other day?' The woman had been dead for years.

She caught his surprise. 'I've only just persuaded Alan to let me sort out Claire's things. And I'm not stopping at the house. There's cars in the garage he hasn't driven since Claire died. A sports car and

251

her BMW. He hoards things like he's living in a museum.'

'I see.' Harry felt as if he'd spent time in a museum today himself. He didn't think Mr Boothroyd had thrown out any of the late Mrs Boothroyd's things either—and she'd been gone for nearer twenty years than five, according to the daughter. 'So what's made him change his mind?'

'Me,' she said. 'And the letter from Mark. Once we find out how Claire really died he'll be able to get on with his life again.'

Harry thought that might have had something to do with it. After today's experience it was almost a relief to turn to the old dilemma of Claire Scott.

'That DNA result is in,' he said.

'And?'

'It's a match. Mark Presley was definitely in the other car.'

'Oh God.' She looked shocked.

'That's what you were expecting, wasn't it?'

'Yes, but I can't help feeling funny. If only Alan or I could have spoken to him before he died. We were so close to hearing the truth.'

Harry understood. It was one thing to hold to a theory but to see it proved was sometimes a shock.

'Now we know that's the case, I'll get on to the jockey school and see how Presley could have been out on the lash when he was supposed to be locked up. And I'll make a point of talking to Mr Eliot's aunt.'

'Actually, Harry, I have a pretty good idea what she's going to say to you.'

'What do you mean?'

She was looking a bit sheepish, but also full of herself. He could guess why.

'Don't tell me,' he said, 'you've been bending her ear already.'

'There's no law against it, is there?'

No, there wasn't, but it was irritating all the same.

'I made a note of her name last night. Did you think I didn't take you seriously?'

'Sorry. Well, I'm not really. I know you've must have a million other urgent things on your plate and this is important to Alan and me. I couldn't wait. Don't you want to know what I found out?'

*　　　*　　　*

Robin refused a top-up of champagne which caused Gloria's eyebrows to ascend magisterially.

'It's very restrained of you, darling. You know you're staying the night.'

He'd only once before slept over at Gloria's place, and that had been in the early heady days of their affair when lust had overruled prudence. Usually they spent their all-nighters at his small flat though lately she'd taken to complaining about its unwholesome nature and had insisted on being taken to a hotel. He wasn't sure what had brought about the invitation for this evening.

'All the more reason to pace myself,' he said.

'And all the more reason why I shouldn't.' She raised her glass and took a healthy gulp.

They were sitting in a living room that looked as if it had been designed by some bloke off the telly who wore ruffled shirts. Robin knew from his first visit that the white leather sofa on which Gloria perched made distracting sticky rubbery noises if used as an impromptu bed. From where Robin was sitting, his eyeline was attracted to the plunging neckline of Gloria's emerald-green dress. She looked at him with a glint of amusement in her eye. The invitation to make use of the sofa was evident.

'How come I'm now persona grata?' Robin asked. 'Are the nosy neighbours on holiday?'

She shook her head and drank some more. All amusement had vanished from her features. 'Clive's moved in with a fancy woman in Leeds.'

'Ah.' He rather wished he hadn't asked.

'Turns out that all those trips to Barcelona and Berlin were really bunk-ups on the Harrogate Road. So, why shouldn't I entertain who I like?'

'You had a row with Clive?'

'Of course I had a flaming row. I found credit card bills from restaurants all over Yorkshire when he wasn't supposed to be in the country. The arrogant swine didn't even bother to lie. He said he was in love.'

'Oh dear.' He was aware it was an inadequate response. But he wasn't sure that he was equipped—this evening in particular—to offer the kind of solace that would help.

She drained her glass and leant forward to place it on the coffee table, her dress gaping. She lifted her unhappy face and stared at him. 'Come here, you daft bastard, and give me a hug.'

He was cradling her large sobbing body in his arms when the phone in his pocket went off.

'Sorry, darling,' he said as he saw who was calling, 'I won't be a moment.' And he rushed from the room before she could stop him.

*　　　*　　　*

254

Alice knew she should have kept the lid on her urge to tell Robin 'I told you so' but their conversation that afternoon still rankled. As Harry went up to the bar to fetch another round, she made the call. When Robin came on the line he sounded a bit flustered.

'What is it, Alice?'

'I'm just having a drink with Harry and he says the DNA proves Mark was in the car.'

'That confirms what we thought.' He didn't sound all that impressed.

'And he also thinks I'm quite right to suspect that Eddie Naylor was with him. Do you want to know why?'

'I assume you're going to tell me.'

She ignored his attempt to pretend disinterest. 'Harry's got a list of other students who were on the same course as Mark. He'd already got one of his blokes doing some digging and it turns out a couple of them have police records. And guess what?'

'For God's sake, Alice, spit it out.'

She laughed. It wasn't often she went one up on Robin. 'Eddie Naylor has a juvenile record for nicking cars. Now tell me I was wrong to suspect him.'

There was a short silence on the other end of the line. Finally he said, 'Alice, you're a regular Miss Marple.'

She supposed it was the closest she was going to get to an admission that she'd been right all along. Up at the bar she could see Harry pocketing his change and picking up their drinks.

'Got to go now, Robin.'

'Hang on. Has Harry talked to Naylor?'

'Not yet. He says he's going to get hold of him tomorrow—take him down to the station for a formal interview. After all this time I think we're finally going to find out what really happened to Claire. Isn't that fantastic?'

'It certainly is. Well done, Alice. Really well done.'

At last. As Alice stowed her phone away she savoured the glow of triumph.

*　　　　*　　　　*

'That took a bloody long time.'

Gloria had switched from self-pity to suspicion in the time Robin had been out of the room. She stood, glass in hand, the other on her hip, glaring at him resentfully. But that was OK by him. He wasn't sure he didn't prefer aggressive Gloria to the tearful submissive version—he was more used to the former.

'Medical emergency,' he said, slipping into his jacket. 'A horse I operated on today has had a bad reaction. I've got to get back to the clinic.'

'What? You're going to leave me?'

'I'm sorry, Gloria. I truly appreciate all the trouble you've gone to.'

'Don't do this to me, Robin.'

'I don't want to go but I don't have any choice. We're going to lose the animal if I don't.'

Her eyes narrowed. 'I don't believe you. You've been planning this, that's why you've not been drinking. You're sodding off to that other woman, aren't you?'

Oh, for God's sake. As if he didn't have enough

256

on his plate.

'There is no other woman, Gloria. Believe me, this is a genuine emergency and I wish I didn't have to go. Especially when you're looking so tempting.' A parting compliment was wise in these circumstances. He held out his arms. 'Forgive me, darling.'

To his surprise, and relief, she stepped meekly into his arms. He kissed her comprehensively, for a moment tempted to stay and put the sofa to use. But that would hardly be the behaviour of a conscientious medical man en route to an emergency. He broke off the kiss but allowed her to cling tightly to his chest, her head on his shoulder. Just a few seconds more and he'd disengage. Then he became conscious of her fiddling with something behind his back.

'What are you doing, sweetheart?'

She shoved him away viciously, so that he stumbled on the chair behind him and fell onto the sofa.

'You really are a devious slime ball,' she shouted, her face puce with fury.

She was holding his phone. She must have fished it from his pocket while they were embracing and flipped it open behind his back. 'You weren't talking to any client, you were talking to Alice. It says so.'

'But Alice works with me at the clinic, Gloria.'

'So? She's like any other little slut after hours, isn't she? I should have known you were screwing her. You shit. You're the same as Clive and every other effing man I've ever been mad enough to invite into my bed.'

'Gloria—'

257

He knew she was going to throw the phone at him before it came hurtling through the air.

'Bastard,' she shouted. 'Just sod off and get lost.'

A champagne glass came flying at him next and he ran for the door before she chucked the bloody bottle at him too.

*   *   *

Robin drove to the nearest phone box—he didn't want his next call to be traceable. Following Alice's example, he had done some research of his own on the internet. Eddie Naylor, budding entrepreneur and thrusting twenty-first-century company owner, had his own website, packed with personal information and contact details, among them a mobile phone number.

Before he dialled, Robin took a moment to reflect on his pitch. Naylor plainly fancied himself as a businessman. If he was offered a big enough carrot surely he'd be happy to discuss a deal out of office hours. As it happened, Robin wouldn't even have to stretch his imagination to offer a plausible proposition. The Silston clinic regularly stabled horses and was always in the market for equine supplies, including bedding material. And he'd throw in the name of a mutual friend to smooth things along. Alice said Luke Eliot had been at a riding school with the fellow—that should do it.

Frankly, it didn't matter what story he came up with just as long as he got to Eddie Naylor ahead of the police.

*   *   *

258

Eddie hadn't heard from Martine and hadn't been able to raise her on the phone. He suspected she was ducking his calls. Surely she must have spoken to her father by now. He'd made arrangements to transfer the money to Moreau's bank but fifty grand was a hell of a lot of lolly to whang off into the blue without something in writing to go with it—like a letter agreeing that the money was a final settlement of an unfortunate misunderstanding and in no way implied any liability on his part. He hoped Martine had made all that clear. Otherwise her Froggy father could whistle the *Marseillaise* out of his jacksie and he'd not see a penny.

These thoughts swirled around Eddie's head as he loaded paper and stacked bales in the old barn. At least he was doing something useful. Things had got rather behind since the French delegation had turned up. Not least because of Joe's defection. He tried his best to get his former manager back on the job but he wasn't having any of it. The Frogs had well and truly put the wind up the old feller. Eddie suspected that they'd also put in the poison about the size of his cut. He'd paid Joe five hundred for his day out at Tattersalls and told him his own end was only ten per cent. If Moreau had told Joe that Eddie and the dealer had split nearly half a mil, that would explain why the old fool was so hacked off. Jesus, you tried to do a bloke a favour and he kicks you in the teeth. When had a sad sack like Joe Clegg ever earned five hundred pounds in one day?

Still, he wished the old bugger was down here with him now. Maybe he should have offered him a cash incentive to come back to work. It was a bit creepy being in here on his own.

He'd locked the barn door which, as a rule, stood open to let the dust and noise out. He had a twenty-four-inch leader wrench tucked under the work bench and a shotgun stashed behind his office door. He'd cleared a way through to the emergency exit at the back of the barn; if Moreau's heavies turned up at the front he could be out the back and away down the footpath on the old bike now hidden in the bushes. It wouldn't get him far but he reckoned that, once away in the woods, he'd be more than able to give the slip to some lumbering thug from the city.

Part of him felt pretty silly about the whole thing. Jean-Luc Moreau was the kind of businessman who got profiled in the money pages of the broadsheet newspapers. He was well known because of his racing connections and was wheeled out regularly on radio and TV when he had a runner in the Arc or the Derby. He might be tough but he had a legit reputation. Surely he wouldn't want to chuck all that away by behaving like some gangland boss. Logically, Eddie would have had more to worry about if Moreau had not turned up in person. No matter how angry the Frenchman might be, Eddie couldn't believe he would seriously dirty his hands.

All the same, he thought of the French bruiser by Moreau's side the other evening, his eyes as dull and expressionless as old centime coins. He looked capable of tearing a man's arm off with his bare hands, whatever Martine might say about him. Lovely Uncle Gaston my arse.

As he was checking that the shotgun and wrench were in place for the umpteenth time, he was startled by a sudden noise. The ringing of his mobile. He really had to pull himself together.

'Mr Naylor?'

He didn't recognise the voice but it sounded cultured—certainly not French, which was a relief.

'Who wants him?' he replied.

'I'm a vet. You don't know me but we have a mutual friend, Luke Eliot. He tells me you specialise in equine bedding. I do apologise for ringing out of hours.'

'Not out of hours for me, mate. I'm still at work.'

'Marvellous. Maybe you can help me out, I'm in a bit of a spot.'

Eddie was fast concluding his plummy-voiced caller was a twit, not that he had any objection to doing business with him. Especially when he went on to explain that he was a partner in a Doncaster veterinary business with overnight stabling facilities.

'You see, our regular supplier has rather let us down. Sent us some really shoddy stuff. Luke says you're top-notch. I was wondering whether I could get some samples to show our yard manager.'

'No problem. I can get over to you tomorrow.'

'That's frightfully kind of you. But suppose I drop by this evening? I've just finished a call near Selby—that's close to you, isn't it?'

Eddie agreed that it was.

*   *   *

Robin drove down unlit country roads with no signposts, missed turnings and doubled back twice. Finally he located the correct turn. There were lights on in the big barn and the sound of machinery. *Found him.*

He put on a tie and checked his appearance in the driver's mirror. He wanted to look respectable. Unthreatening.

He had his vet's bag in the boot. He took an item from it and placed it carefully in his jacket pocket.

He just hoped Naylor was on his own.

*　　　*　　　*

Eddie might not have heard the banging on the door if the shredder had not come to a halt. For a moment he was frozen in shock. Was this it? Had the French hitman come for him?

'Hello! Mr Naylor?'

An upper-class English voice—that vet bloke. He'd certainly taken his time. Eddie unlocked the door and yanked it open.

The fellow in the glare of the floodlight looked perfectly benign, baggy jacket, collar and tie—what you might expect from a vet, to be honest. What's more, he was on his own. Eddie felt a bit silly.

'Come in,' he said. 'Sorry you had to shout through the door but I'm here on my own. We get lads out thieving sometimes.'

The man looked at the bales of paper quizzically. Probably thinking you'd have to be some desperate thief to want to take those. He smiled and held out a business card. 'Robin Scott. How do you do?'

Eddie peered at the card. Scott appeared to have a whole alphabet of letters after his name and was a partner at some place called Silston Equine Hospital. Impressive.

'You know Luke?' he asked.

'Not well but he's been around the surgery recently. I had to do a tie-back op on a horse he rode at Beverley. Luke spotted his breathing difficulties, which was smart of him.'

'And he gave you my name?'

'Sang your praises loud and clear.'

Fancy Luke putting some business his way. He owed him one.

'Do you want to have a quick look round then?'

'I'd be fascinated.'

Eddie led his visitor inside and launched into an explanation of the shredding and bundling procedure, complete with a demonstration. The vet seemed genuinely interested.

'That's impressive,' he said over the noise of the machinery as the first bundles of paper appeared, wrapped and ready for transportation.

Eddie allowed the load to pass through and then shut the shredder down. He'd done enough for the night anyway. Once he'd dealt with this guy he'd be off home.

He pulled up a couple of rickety chairs and they sat by the bench. 'What else can I tell you?' Eddie said.

'There's one thing. The most important thing.'

'Fire away.'

'Were you involved in a road accident on the night of the twenty-fifth of October two thousand and two?'

The barn seemed to tilt sideways. It was about the last thing Eddie had expected him to say.

The man leaned forward, thrusting his head into Eddie's personal space. He no longer looked benign.

He spoke again. 'Were you in a car on a country

263

road south of Doncaster that hit a BMW and forced it off the road?'

'I don't know what you're talking about.'

'I think you do. You were a student at the Hands and Heels Academy and you went out with your room-mate Mark Presley. The pair of you ended up stealing a Mondeo in Doncaster. He had a plaster cast on his foot, so you were driving when you hit the other car. Then you drove off without reporting it and the woman in the BMW died. You must remember surely.'

'No.' His face was flushed. This man was staring at him with eyes like searchlights, reading the guilt there. Who was he? Some kind of private detective? 'I don't know where you got this but it's a complete lie.'

'So you didn't share a room at the HHA with Presley and you didn't help him when he injured his foot?'

'I wasn't with him that night, I swear. I know nothing about it.'

'Come off it, Eddie. It's obvious you're lying. If I can see it that clearly, imagine how it's going to be when Detective Inspector Giles of the South Yorkshire Police gets hold of you. He's coming to arrest you tomorrow, I believe.'

'Clear out. Just go away. You're freaking me out.'

'I intend to. I want you to fully understand the position you are in. You have been living a lie for five years but it's all about to come out in the open. The police have DNA evidence from the Mondeo you stole.'

Oh shit.

'What the bloody hell business is it of yours?'

264

'You haven't been paying attention, Eddie. My name is Scott. My sister-in-law was called Claire. My brother Alan has never recovered from her death.'

Oh shit, shit.

'Look, I never killed her.'

'So you admit you were in the Mondeo?'

'I'm not admitting a thing.'

'Give it up, Eddie. I'm not the police. Poor Claire is gone. I just want my brother to feel better about his life. You help me and maybe I can help you.'

Eddie had been rapidly calculating. There was the shotgun in the office—he could blow this guy's head off. But what was the point if the police had his DNA from the car? Horrible though it was going to be, holding his hand up for driving away from an accident five years ago would not be the end of the world. Unlike going down for murder.

'How can you help me?'

Scott seemed to relax a fraction, he leaned back in the chair, his demeanour less threatening now he'd received a tacit admission of Eddie's involvement.

'As a family, we've never had any details of the accident. That hurts. I want to be able to tell my brother what really happened. Neither of us is interested in persecuting a couple of kids who panicked and drove away from the scene. Frankly, I can understand how someone would do that.'

'So how could you help me?'

Scott considered his words before he spoke. 'Claire has a sister who this policeman, Giles, is rather sweet on. If Alice goes to Giles and begs him not to take it any further, he might listen to her. I can assure you that the family don't want a court case. They don't want the whole business aired in public again. Even if Giles pursues you, I reckon we could persuade him not to drag you into custody. Maybe there's a way of dealing with the matter in a low-key way.'

Eddie was struck dumb. Was it possible he could wipe the slate clean on the whole sorry business? That would be fantastic.

'OK, I'll tell you what happened.' What had he got to lose? 'First off, you've got to realise it was a genuine accident. It was a nasty bend and we were both going fast. She came straight at me.'

'So you were driving?'

'Yes. I swerved and we clipped each other and she went off the road. I pulled over further down. I was going to get out and see if she was OK when another car came along and stopped.'

'What kind of car?'

'I don't know. Some old-fashioned sporty thing. A bloke got out and went to look at her lying on the ground. We reckoned there was nothing we could do so we drove off. Bloody stupid I know, but we panicked.'

Scott nodded. 'That's understandable.'

'I'm not proud of it. We should have stayed and reported the accident but we reckoned the other fellow would do that. And considering we'd nicked our car, we thought we'd better scarper. We didn't know she was going to die. I was amazed when I heard it on the news. Honestly, we were not responsible for her death.'

'For what it's worth, Eddie,' the vet said. 'I believe you.'

Confession is good for the soul—Eddie had

never pondered the truth of that before. He did now and the pent-up emotion of five years overwhelmed him.

'Jesus, I'm sorry,' he said as he closed his eyes to hold back the tears.

So he didn't see what hit him.

CHAPTER THIRTEEN

Harry was glad he wasn't doing the driving. The task of finding Black Croft Equine Services belonged to DS Gerald Ferry of the Cold Case Review Unit. Ferry—who, naturally, everyone referred to as Bryan—was approaching the end of his time on the job, though such was his expertise in shedding light on unsolved crimes that Harry had no doubt they'd be hauling him back as a civilian investigator before he'd get a chance to put in any serious work on his golf handicap.

Harry had told Alice about the Cold Case team last night in the pub and she'd been thrilled to hear that they were taking another look at her sister's death. 'But you'll talk to Eddie personally, won't you?' she'd asked.

'I certainly will,' he'd said.

So here he was with Bryan at eight in the morning bumping down an overgrown and rutted country lane without signposts.

'You could always turn on the GPS,' Harry suggested.

Bryan gave him a lugubrious look through his thick-rimmed spectacles. 'And end up in the bloody river?' he muttered. 'No thanks.'

They'd been on the road for an hour already, having paid a visit to Eddie Naylor's home address, a development on the outskirts of Castleford where the cars in the forecourt were no more than two years old and there was not a child seat in sight. Harry had pegged the place as a haven for aspiring singletons. Their quarry had not been at home.

'Bet he's overnighting with some bint,' had been Bryan's opinion, reviving a term Harry had not heard for some years. But Bryan was a bit of a dinosaur in most respects.

Naylor's place of business turned out to be a looming old barn next to a muddle of clapped-out farm buildings and identifiable only by a small white painted sign pointing off the road. Bryan turned into an area of unpaved dirt and gravel and parked next to the only other vehicle, a black Audi convertible which looked utterly out of place in these bucolic surroundings. Naylor's car—it had to be.

There was no bell by the door and the low thump of machinery from within the building masked Harry's knock. He banged louder. The door yielded under his fist and eased open an inch or two. Harry gave it a good shove and stepped across the threshold.

'Hello! Mr Naylor!'

Striplights blazed overhead despite the sunlight flooding in from skylights set in the roof. They were confronted by what looked like a labyrinth of newspaper stretching towards the back of the barn, a grubby forklift truck barring the path into the maze. Harry took in a work bench, a conveyor belt on the move and a flimsy partition wall but there was no sign of Naylor. The air was thick with hanging particles and dust lay upon every surface. The whole place stank.

'Strewth, what a tip,' Bryan murmured.

Harry strode across the filthy floor to a door in the wall. Here was Naylor's office, with desk and filing cabinet of the bog standard variety, a garage giveaway girlie calendar on the wall and a dartboard on the back of the door. And something more ominous leaning against the wall.

'Here, Bryan, look at this.'

Harry supposed it was reasonable a man might keep a shotgun by his desk in this setting—you could probably pot a rabbit in the car park. It ought not to be left out like this, of course.

'Bryan!' he called again.

The sergeant finally appeared. His face was as impassive as ever as Harry pointed to the shotgun.

'I wonder if he's got a licence? And I don't see a gun cabinet anywhere. Might be a bit of leverage if he's not keen to answer questions in the Scott case.'

Bryan said nothing in reply, which was odd. He was never short of an observation.

Harry looked closer at the other man. His face was not so much impassive as rigid with emotion. Harry realised Bryan was struggling to speak.

'Are you all right, Bryan?'

'I found Naylor.'

'Good, where is he?'

Bryan turned back into the barn and pointed to the rattling machinery. Harry was confused. There was no sign of Eddie.

'It's an industrial shredder, guv. Turns paper into bales of horse bedding.'

269

'Yes?' Harry was walking towards the thing. He could see a moving belt, though it carried no load, some metal casing and a Perspex cover. 'So where is he then?'

Then his eye fell on the Perspex but he couldn't see through it. It seemed streaked and spattered on the inside with a dark substance. Oil maybe? But flecked with red and black specks. At the same time the odour that had enveloped him from the moment he'd stepped into the barn thickened in his windpipe and he knew with horrible certainty what had petrified his companion.

Licence or no licence, Eddie Naylor would not be answering any of their questions.

*   *   *

The phone call from the auctioneer's took Alice by surprise. She'd forgotten about the mystery of Claire's painting.

Mr Craig Senior sounded very remote from his colleague, in years and style and, it transpired, in location.

'I'm sorry it's taken so long to get back to you,' he said. 'They had to forward your letter from the office. I don't go into London much these days.'

Alice wondered whether this old codger was going to be much use.

'You say you want to discuss a painting by Peter Rawdon that we sold a few years ago.'

'That's right.' Alice had not gone into much detail in her letter. 'It was called "Great Minds". A man on a horse looking at a girl with her dog.'

'Oh I remember that one. A lovely thing. Some might say it's a bit pretty in a Victorian story-

270

telling way. But I think it's got an underlying edge to it that's typical of Rawdon. The horse is looking at the dog as if it's wondering whether to kick it and the man is looking at the girl in a similarly predatory fashion. It's not the idyllic scene it first appears—there's trouble in Paradise, just as there was in 1914 when it was painted. I'm sorry, I'm bumbling on a bit.'

'No, Mr Craig, I'm delighted you remember the picture so well.'

'Rawdon's always been a favourite of mine. So, how can I help you, Miss Young?'

'What's puzzling me is that I am sitting in a room in Silston Hall in Yorkshire and on the wall is, as far as I am aware, the original painting called "Great Minds" by Peter Rawdon. Yet I have just discovered a Cadogan Craig catalogue of October 2002 offering the same painting for sale. I'm sure you can understand my confusion.'

She waited for an answer. When it came Mr Craig did not sound as perplexed as she might have imagined.

'I'm just looking up the sale,' he said. 'I have my own records, don't worry. Though the most reliable, if you forgive me, are maintained in my own head. Yes, here we are. Rawdon's "Great Minds" was sold at auction in the autumn of 2002 for six hundred and twenty-five thousand pounds.'

'How much?' she blurted. She'd always admired the painting but she'd not realised it was that good.

He repeated the figure. 'It was a fair price. There aren't that many Rawdons around and it is believed this is the last picture he made before he enlisted. I would imagine it would go for rather more if it came on the market today.'

271

'Is there any chance the picture you sold was a copy of the one here now?'

'Not in my opinion.'

Alice pondered. She wondered how reliable he might be. 'I suppose I could get another opinion.'

'Oh, certainly. But,' a soft chuckle punctuated his words, 'though it is immodest of me to say so, I believe I am the foremost authority on the artist. And what I saw, I am convinced, was by his hand.'

There seemed no arguing with that.

'Can you tell me who sold the painting?'

'We were acting on behalf of Mr Scott—of Silston Hall. You will be acquainted with the gentleman, I assume.'

'He's my brother-in-law.'

'In that case, I suggest you address any further queries to him. I might add, however, that this situation is not unfamiliar to me. I have come across people who wish to sell their art but cannot bear to have it vanish completely from their walls. So they commission a copy and discreetly sell the original. Sometimes their nearest and dearest don't discover the subterfuge until after the seller has passed away.'

Alice put the phone down, lost in thought.

*　　　*　　　*

After reporting Eddie Naylor's death, it had taken Harry half the day to extricate himself from the clutches of the local police. Naylor's horse-supply factory was in Selby District, part of the neighbouring North Yorkshire Police. Fortunately, the senior detective on the investigating team, DI Appleyard, turned out to be a pal of Bryan's.

'You think you've come across everything in this business,' he had said, 'but I've never seen a bloke turn himself into eighteen-inch cubes before. He might have spared a thought for the poor sods who have to clean up afterwards.'

'You think it was suicide?'

'I think the daft ha'p'orth tried to unjam the compressor rod without turning the machine off. But we mustn't rush to judgement, must we?'

There had been much in his ponderous manner that reminded Harry of Bryan.

'Dave Appleyard,' the sergeant was saying as he carefully laid a selection of photographs across his desk back at Durnside, 'used to be on my darts team down here until he transferred out. Must be eight or nine years ago.'

'Just get on with it, Bryan.'

Harry was in a rush because he'd just had word that Arthur Boothroyd had died in hospital that morning so he was now part of a murder inquiry. He had only five minutes to spare on the Claire Scott review.

Bryan finally regarded his display with satisfaction. 'I went through the post mortem report last night.'

'Really?' Harry hadn't paid much attention to that. The poor woman had hit her head when she'd been thrown from her BMW and had died from the wound. It had been dealt with at the inquest.

'The pathologist was Professor Desmond. That mean anything to you?'

'Not much. He retired years ago, didn't he?'

'He retired in January two thousand and three. Rather hastily. There'd been a couple of blips and he was pushed out of the door smartish when they came to light. The poor old boy was in the early stages of Alzheimer's and his last few months on the job were, let's say, a bit slapdash. Recently I've been looking at one or two cases in which he was involved.'

'And?' Bryan liked to take his time and Harry didn't have much of that to offer.

'Basically, he says Claire Scott died as a result of striking her head on the ground when she was thrown from the car.'

'Yes. The BMW crashed through a wooden fence on the side of the road, hit a tree and turned over. She was thrown out of the car and found beneath the trees.'

'At the beginning of the report he says there were wood splinters from the fence buried in the wound but he doesn't mention them in the conclusion.'

'So? The splinters were on the ground where she hit her head.'

'But the wound was two inches at its deepest and sharp-edged.'

Harry was puzzled. 'Are you saying that her injuries couldn't have been caused by her being flung onto the ground?'

'I'm just wondering how she could be found with splinters from the fence buried in her head when she was inside the car when she hit it.'

Bryan pulled a couple of photographs from the file. Harry was familiar with the pictures of the scene. Claire was lying on her back on the grass. The ruins of the broken fence lay all around.

'You're telling me you think someone whacked her over the head with a piece of fence timber after she was thrown out?'

The sergeant allowed himself a small smile. 'It would account for the nature of the wound, guv.'

So it would.

*   *   *

Luke heard about Eddie's death from the gateman as he arrived at Newmarket. Rumour flashed around the changing-room like sparks in a sun-baked forest. There was no other topic of conversation.

Luke kept his mouth shut. Eddie was dead. He couldn't think straight. It was as if his thoughts could not hurdle that impossible fact. Eddie was larger than life, a personality who breezed through the world and made light of its burdens. He wasn't someone who was stupid enough to fall into a paper-shredder.

Around him, the shock was wearing off and the jokes were being cracked. References to Eddie no longer being too big for his boots, about his affairs being wrapped up and him finally being cut down to size. Black humour—that was one way of dealing with the situation.

Luke avoided joining in and the others respected his silence. They knew he was a friend of Eddie's, closer to him than anyone else in the room apart from Seb—and Seb was absent, serving out his ban for misuse of the whip.

Luke was profoundly grateful that Seb was not sitting opposite him today. He'd steered clear of him since Leicester, when Seb had told him to keep his trap shut. And he'd observed at a distance what looked like a similarly bad-tempered exchange between Seb and Eddie at Nottingham, just after he'd earned his ban.

But suppose Seb wasn't just reacting to the ban when he'd rowed with Eddie? Suppose he'd told Eddie to keep his trap shut too, and Eddie had told him where to shove it? It wasn't impossible to imagine the two of them falling out. Since the death of Mark's wife, everything had gone a bit pear-shaped.

The thing was, it all came back to the car crash that had killed Claire Scott. Four of them had kept the secret for five years but now, suddenly, two of them were dead.

Was that just a coincidence?

Luke was damned glad Seb was not anywhere in sight. He'd changed recently. As he'd got more successful he'd got more ruthless.

Ruthless enough to kill two of his friends?

Luke couldn't say for certain. But the thought was there and subconsciously the whole business affected his riding, sapping his concentration. He was slow out of the starting stalls in the first race and never made up ground. In the second he got boxed in and made a vain attempt to go up the inner which came to nothing. In the last race of his afternoon, he left his bid too late and was second on the line. 'Not your afternoon,' said Peter Lloyd as he helped Luke dismount.

He apologised, ashamed of his performance but also uncaring. How could he be expected to concentrate on riding when he felt he was a marked man?

Just he and Seb were left alive from the four who'd shared the secret. If Seb got rid of him then his position as champion jockey and everything that went with it would be secure. Was Seb tough enough to do such a thing?

He wouldn't bet against it.

Luke sat in his car at the end of the afternoon and debated where to go. He'd be a bloody fool to go home. Seb knew where he lived.

*   *   *

Alice had spent the afternoon at the clinic, trying to put the matter of the painting to the back of her mind as she worked. But the issue wouldn't go away.

Should she speak to Alan about it? She didn't want to embarrass him and, if he had sold the original, he was entitled to do so. But it was listed in the insurance policy along with the other art and there didn't seem much point insuring a copy. She'd helped him with the paperwork so she knew the sums involved weren't negligible.

But that was a detail. She wanted to know why he had sold Claire's favourite painting but she wasn't sure she had the nerve to ask.

She waited till Robin was finished with his appointments and then she made them both coffee.

'I need your advice,' she began. She laid the Cadogan Craig catalogue on his desk, opened to the Rawdon page.

'I found this among Claire's papers.'

He raised an eyebrow and sipped his coffee.

'You may or may not remember, but this painting is hanging in Claire's old study—at least something similar is. I've been on to the auctioneers and they say they sold the original. On behalf of Mr Scott of Silston Hall.'

He nodded. 'I see.'

'I don't know what to do. Should I mention it to Alan? I don't want to upset him—it was Claire's favourite picture.'

Suddenly he grinned. 'Good copy though, isn't it?'

'You know about it?'

'Of course. I'm the Mr Scott who sold it.'

'I don't understand.' And she didn't. She sat down heavily in the chair on the other side of his desk and tried to formulate the right questions. He saved her the effort.

'It was Claire's idea. When Alan took her off to Italy that summer she asked me to have it copied and get the original off to the auctioneers. The copy was in place by the time Alan and Claire got back. He never suspected.'

'But why?'

'She wanted the money.'

'What for?' But as she asked the question she had a good idea what the answer would be. 'Was it the art gallery?'

He nodded. 'She'd found a place in Leeds. Good space, good area, good terms on the lease. But Alan wouldn't cough up the money so she came up with this scheme.'

'I didn't realise she'd got that far. I thought it was just a dream, something she might get around to doing if she never had children.'

He shook his head. 'She was dead serious. We talked about it quite a bit. She was going to show some old stuff of your father's and a couple of new kids she'd discovered. She was hoping that maybe you'd take your art more seriously and produce some pieces for her.'

278

'She never said anything to me about that.'

'It was going to be a surprise.'

She stared at him, lost for words and, in a funny way, jealous. Why had Claire confided in Robin about this and not her?

Because Robin could fix it for her. He was a most plausible Scott of Silston Hall. Also, and sometimes she had to remind herself, Claire and Robin had a history. It was Robin, not Alan, she'd gone out with first and she was well aware of Robin's louche past. If she'd wanted to pull off a painting scam it made sense that she'd turn to her brother-in-law.

'But how did she think she could get away with it?' Alice asked. 'Alan would have gone mad if she'd gone against him like that. And she was pregnant. How did she think she could get an art gallery up and running with a new baby to look after?'

'Everything was already in hand by the time she found out about the baby. She was determined it wasn't going to stop her. Sure, Alan would have kicked up a fuss for five minutes but she'd have got round him in the end.'

Alice reflected that that was probably how it would have been. They were always having rows. Alan was famous for blowing his top but Claire was used to weathering the storm, and when it had blown over, she was invariably the one who had got what she wanted.

All the same, to steal the picture from her husband was not what Alice would have expected of Claire. It was underhand.

Her disappointment must have shown in her face.

'I'm sorry,' said Robin. 'But you've always put Claire on a pedestal.'

She didn't argue the point. 'How was she going to explain to Alan where the money for the gallery had come from?'

'From Edwin.'

'But my father doesn't have money. His pictures don't sell any more. They make about enough to keep him in materials and pay the Grovelands bill.'

Robin smiled wolfishly. 'You know that but Claire was going to convince Alan that some eccentric old art lover had come up with a new commission. A millionaire recluse from Texas or someone suitably unavailable. He'd have fallen for it.'

'What were you going to get out of it?'

'Half what it sold for. I was post-divorce at the time. Financially wounded, so it was tempting.'

'And what happened to Claire's share when she died?'

'I didn't know what to do. I mean, I couldn't give it back or pass it on to Alan without him getting suspicious. What I've tried to do over the years, honestly, is plough the money back into this clinic.'

'And that's where it's gone, has it?'

'Some of it, yes. But I had to get myself straight. There were debts, and the school fees and the settlement and everything. Money is like water, isn't it? Somehow you can't keep it in your hands.'

'Robin, the painting sold for over six hundred thousand pounds!'

'Was it that much?'

'You're hopeless, you know.'

He shook his head and sighed. 'I'm sorry. Promise you won't let on to Alan.'

280

How could she? She would be tarnishing the memory of the woman he'd worshipped for so long. She fervently hoped that he would never ever take too close a look at the painting that had once been Claire's favourite.

'I promise,' she said with ill-concealed bad grace.

*   *   *

Luke luxuriated in the familiar pleasures of his aunt's home. Hot tea, homemade cake and new-born puppies were familiar to him from his youth and couldn't be bettered.

Lily had not shown any surprise when he'd turned up unannounced at the door.

'I'll put the kettle on,' she said after he'd kissed her. 'Sheba's down the end with her new brood. Go and see for yourself.'

The dogs were brilliant, as always. He particularly liked the little one who tried to chew off his finger.

'That's Scrap,' said Lily as she brought in the tea. 'At least, that's what your lady friend called him.'

Luke stopped tickling the little fellow's tummy. 'What lady friend?'

'Oh. So she hasn't told you about her visit? Blonde girl, messy hair, pretty enough. You could do worse.'

'Alice.'

'That's the one. She came here to give me the once-over, pretending she wanted to buy a dog. Then she had me fishing out old photos and I thought she was interested in you, but I might have

281

got that wrong too.'

'What do you mean?'

'The photos she wanted to see were taken at the Academy when you were there. She had lots of questions about who roomed with who and who palled up together—that kind of thing. She was very interested in poor Mark Presley. You know why, don't you?'

'No, Aunt. She must just have been curious.'

'Don't you treat me like a fool, Luke.' The tone of reproach was familiar. 'She's not the only visitor I've had asking about what went on at the Academy five years ago. I've had a policeman here for an hour this afternoon eating my cake so you'll not get seconds.'

Jesus, Harry Giles had been here?

'What policeman?'

'Does it matter? Here's his card. Detective Sergeant Ferry.'

The name meant nothing to Luke.

'And what did he want?'

'He said he was reviewing the death of a woman who had been in an accident with a stolen car at the time you and these other lads were at the Academy. Did I remember it? I told him of course I remembered. The warden gave a statement to the police that none of our students could have been involved because the accident took place after lock-up at half past ten. She made that statement on my say-so.'

Luke nodded. This was getting uncomfortable.

'And I gave that say-so, now I look back on it, on the word of my nephew. Four of you had the end rooms and you told me the others had turned in. Now I understand that at least two of them had

282

gone off to Doncaster. More fool me but I never checked with my own eyes. But then I didn't think the boy I knew would lie to me. I'd have sworn on my mother's grave, Luke, that you would never tell me a deliberate lie.'

Luke took a deep breath. 'I'm sorry.'

'Sorry? Sorry is not good enough. A woman died and you were part of it. You covered up a crime. You can't make it better by saying sorry to me.'

'I know that.' He reached for the policeman's card that she held in her hand. 'I'll call Sergeant Ferry tomorrow.'

'No more lies, Luke. Tell him everything you know. I suppose you thought you had to stick by your friends but they should never have asked you. To my way of thinking, they weren't friends at all.'

He turned the slip of cardboard over in his fingers. She was right. They weren't true friends. And now two of them were dead. And the third was probably scheming how to take him out of the picture too.

'Can I stay here tonight, Aunt?'

For a moment he thought she was going to say no. He really was in the doghouse.

*   *   *

Turk had to hand it to Scab—or Les as he'd promised to call him tonight. Just when you decided he was the world's biggest loser, no question, he did something that amazed you. Like when he'd whacked that ginger-headed van man with his clipboard or mooned the girls on the coach. But tonight was his best ever.

Scab had talked Turk into coming to this poxy

kiddy club, said it was a good place to score and the lasses were tasty. Well, they'd missed the chance of getting hold of any dope. There'd been a raid a few nights back and so there was nothing to be had, which meant getting through the evening on orange juice or Coke, since they didn't sell any proper booze. And, in Turk's opinion, the girls were no better. They might look all right at a distance but up close they were just yappy Year 8s, some almost as spotty as Scab.

Then, just as Turk was thinking they should leg it, Les pulled one of his strokes. When Turk got back from taking a leak, he found the scabby one sandwiched between two stonking hot lasses. As he welcomed Turk he tried to act as if he was used to hanging out with girls with legs up to their armpits and lads-mag front bumpers but Turk knew better. Not that he was complaining.

The girls talked funny—they were Poles, said Scab. Ola and Kassia. Ola, the taller of the two, seemed to have attached herself to Scab and was already leading him off to dance. Which left the flaxen-haired one with freckles for Turk. Life was no hardship sometimes.

The girls could put it about on the dance floor, which was fine by Turk who was pretty nifty himself. Scab looked his usual shambolic self but Ola didn't seem bothered. It was a right laugh.

Back in the bar things got even better.

'You want?' said Kassia, holding her hand open to show some small white pills.

'What are they?' asked Scab.

Magic beans. Disco biscuits. Ecstasy. Must be.

She giggled. 'We all take one?'

'Yeah, sure,' Turk said and popped one into his

mouth.

Scab pulled a why-not? smile and gobbed a pill too.

They looked at the girls.

'I need a drink,' said Ola, 'to swallow.'

She looked appealingly at Scab who took the hint.

The two boys pushed their way to the bar. 'Got to hand it to you, Les,' said Turk. 'You've enhanced your reputation tonight. How did you hook up with them?'

Scab was grabbing bottles of mineral water off the counter.

'She just came over to me, then she called her friend. Call it animal magnetism.'

Just at that moment Turk would have called it whatever Scab liked.

The girls were keen to get back to the dance floor.

And that was where, in a kaleidoscope of whirling lights and sounds, amidst a mass of heaving bodies, things went tits up.

Turk's head was hammering to the music and his arms and legs were jerking—at least he thought they were until he looked down to find he was standing still. These were funny kind of Es—they seemed to make you sleepy.

He was bumped and jostled and found himself falling. It was interesting. Took him a long time to hit the floor. He was resting on top of someone else. Kassia would be nice. Not Kassia though, or Ola—scabby old Les, worse luck.

'Where the girls go?' he asked. But Scab didn't answer. Jesus, he looked like shit. Like he'd fainted or something.

Then hands grabbed him. Strong hands lifting and carrying him away from the lights and noise.

He hoped they'd put him somewhere he could sleep.

CHAPTER FOURTEEN

It was a rare day that Harry Giles's belief in the essential goodness of human nature was affirmed. But this, praise be, was turning out to be one of them.

First off, after twenty-four hours of wrestling with her conscience, a woman had turned in her younger sister's boyfriend for the murder of Arthur Boothroyd. Since the man had arrived at her house covered in blood at four in the morning and ordered her to mind her own business or her kids would get it too, Harry wondered what had kept her so long. He and the rest of the team were grateful, nevertheless. The burglar had been arrested with Arthur Boothroyd's wallet in his possession and would be charged within twenty-four hours.

As a result, he'd been able to join DS Ferry in the interview room to hear what Luke Eliot had to say. The jockey had appeared by appointment with a solicitor in tow, recommended, Harry gathered, by his aunt who had been instrumental in urging the lad to come and tell his story.

It was a good day for the public conscience, for once.

Harry injected plenty of warmth into the welcome he gave Luke. Though this was a formal occasion, they were acquaintances and had friends in common. He thanked Luke for volunteering to help the inquiry without adding that it would have been even more helpful five years previously—but they all knew that.

The jockey began his tale without apologies or a hand-wringing preamble. Good. Enough time had been lost in this matter already.

'There were four of us on the course at the Academy who sort of teamed up. Mark Presley, Eddie Naylor, Seb Stone and me. To be honest, I rather tagged along. I was sharing a room with Seb who was a pretty experienced rider already. I was a bit in awe of him but he was really good to me. It got to the end of the second week and Mark had an ankle injury—his foot was in plaster. He was having a miserable time so Eddie suggested they take him out to cheer him up. Seb asked me if I'd mind covering for them and I agreed.'

'What did that entail?' Bryan asked the question.

'Lock-up was at ten thirty and we were supposed to be in bed. All I had to do was stop the warden on duty from finding out that the others weren't in their rooms and leave a window open for them to get back.'

'And the warden on duty was Lily Dougherty?'

'That's right. My aunt. So it was easy for me to tell her that the others were in bed at lock-up time. She believed me—she had no reason not to.'

'What time did the others leave?'

'I should think they were gone by eight. They'd arranged for a taxi to pick them up out on the road.'

Harry frowned. The investigation had slipped

up there. They should have located that taxi driver.

'And what time did they return?'

'It was around midnight when Seb got back with Mark. I was in bed but I heard them come in so I got up. Mark was in a bit of a mess because he'd fallen when he'd got back in the grounds. They were obviously a bit drunk, I had to tell them to keep the noise down. I asked where Eddie was and they said he'd be along soon. Then I went back to bed and Seb said he was going to talk to Mark. I heard him coming back into our room at about four in the morning and I asked if Eddie was back yet and he said yes. All three of them were there at breakfast and seemed OK.'

'Did they tell you what they'd been up to?'

'Not really. I gathered they'd done a round of the pubs and tried to chat up a few women.'

'Did they say how they got back to the Academy?'

'The night before, when I asked, Mark said they got a lift and Seb said, "An Eddie sort of lift," which they both thought was funny. I assumed that maybe Eddie had found a girl with a car who'd dropped the other two off and then he'd got off with her—which would explain why he didn't get back till later.'

'Go on.'

'The next day we heard about the road accident and a woman dying. I didn't make the connection. Seb came up to me that afternoon and told me to keep my mouth shut about them going on the lash, which I thought was a bit out of order because I'd no intention of saying anything. Then later on the three of them got me on my own and said that things had got a bit out of hand when they were

288

trying to get back and that if I let on they'd been out the night before I would basically stuff their careers and ruin their lives. I asked what had happened and they said it was best I didn't know. By then I'd guessed it was to do with the crash and said something like, "So Eddie nicked a car, did he?" and they went dead quiet. So I knew then that they'd been in the car that had driven off from the accident. I freaked out because they were saying on the news that they had left a woman to bleed to death by the side of the road and maybe if they'd at least called in she would have lived. But they told me it wasn't like that.'

Luke paused and the solicitor, a senior gent with an avuncular air, asked him if he was OK to continue. Bryan quickly offered a cup of tea but Luke shook his head.

'They told me that this other car was going too fast as it came round the bend and they couldn't avoid it. They clipped sides and the other car went off the carriageway so they stopped further down the road. Then they reversed back to see what had happened. I think a few minutes had gone by, because they'd argued over whether to go back or not, and by the time they got back to the bend, there was another car there.'

'Another car?' Bryan's tone was casual but Harry could tell that he was intent on every nuance of the jockey's voice.

A third vehicle. There'd never been any suggestion of such a thing. This was significant.

'Another car had stopped by the first, which was now off the road under the trees. They said the driver had been thrown out and was lying on the verge. And as they sat there wondering what to do, a man got out of the second car and knelt down by the person on the grass. Seb said he was sure he saw the person move and when he said so, Eddie just drove off. They were worried about being in the stolen car, over the limit, which is bad enough I know but it's not like callously leaving someone to die—which is what was being said on the news.'

'Did you suggest to them,' said Bryan, 'that they should come forward and give their side of the story?'

'In a way, I suppose. But they weren't up for it. It was much easier for everyone to keep quiet about it. So we made a pact, all of us, not to say anything. And, believe me, I bitterly regret it. It's been like a curse hanging over us—that's what Mark thought anyway, especially after Jeannette died. And now he's dead and so is Eddie. I even started thinking that Seb was going around bumping them off so they didn't talk.'

Bryan made a note on his pad. 'Are you alleging that Seb murdered Mark Presley and Eddie Naylor?'

Luke smiled for the first time. 'No, I'm not. It's ridiculous. But I panicked a bit yesterday when I heard about Eddie. All I could think of was that Seb and I were the only ones left and if I died his secret would be safe.'

'In which case,' said Harry, 'you've done the right thing in coming to see us. There's no point in killing the cat when it's out of the bag, is there?'

Luke thought about that for a moment and laughed nervously. 'But that's not why I came. I just wanted to make a clean breast of everything.'

The solicitor spoke up. 'My client is aware there may well be repercussions to his statement and is

290

fully committed to helping the police in their inquiries.'

'It's a pity it's taken him so long to come forward then, isn't it?' Bryan's tone was pleasant but there was no overlooking the sting in his words.

'That may well be, officer, but you must bear in mind his age at the time—he was only sixteen. And though his loyalties might have been misplaced, it would have been very difficult for him to lay evidence against his older, more influential friends.'

'Bollocks,' said Bryan.

There was an awkward silence broken by Luke. 'Look, I've done it now and I'll take the consequences. May I go?'

'Not just yet, Mr Eliot.' Bryan turned the page of his notebook. 'Would you like to tell us a bit more about this other car?'

*   *   *

Martine's mind was not on the horse she was riding. She should have cried off sick this morning or made some other excuse to Marsha. As it was, she'd set off too fast and was labouring a long way before the end of the gallop. She was inclined to blame her mount—Tartuffe, the object of so much grief. First, disappointment on the racecourse, then the discovery of the price-fixing scam at auction and now this—Eddie's murder. It was ironic. If Tartuffe had been as good as he was cracked up to be, none of it would have happened.

The newspapers and television weren't referring to Eddie's death as murder; so far it was just a 'bizarre accident' but she knew better. Soon, she had no doubt, they would be calling it what it was.

Martine vividly remembered the dinner in the restaurant when Seb had described Eddie's paper-shredding plant with so much glee. At the time she'd been irritated—it was in such bad taste. But Papa had been amused. He would not have forgotten.

Eddie had told her himself that Papa had threatened to throw him in the shredder. Those had been his words and that was exactly what had happened to him. Good God, what a way to die.

She'd never honestly believed her father would carry out his threat. How could she? It was barbaric and Papa was not a barbarian.

But he could be cruel and he never backed down from his threats, as she knew to her cost from many small events in her childhood. Though having her new birthday dress cut to pieces in front of her eyes was not a small thing when she was nine. And there'd been other punishments which had served their purpose over the years, for she had learned never to disobey Papa.

Was it possible her father could have carried out his threat against Eddie? Not personally, of course, but there were men like Uncle Gaston who were used to bending their backs for him.

But Papa had reassured her that his threats were just talk—tough talk. Could Gaston have taken Papa's words literally?

She'd tried to intervene, not to get Eddie off the hook but to persuade her father to deal with him in a civilised fashion. And Papa had dismissed her. 'Let me handle this matter my own way,' he'd said. She was afraid that that was just what he had done.

The worst thing was she had nobody to talk to.

Marsha was on hand and a good friend. Martine looked on her almost as her English mother. But Jean-Luc was off limits as the subject of any intimate conversation. Martine had learnt early on not to notice where her father slept when he stayed overnight at Marsha's farmhouse. And Marsha never discussed her personal relationship with the man who owned many of the horses she trained. She was even more blindly loyal to Papa than Martine was herself. So it would be foolish to suggest to Marsha that Jean-Luc might have had anything to do with Eddie's death.

Of course, the one person she ought to be able to rely on was Seb. If only she had not taken her bad temper out on him, then he would have been her confidant. He could have reassured her and soothed her and told her she was being silly to think such terrible things.

She deeply regretted the way she had treated Seb. He had proposed marriage to her and she had slapped his face. For no reason really—except that she was angry she'd been fooled by his friend and that Papa blamed her. So she'd told him he was not good enough for her. That was funny, considering she was probably now the daughter of a murderer.

Eddie would have talked to Seb. He'd have told him about Papa's visit and his threats. So Seb would be aware of the truth—and he wouldn't want to know her now.

She'd acted like a fool but that was nothing compared to what her father had done.

Poor Eddie.

*　　　*　　　*

Alice hadn't heard from Harry and that bothered her. Their drink in the pub had turned into dinner in the upstairs dining room and their conversation about DNA and Lily Dougherty had become a discussion about abstract expressionism.

'I'd like to meet your father,' he'd said as he pushed his empty plate aside. He needed the food since, as he confessed, he'd been surviving on sugared tea and digestives. He refused to go into the case he'd been working on—'Can't you forget I'm a policeman for a bit?' he'd asked. She'd complied and it had been worth it.

'You can come with me one Sunday if you'd like to meet Edwin,' she said. 'He won't talk to you, though—doesn't even talk to me.'

'It would be nice to be in the same room as a major artist. I've seen his paintings in galleries.'

She wondered if he'd been spinning her a line, but he hadn't. Edwin's work was still shown in Liverpool and Glasgow but only the stuff from the sixties. It was a pity he'd destroyed so much of it.

'I've sometimes thought,' she said, 'that he'd have been better off dying forty years ago. Everyone has hated his work since then. It's driven him mad.'

Harry had surveyed her thoughtfully. 'If he'd died forty years ago, you wouldn't exist and that would be a shame.'

She liked Harry a lot, she decided. Though it was confusing wondering how she ought to think of him. Was he simply a friendly professional investigating her sister's death or was he becoming a real friend?

She'd not rung him since the other night and he'd not called her. What was she entitled to expect in these circumstances?

When they'd parted company he'd been intending to interview Eddie Naylor. But Eddie was dead in a grotesque fashion which the press had played up gleefully. She wanted to know from Harry what he thought about this unfortunate coincidence, but was she entitled to harass him to find out? He knew her interest and he'd be in touch when he could, surely. She didn't want to add to his burdens.

The door to her office banged open, interrupting her train of thought.

'I want a word with you,' announced an angry voice. A tall figure with wild red hair and pink flushed cheeks confronted her from the doorway. Gloria. 'What have you done with him?'

'Do you mean Robin, Mrs Harper?'

'Of course I bloody do, you little tart. You're screwing him, aren't you?'

Oh, for God's sake.

'No, I am not.'

'What about the other night then? You rang him and he came running. And that's not the first time I've been left in the lurch while he's gone off with you.'

'I don't know what you mean.'

'Bitch.' Gloria took a deep breath, as if she were restraining herself with great difficulty. It seemed to Alice that she was torn between hurling herself at her with murderous intent or collapsing in tears.

She did neither. Instead she turned for the door. 'Just tell him, I'm expecting him,' she said softly. All the aggression seemed to have left her as she stumbled out.

What a flake. Alice was sorry for her but, all the

295

same, it was ten minutes before her hands stopped shaking.

*   *   *

Seb couldn't believe it had come to this. Mark dead, Martine gone from his life and now Eddie. Mangled to death in that grim paper machine he'd been so proud of—just as he had feared.

In the light of that it didn't seem such a disaster that two detectives sat in his living room questioning him on the subject that he'd dreaded discussing for five years. In the shadow of recent terrible events he could even understand why Luke had crumbled.

They'd told him that at the outset.

'This morning Luke Eliot made a voluntary statement concerning the death of Claire Scott in a road accident in October two thousand and two. It's only fair to tell you that he was accompanied by a solicitor and that your name was mentioned.'

Seb heard what the sergeant with spectacles said but his eye was on Harry Giles, the copper who'd been at Mark's funeral. He'd seemed a reasonable enough guy then, keen on racing at any rate.

Giles spoke. 'What we're saying, Mr Stone, is that we can do this down at the station and you can have a lawyer present. Or you could give us your version of events here and now in more relaxed circumstances.'

Seb didn't think about it for long. He didn't want to be spotted going into a police station if it could be avoided. It would only take some sharp-eyed fellow on the desk to lift the phone and all the papers would have it. Champion jockey arrested. It wouldn't stay on the racing pages either.

So here he was, finally about to spill the beans about that stupid accident. He wondered what Luke had told them. His side of it, Seb supposed, though that wasn't much. Luke's involvement had been second hand. Seb was the only one left alive who'd actually been in the crash.

He told them the truth. Eddie had nicked the car, just spotted the keys to the Mondeo left in the driver's door. Short of leaving a sign saying 'Steal me', there couldn't have been a bigger invitation to take it. Since they'd failed to find a cab or a bus and with Mark limping along on a crutch, it was a temptation they couldn't resist.

'Eddie just took charge and pushed us inside. It felt like a lark, really. He said he'd drop me and Mark and then dump the car some distance off from the Academy. We asked how he was going to get back and he told us not to worry. He'd nick a bike or hitch a lift. Anyway, he did the driving. He must have been a bit pissed—we all were—but it seemed like he did OK.

'He had his foot down a bit when we went round that bend and it was bloody lucky we didn't end up off the road as well. Mark was in the passenger seat and I was behind Eddie, looking over his shoulder, so I saw these headlights coming straight at us in the middle of the road. They were coming quick and we couldn't get out of the way. There was a crunch behind me, a loud horrible metal bang and I knew we'd collided. We swerved towards the verge on our side but Eddie managed to keep us on the road and we came to a stop about a hundred yards on where there was a lay-by. He pulled in and we just sat there. I was suddenly stone-cold sober. I remember thinking, oh my God I nearly died. I've ridden lots of horses and had one or two falls where I've lain on the ground and thought I was paralaysed for life, but I've never been as terrified as I was in that car.'

Harry looked suitably impressed. The other one, Bryan, just said, 'Then what happened?'

'We discussed whether we should go back. Eddie had turned off the headlights when we stopped. Mark said we ought to go back but Eddie was paranoid about being caught with the car. He said he didn't want to get involved with the other driver because they'd want insurance details and things—even though it wasn't really our fault. While we were talking I was aware that another car came past, really quick, from the same direction as the one we'd hit. I don't think the other two noticed, they were busy arguing. Anyway, we decided to reverse and see if the car we'd hit was OK. So that's what we did.'

'Without lights?' Bryan asked.

'Yes. Eddie didn't want us to be seen. And he was driving so it was up to him. Anyhow, we got close enough to see there was another car already there. It must have been the one that passed us while we were off the road.'

Seb thought they might have been surprised by this revelation but they weren't. He'd kept his eyes on Harry and got the impression that this was what he was expecting. So Luke had already passed on the information.

'There was a woman lying on the ground and a man kneeling beside her. I assumed the woman had been in the car we hit. The man looked quite tall, plenty of hair, could be thirty or forty. It was hard to tell. Once we saw he was there, looking after the other driver, we drove off. In retrospect, it was an enormous mistake but Eddie said we mustn't hang around.'

'You didn't think of coming forward the next day, when you'd had a chance to reconsider your hasty departure from the scene of an accident?' Bryan's tone was gentle but his eyes accused.

'We were too scared. We'd have been hung, drawn and quartered.'

Harry stepped in. 'Can you describe this man's car?'

Seb was on safer ground. 'A sports car—very nice. Two-seater convertible, low on the ground, with a long front. White or yellow, I'd say—a light colour anyway.'

'Do you like cars, Seb?' Harry looked interested.

'Sure. I've got an Alfa Romeo though I wouldn't mind an Aston Martin.'

He caught the look on Bryan's face and wished he'd kept his mouth shut. The boring sod probably drove a Mondeo like the one they'd nicked.

'What I mean is,' said Harry, 'do you know enough about them to recognise the car this man was driving?'

Seb didn't mind blowing his own trumpet. If he ever went on *Mastermind* he'd be better on cars than horses. 'I reckon it was a Morgan. A plus four or plus eight—it had that kind of look.'

'Thank you, Seb.' Harry got to his feet. 'You've been very helpful.'

Bryan looked like he was just getting going with the third degree but he reluctantly closed his notebook.

'Is that it?' Seb asked.

'For the moment. It's not over, however. We'll be wanting to talk to you again.'

He'd get a lawyer next time. Seb was beginning to regret having allowed this informal conversation to go ahead—but there had been reasons.

'Can I ask you about Eddie?' he said.

'What about him?'

'I mean, was it really an accident?'

'Have you any reason to think it wasn't?' Harry said.

This was his opportunity. He could tell the police that Jean-Luc Moreau had had Eddie killed because he'd swindled him over the purchase of a horse. But he didn't. Start that kind of talk going and he'd find himself caught up in a price-fixing scandal. It was going to be bad enough when this crash story came out. And there was another reason. Despite the way she'd treated him and his fear of Moreau, he loved Martine. If he had any hope of ever mending their rift, it could not be him who pointed a finger at her father.

But he still wanted to know about Eddie.

'No reason at all,' he said in response to Harry's question. 'It's just that first Mark dies in a fire, then Eddie in this weird accident. I'm the only one left alive who was involved in the crash with Claire Scott. It makes me feel a bit . . .' His words tailed off.

Bryan grinned. 'I think I'd be a bit worried in your position too, Mr Stone.'

'We'll be in touch,' said Harry. He was grinning too as he made for the door.

*   *   *

'That was a bit naughty of you, Bryan,' said Harry as they drove back to Durnside.

'He deserved it. He's only interested in saving his own neck.' There was satisfaction in Bryan's tone.

'He's got a point, though, about the other two lads. It seems a mighty big coincidence that the pair of them should die within a few days of each other.'

'Bad karma. What goes around comes around.'

Harry considered his colleague's words. 'You sound remarkably like Alan Scott. The way he used to talk about the driver who'd left his wife to die, he'd have been happy to administer that kind of karma personally.'

Bryan flicked a glance at Harry as he drove. 'What are you saying?'

'Nothing really. The fact is that we know now that, however stupid and selfish those boys were, they didn't kill Claire.'

'The driver of the sports car, you reckon?'

'It has to be.'

'But why?'

'Quite. You'd have to be a complete fruitcake to stumble across a road accident victim and whack them over the head for fun.'

'Plenty of fruitcakes in the world, guv.'

They drove on in silence, Harry's thoughts working overtime. 'The BMW was going fast. The sports car was also going fast from the same direction.'

Bryan was following him. 'You think one car was chasing the other?'

'It's possible, isn't it? If Claire was trying to escape then the accident stopped her getting away.

301

The man in the sports car was able to catch her.'

'And seized his chance to kill her?'

'Yes. He sees her lying on the ground, picks up a handy length of timber and smashes her head in. And the lucky bastard gets away with it until now.'

Bryan slowed for the traffic. They were approaching the station. 'Why now, do you think, guv?'

'Because Mark Presley wrote to Alan Scott. After the death of his own wife in a car accident.'

'So I'm right,' said Bryan as he pulled into the station car park. 'Karma. What goes around comes around.'

Harry couldn't disagree. There was a link here and he had to find it.

'Do me a favour, will you?' said Harry as they headed for the CID room. 'Find out the latest in the Eddie Naylor investigation.'

Maybe Seb Stone was right to be fearful for his life.

*   *   *

Robin felt like a man with a leaky roof and one bucket. No sooner had he rushed to stem the flow in one place than trouble rained down in another.

So far there had been no repercussions from his visit to Naylor's bedding factory. The story had even disappeared from the day's headlines and a police news conference announcing a murder inquiry had not come about. So maybe he'd got away with it—again.

But no sooner had he stopped the flood there, than there was another breach. Alice and her bloody tidying up. He'd not thought there would be anything incriminating in Claire's things. It was infuriating to think that at almost any time in the past five years he could have walked into her study and removed that catalogue from her desk. But he'd not known it existed.

Well, he'd done his best with Alice. She'd not want to blacken her sister's name with Alan and so she'd keep her mouth shut. She'd better.

His flat was a pigsty, he was happy to admit, but domestic housekeeping was not high on his agenda right now.

So where had he put that carrier bag? Somewhere safe, he knew that. Even in the desperate exhaustion of the moment when he'd got back from Presley's place, he'd placed it out of sight.

The doorbell rang. That was all he needed. He ignored it—he had no time.

Had he put the bag under the bed? He pulled out a box of books and shoved aside a jumble of shoes and trainers. No.

The bell was ringing again, loud and insistent. This was no casual canvasser or passing tradesman. He heard a voice shouting through the letterbox at the bottom of the flight of stairs.

Gloria. He might have known.

He'd been ducking her calls and counted himself lucky he'd not been in the clinic when she'd turned up and bad-mouthed Alice. But he'd been fooling himself to think the woman would give up. She was hardly the type.

'I know you're in there,' she was shouting. 'I can see your bloody car.'

He had no choice. Maybe he could just keep her on the doorstep.

He opened the door and blocked her entrance. 'Gloria, sweetheart, this isn't a good time.'

'Why not?'

'I'm in a rush. I've just got to pick something up and get back to the clinic.'

'Another medical emergency?'

God, she looked a mess. He didn't think he'd seen her without make-up for some time. And that hair! Wild did not cover it.

Though he was prepared for her to demand to be allowed in, he had not thought she would simply charge between him and the doorjamb like a prop forward. He found himself staring at her considerable rear disappearing up the stairs as she shouted, 'You've got that little slut up here, haven't you?'

He closed the door and followed her upstairs. There was no point in running after her, she'd find out soon enough that the place was empty.

He reached the landing as she entered his bedroom and watched from the doorway while she dragged the covers from the bed, as if she might discover Alice cowering there. Then she bent to peer beneath the bedstead, much as he had done a few minutes earlier. She stood up, eyes blazing with fury and frustration.

'Satisfied?' he said.

She threw herself at the wardrobe, yanking open the door so hard that he thought it might topple on top of her. With a sweep of her arm she thrust a curtain of clothes to one side. A carrier bag pitched from the bottom shelf onto the carpet, the white plastic rolling across the floor propelled by its contents. That solved one mystery at any rate.

She turned to face him. 'Where have you been?'

she demanded, seemingly forgetting the purpose of her rampage now she'd failed to find the evidence she was after. 'You don't answer the phone. You haven't come to see me. You can't walk out on me now.'

Robin resisted the obvious retort, that she had thrown him out of her house and thrown a few other things too when they'd last met.

'Look, Gloria, don't you think you'd better forget about me for the moment? Do you really want your marriage to go down the drain?'

'It's over. Clive's gone for good.'

'How can you be so sure? How long have you been together? It must be worth trying again.'

She sat heavily on the mattress and buried her face in her hands. Robin hoped she wasn't going to start weeping. He didn't have the energy for her hysterics.

She looked up at him. 'Twenty-six years,' she said. 'I married him when I was eighteen.'

'That's a lot of time to just throw away,' he said, placing a consoling hand on her shoulder.

'You don't understand,' she spat, the old venom returning. 'Clive's told me he's talking to a solicitor. And the children are on his side. Melissa had dinner with him and the Harrogate road bitch last night. She rang and said Faye was "really nice" and "good for Dad" and asked me to be mature about it. Jesus!'

That must have hurt. Melissa was a trainee accountant and discussed ISAs and personal pension plans with her father on a regular basis. She was twenty-four going on sixty and sounded insufferable.

'I'm sorry, Gloria,' he said and he was, up to a

point.

'Don't you dump me too,' she howled suddenly, grabbing his hand. 'He's leaving me the house—you can move in.'

'That's not the way to do things, Gloria. You've got to consider your next step calmly.'

'But I can't stay there by myself. Anyway,' she looked round at his apology for a bedroom, 'why would you want to live in this horrible tip?'

He could think of many reasons but whatever he said would be considered provocative. As was his silence.

She shoved him away from her and got to her feet. 'It's because you want somewhere to screw your other women, isn't it?'

'Gloria, I've told you. There are no other women.'

'Come tonight then. I can't stand the thought of being there by myself. Please.'

This time she did start with the weeping. He'd always found that hard to handle.

There was only one way to get rid of her and he took it.

As he led her out to her car she was rabbiting on about what she'd make for dinner.

'For God's sake, Gloria, what does it matter?'

She looked like she might start crying again but held herself in check. With considerable relief he watched her get into her car and start the engine. She rolled down the window for a parting shot.

'If you don't come,' she said, 'I'm going to kill myself.'

As she drove off, it occurred to Robin that that might solve one of his problems.

He went upstairs and retrieved the plastic bag. It

306

contained a bottle of vodka and a receipt from Mark Presley's local supermarket. He'd bought two bottles at the time but, the way things had turned out, one had been enough to put Presley to sleep.

It had been stupid to keep it, it was highly incriminating, but who throws away perfectly good vodka? But now, with things getting out of hand, he was glad he hadn't chucked it.

He drove back to the clinic and hid the bag in a new place. By way of insurance.

CHAPTER FIFTEEN

Bryan appeared positively jolly as he approached Harry's desk. Harry knew that look, the sergeant had unearthed some information that he considered significant.

'I've just had a chat with Dave Appleyard. Did I tell you he used to be on my darts team?'

'Yes, Bryan.' The sergeant could have made Job impatient. 'Now cough it up, will you? Was Naylor murdered?'

Bryan pulled a face, as if it hurt him to divulge the destination without making the most of the journey. 'Looks like it. They found anaesthetic in his blood. They think it's some stuff called Somulose.'

'Suppose he administered it to himself then jumped in the machine—suicide.'

Bryan shook his head. 'You inject the stuff into the bloodstream. Apart from the fact he had enough in him to render him incapable of movement within seconds, there's no sign of a syringe. They've had a good look round his flat and his car.'

Another murder. Harry was an experienced officer but a moment like this still quickened the blood.

'So,' Bryan continued, 'it looks like a person or persons unknown rendered Naylor unconscious and dumped him in the shredder. Funny thing is, it appears Eddie was expecting whoever killed him. He had just put in some security precautions—a light over the door and a spyhole in the door. Then, of course, there's the shotgun.'

Harry nodded, he hadn't forgotten. 'Was it loaded?'

'Both barrels. But after all his precautions, it seems he just let the killer in. Scenes of Crime are still poring over the place, God knows whether they'll get any useful DNA evidence. They've got some tyre tracks in the yard, though, that don't match Eddie's car.'

'Or ours?'

Bryan grinned. 'Don't worry, guv, I've sorted that out.' He was looking pretty pleased with himself, as if he had more to divulge—which he did.

'There's a guy down the road who used to work for Naylor. He says Eddie was visited by two French gentleman the other evening who threatened to stuff him down the shredder unless he paid them some money he owed them over a horse deal. Even as we speak, the Frenchmen are being brought here for questioning. Some character called Moreau and his chauffeur.'

'Jean-Luc Moreau?'

Bryan consulted his notes. 'That's right.'

'Jesus Christ. Have the press got this yet?'

'They haven't even been told it's murder. I think the idea is we wrap it all up quick before there's a hullabaloo.'

Harry laughed. There'd be a hullabaloo all right if France's leading racehorse owner was put on trial for murder.

'This Somulose,' he said, 'is it easy to get hold of?'

'It is if you're a vet. They use it to knock out horses.'

That was food for thought.

*   *   *

Alice hardly knew Martine at all but she could tell she was distressed. They'd had no problems chatting on the phone following the race at Doncaster—hence this invitation to supper. But now she was here, something obviously wasn't right.

As Alice poured them both a generous measure of wine, she said, 'What's the matter?'

The French girl grabbed her glass and drank eagerly.

'I cannot tell you.'

'Why not?'

'It is such a terrible thing. And I do not know you very well.'

'Sometimes it's better not to know the person you're dumping on. I don't have an axe to grind. I'm completely impartial. Try me.'

Martine looked at her, weighing up the offer. She drank some more and then said, 'It is a very big secret. You must not tell.'

'Or you'll have to kill me, right?'

Martine's face dissolved. Oh my God, what had she said? The girl was going to cry.

'I'm sorry, Martine. It's just a stupid joke. We English make jokes when we shouldn't to lighten the mood.'

But it was too late, Martine had thrown herself full length on the sofa and was sobbing into the cushions. Alice knelt down next to her and put her arms round her heaving shoulders. What else could she do?

Eventually, the storm passed. Martine sat up and mopped her face with the tissues Alice had supplied.

'My father has just been arrested,' she said.

Good Lord. Jean-Luc Moreau arrested—that was a shocker. It was also big news.

'I haven't heard about that.'

'No one knows yet, that is why you must keep the secret. His lawyer rang me as I was driving here and told me. I wanted to go to Papa but he forbade me to do so. He said I must wait. So I am sorry I am not good company.'

Alice ignored the apology, it wasn't the point.

'Why have they arrested him?' Some City fraud, no doubt.

She couldn't have been more wrong.

'They think he killed a man called Eddie Naylor. He had a terrible accident at his factory.'

'Yes, I know.' Alice's mind was racing. It was an extraordinary coincidence that Jean-Luc Moreau should be involved with Eddie and it was hard to take in. One thing shone out, however—the police must be treating Eddie's death as murder.

'Martine,' she said, 'why on earth should the police think your father murdered Eddie?'

That started the tears again but also a rigmarole of a story involving the sale of a horse at Tattersalls and Martine's past relationship with Eddie and her current one with Seb Stone and who'd said what to whom and a person called Uncle Gaston who was a big man but very gentle really. As Alice listened, and she did her best to take in the details, she couldn't help wondering whether it had anything to do with Eddie's death at all.

If he'd been murdered, might it not have been because someone didn't want him to talk to Harry about Claire's death? She pondered this as she served Martine supper—for a girl in distress she had a fair appetite—and made up a bed for her on the sofa. Too much wine had been drunk to allow her to drive home and the French girl did not protest.

Later, when she was on her own, she tried Harry's mobile number. She was fed up with being kept in the dark.

'Hello?'

'It's Alice. I know it's late but just answer me a couple of questions.'

'Ask away.'

'You are aware that Eddie Naylor was murdered, aren't you?'

'How do you know that?'

'I've promised to keep my source a secret for the moment—it's nothing sinister. But don't you think it's odd that Eddie was killed just as you were about to interview him about Claire? I mean, when Alan was on the point of talking to Mark Presley

311

about Claire, suddenly Mark died too. It seems fishy to me.'

A heavy sigh came down the line. 'Alice, lots of things are fishy in all this. There's things I can tell you and things I can't—do you understand?'

'I suppose so.'

'Good. Promise me you'll keep all this to yourself. I'll see you very soon.'

And that was it, he put the phone down. She supposed he had to be cagey but it was bloody irritating all the same.

She dialled one last number. She'd pinched it off Martine's phone and she was conscious that this could be an even riskier call than the last.

The phone rang for ages and she almost gave up before it was answered.

'Is that Seb Stone?'

'Who's this?' The voice bristled with suspicion.

'I'm a friend of Martine's.'

'Oh.' The tone changed in an instant. 'Is she all right?'

'Not really. That's why I'm calling. Just answer one question—do you still love her?'

The pause dragged on. 'Yes. But what business is it of yours?'

'I told you, I'm a friend. But she needs more than a friend right now. Just listen to what I'm going to suggest.'

*   *   *

Harry couldn't sleep. He'd been musing about Mark Presley even before the surprise phone call from Alice. Though the inquest was yet to take place he'd been expecting the coroner to find for

312

accidental death. But the murder of Eddie Naylor threw that into the balance. Not to mention how Claire Scott had met her end.

He felt guilty about Alice. He wondered how she was going to take it when she discovered that her sister had survived the road accident but had then been deliberately killed by a supposed rescuer. She probably wasn't going to thank him for telling her—the messenger is never completely innocent. Especially in this case when, as he now suspected, the person responsible for all these deaths turned out to be someone she was so close to.

*   *   *

It was too early in the morning for Seb to be able to buy flowers but he had the ring in his pocket— the ring he'd intended to present to Martine at the dinner that had backfired. With that fiasco in mind, it was probably just as well he wasn't about to arrive bouquet in hand.

Thoughts of rings and engagements were far from his mind as he followed the directions he'd been given over the phone the night before. This Alice had said Martine needed him—she was in trouble. Seb could guess what kind of trouble that might be. There had still been no news about Eddie's death but it was likely, surely, that the police had heard of Jean-Luc Moreau's threats. They hadn't heard them from him, though, and he could say so to Martine with a clear conscience.

Whatever happened with her father, she would have no inkling of his own imminent disgrace. When the facts of the road accident came out, as they were bound to, his stock would hit rock bottom in her eyes. At least this way he had the chance to come clean to her first.

Somewhere in his mind he noted that Silston Hall was impressive but he wasn't interested in sweeping drives and handsome country mansions at the moment. As he parked at the side of the big house, a door opened and a girl in jeans with untidy blonde hair beckoned to him.

Last night, when she'd told him her name and address he'd made the connection with Claire Scott. Coming here took courage in more ways than one.

He didn't know how to greet her but she offered her hand to shake and led him inside, past some gloomy shapeless paintings, into a bright little kitchen.

'Martine is still asleep,' she said. 'I've made some coffee so why don't you sit here and wait for her? I'm going down to the clinic.'

He agreed. She appeared to have thought it all out.

'Does she know that I'll be here?'

'No.'

She must have read the anxiety in his face for she added, 'Good luck,' as she went.

He was going to need it.

*　　　*　　　*

'That's a nifty-looking little car over there, don't you think?' said Harry.

They were approaching Silston Hall up the long driveway and the smart scarlet sports car parked at the side of the house was in plain view. Bryan

314

slowed to a crawl, causing the other police car behind to jam on its brakes.

'Looks like an Alfa Romeo 147 to me,' said the sergeant. 'Stylish but the rear accommodation is only so-so. I don't think the missus would approve.'

Harry allowed himself a grin. Once you got used to him, Bryan wasn't such a dry old stick.

'I didn't know you were much of a petrolhead.'

'I could say the same to you, guv.'

That was true, but they'd both had to start mugging up on sporty motors over the past twenty-four hours.

As far as the red car went, the pair of them had noticed it parked in the driveway of Seb Stone's house on their visit the previous day.

'God knows what Stone is doing here,' Harry now said. 'But it could be very useful.'

They parked beyond the red vehicle and, after telling Anderson and Carter in the car behind to make sure Stone didn't leave, Harry led the way to the door at the rear of the house.

Alan looked surprised to find them on his doorstep. He looked even more surprised when Harry told him he was required for interview down at the station. Surprise turned to barely suppressed anger when he was informed that the police had a warrant to search his premises.

'Good God, Harry, are you arresting me?'

'I'm sorry, Alan. We just need to clear a few things up about Claire's death.'

'What things? What's this about?'

'Claire wasn't killed in an accident, Alan. She was murdered. And I have reason to believe you did it.'

315

Robin watched the two cars drive past the clinic and up to the house. Giles was in the first one, so there was no doubt it was the police arriving mob-handed. Ten minutes later one car returned and he plainly saw his brother sitting in the rear alongside an officer he didn't recognise.

That it should come to this. He'd done all he could to look after Alan's interests—getting rid of two of the joyriding scum involved in Claire's accident had been acts of brotherly devotion, after a fashion. Seb Stone didn't know how lucky he was—but there was no point in going after him now. Things had progressed beyond that.

Alan couldn't be saved. He'd just have to take his medicine for all those years of being the elder brother, the dispenser of cheques and patronage, the superior human being inspired by the love of a virtuous woman.

Claire had been virtuous, all right, and look where it had got her. If she'd been less virtuous he wouldn't have had to shut her up before she spilled the beans to Alan about the painting.

He'd thought at the time that if she spotted the swap he'd be able to talk her round. He'd have been prepared to give up half the money so Claire could start the gallery she wanted—he hadn't lied to Alice about that. And, with her cooperation, they could have pulled the same stunt on the other musty old paintings cluttering up the walls of the Hall. With a brilliant copyist available and a source of valuable pictures to hand, they could have cleaned up. Alan would never have noticed.

But Claire had changed since he'd first met her

316

as a gold-digging promotions girl in a thigh-high dress doling out aftershave samples in a department store in Leeds. She'd been happy to dole out more than that after he'd made her laugh and dropped in the Silston Hall connection. Then, typically, she'd moved on to the owner of the Hall himself—his wealthier, more successful big brother. Robin supposed that as he was, technically, still married at the time of her wedding to Alan he couldn't complain.

And though, with regret, he'd agreed that their intimacy should be curtailed, there had always been a friendship between them. It was a pity she'd not understood how much he needed the money from the painting. But then she didn't owe two hundred grand to a bookmaker who had threatened to cut her fingers off. He wouldn't have been doing much surgery after that.

So, in a manner of speaking, it was her own selfishness that had got her killed. If she'd just listened to reason on the night she'd come storming into his place she'd be alive yet and they'd all be living happily, instead of Alan sitting like a miser on his gold and the rest of the world kissing his feet. But Claire had discovered the Cadogan Craig sale and guessed at once that he had fixed it—and how. She'd called him a crook and a sponger, a moral bankrupt who leeched off his brother and betrayed every other human being who ever trusted him.

She'd been really quite insulting, so it was no surprise they'd both lost their tempers. If he hadn't been so angry, he doubted if he could have done what he did.

In the end she'd screamed that she was off to

tell Alan about his treachery and she'd see to it he was never made partner and she'd do all she could to get Alan to chuck him out of the practice altogether. She'd got a head start on him by the time he worked out his best bet was to follow and put his case to Alan before she blackened his name completely. And before Alan asked for the return of his six hundred grand. The bastard would have been quite capable of calling in the police if he didn't cough up.

But he'd never got as far as the Hall. Claire's BMW had gone off the road on a bend—the silly tart was driving too fast. As he'd pulled up and got out, the thought had appeared fully grown in his head: 'Serve her right if she's broken her neck.' But she hadn't, which was a pity. She'd been lying there groaning and her eyes had flicked open and she'd seen him clearly. She'd said, 'Quick. Get me an ambulance,' like he was a thick-headed servant. The tone had refuelled his anger but, if he were honest, he'd decided to kill her anyway.

The piece of wood had been right there by his knee. It couldn't have been more convenient if someone had placed it in his hand.

He'd stayed just long enough to be sure she was dead and as he drove off he'd thanked his lucky stars no other cars had come along. He'd been certain no one had seen him. In the light of recent events, that was a laugh.

*　　　*　　　*

Harry wondered what Seb Stone might be doing at Alice's flat first thing in the morning. He wasn't aware they were even acquainted—but what did he

318

know about Alice's personal life? More than he should, probably, given that he was in the process of trying to nail her brother-in-law for murder. Yet not enough to satisfy his own curiosity.

Bryan caught his eye as they stood by the door, waiting for it to open in answer to their summons.

'I shouldn't worry, guv, I thought I saw Miss Young in the stables as we drove by.'

Harry glared at him. The old bugger could read his mind.

'Blonde girl,' Bryan continued. 'Classy, if you ask me. She had her picture in the paper after that race at Donny the other day. The one you went to, as I remember.'

Harry was about to tell him, with respect, to shut it when the door finally opened to reveal Seb Stone. He was barefoot and still buttoning his shirt.

'Christ,' he blurted out as he glared at them, 'this is harassment.'

'No, Mr Stone, just coincidence,' Harry said.

'What is it, Sebastian?' A dark-haired girl appeared from behind the jockey and clung to his arm. She, too, was deficient in the shirt-button department. She looked familiar.

'Police, miss,' Harry said, 'but there's nothing to worry about. I would just be grateful, since Mr Stone is here, if he would give us the benefit of his expertise.'

'Would you come and look at something for us, sir?' added Bryan.

'Er, sure.' Seb looked puzzled but no longer anxious. 'Stay here, Martine, while I sort this out.'

Martine—the jockey who'd pinched the race from Alice at Doncaster. The girl whose father was

319

currently being questioned over the murder of Eddie Naylor. No wonder she was clinging to Seb Stone like a limpet. But her anguish would soon be over—not that he was in a position to tell her so.

They waited for the pair of them to finish dressing and locate some footwear, then Harry led the way across a small courtyard to a large outbuilding. He knew Alan used this as a garage. Why had he not looked in here five years ago? he wondered. But if he had, he would have learned nothing. He hadn't known what to look for back then.

Three vehicles sat there. An olive green Volvo estate that Alan used every day. A silver BMW that Harry recognised from five years ago. And another car protected by a grey dustcover.

'Would you like to do the honours, Bryan?'

The sergeant considered the grey shape. 'I'm not quite sure how it comes off, guv.'

'It's got underbody straps,' said Seb. He was already on his haunches to release them, his movements eager. Within seconds he had stripped the cover clear to reveal a long, low, cream-coloured two-seater with a sweeping chassis and a high rounded front. It looked to Harry like a caricature of every classic power-hungry sports car he had ever seen. A boy's toy to stir the blood—and not just of boys.

'*Mon Dieu,* it's beautiful,' murmured Martine.

'What do you think?' Harry asked Seb.

'It's a Morgan plus eight. One of the best cars on the planet. What's it doing here?'

'It belongs to Alan Scott. His wife gave it to him on his fortieth birthday but he hasn't driven it for the past five years.'

Bryan flicked a glance at him. Here were some facts he didn't know, things Harry remembered from his first acquaintance with Alan.

'The thing is,' Harry continued, addressing Seb, 'do you recognise it? Could this have been the car that stopped at the scene of Claire Scott's accident?'

Seb considered the question. He walked to the far end of the garage and looked at the car from the rear. He returned slowly.

'Well?'

He shrugged. 'I can't positively identify it. That would be impossible. But Mark always said there was an S on the licence plate.' And so there was.

Harry nodded. 'So you couldn't rule it out?'

'Oh no. The car that stopped was like this. Absolutely. A Morgan shape is very distinctive. But I couldn't swear it was this particular Morgan.'

That would be too much to ask, Harry admitted to himself. So it was either this Morgan or one of the dozens of others that were doubtless being driven towards Doncaster at eleven fifteen on 25 October 2002 with the letter S in the licence plate.

It was good enough for him.

'Guv.' Bryan was calling him, having turned his attention to the Volvo. He'd taken charge of Alan's car keys earlier and was now rummaging in the boot. 'Look at this.'

Bryan was holding open a white plastic bag. Inside was a bottle of vodka, a bog standard brand, and a slip of paper. Harry took it out to examine. It was a receipt for £25.98 from Topsale Stores, Crackington Road, on 11 October of this year.

Crackington Road was a few minutes' drive

from Mark Presley's house. The date tallied too.

'Come on,' he said.

Before he went back to the station and got stuck into questioning Alan Scott about the murder of his wife, he had to speak to Alice. He owed her that, at least.

*   *   *

Alice was in turmoil. Harry had only been in her office for five minutes but what he had said had turned her world upside down.

Claire had not died as a result of a road accident, she had been deliberately killed.

The boys in the Mondeo that had collided with her had seen another car at the scene—a light-coloured sports car similar to the one in the garage at the Hall.

The driver of that car had smashed Claire's skull with a piece of fence timber.

That driver was in custody and about to be charged with murder.

Furthermore, the driver was responsible for the deaths of Mark Presley and Eddie Naylor, both of whom had been killed on the brink of telling what they knew about Claire's death.

And that driver was Alan.

'But why?' she said to Harry. 'Why on earth should Alan kill Claire? He loved her.'

'It's possible she was having an affair. There's a statement on file that doubts the child she was carrying was her husband's.'

'Who said that?'

'I'd rather not say.'

Alice could guess. Alan had been harbouring a

322

snake in his bosom for years by employing Liz.

'I'm sorry, Alice, but it's a sad fact that husbands are more likely to be responsible for the deaths of their wives than anyone else.'

Harry had gone now but her blood was still boiling at that parting shot. Claire and Alan were not a statistic.

She didn't buy all that rubbish about an affair. Just because there was an age gap between them and Claire's pregnancy had come out of the blue didn't mean a thing. It was typical of Liz to try and spice up her own dull existence by making up tales about more glamorous people.

But there was one thing that gave a terrible credence to what Harry had said. The painting. If Alan had found out that Claire had sold off one of his pictures and substituted a fake, swindling him out of £600,000, Alice could imagine that he would be shattered. His faith in his perfect wife would be broken.

But enough to kill her?

And what was he doing driving down the road behind her?

Following her home from an illicit rendezvous?

Robin lived down that road. Was that where she had been—to discuss the picture scam—and had Alan misunderstood their meeting and chased after her?

She felt in her bones that Alan couldn't have done it. She must be able to prove it. She racked her brains.

Through the window she saw Robin crossing the car park. Did he know what was going on?

She ran outside, calling his name.

'What's the matter?'

'They've just arrested Alan for killing Claire and those other men!'

'Good God.'

'It's completely mad. He's not capable of doing anything like that, is he?' She felt on the verge of tears.

He stepped close to her and put a hand on her shoulder. 'Don't worry, I'm sure it will all get sorted out.'

'But surely you don't believe he murdered Claire?'

'Of course he didn't, Alice. But let's be honest, he'd be quite capable of bumping off those guys in the accident. He's said so many times.' He put his arms around her and rubbed her back like he always did, as if she were an overwrought child. 'Look, I'll get him a solicitor right now. I know just the fellow.'

That made sense, she supposed, but Alan already had a good solicitor, so why would he need a different one? She didn't say anything though. A memory was bubbling under the jumble of her thoughts.

Robin released her with a kiss on her cheek and the assurance that he'd fix everything, and headed for the clinic.

She stood there, the bubble still submerged but now fighting its way to the surface.

She remembered the night before their lives changed for ever, when Alan came into the office and chucked his keys on the desk. 'Bloody Robin,' he'd said cheerfully.

'What's he done now?' she'd said.

'Nothing much. I should be used to him borrowing my things without permission.'

That was all the memory bubble contained—but it was important.

She went after Robin.

*   *   *

Gloria had been watching from the cab of her Range Rover. She'd parked up outside the entrance to the clinic car park, debating with herself.

Should she go in and shout at that bastard?

He'd stood her up again. He'd promised to come last night and he hadn't showed. She'd got pissed and gone round to his place to break down the door if necessary. But he'd not been there—of course. Out shagging again—of course. She'd waited for him to come back and finally fallen asleep. She'd been woken at nine by her mobile going off and Clive talking in that ever-so-cool voice he used when he was really angry telling her that if she phoned his precious Faye again to slag her off he'd change his mind about the house and fix it so she got sweet FA out of their settlement.

And now here she was, pondering her options, when Robin had appeared and the blonde bimbo too. They'd posed in the middle of the car park with their arms round each other, all lovey-dovey as if they were deliberately rubbing her nose in it.

If she'd had a gun she could have blown their heads off, but she didn't.

However, she did have a big heavy powerful car.

But she'd missed her chance.

*   *   *

Robin passed Liz's empty desk, heading for his office. He'd make a show of finding Alan a solicitor.

He'd find a way of keeping this whole thing together. Alan's arrest was a lucky break. All he had to do was hold his nerve and big brother would take the bullet he'd been dodging for five years. There was a certain happy symmetry in that.

He heard the door bang and Alice was bearing down on him.

'You borrowed Alan's car that night, didn't you?'

The words hit Robin like a wave of cold water.

'What on earth are you talking about?' he said.

'The night Claire died—you were driving the Morgan, weren't you?'

'No.'

'You were. I remember it distinctly.'

'You've got it wrong, Alice.'

'No, I haven't. You took Alan's car without permission—like you always did.'

She blocked his path. He recognised fury blazing in her spectacular green eyes—he'd never seen that before. Sweet, biddable, trusting Alice wasn't going to back down.

The accusations continued to tumble from her mouth. Her face turned red and blotchy, ugly with passion. 'It was you in the Morgan at the crash site, wasn't it? You could have helped Claire. You could have saved her life!'

'Don't be silly, Alice—that wasn't how it was at all.'

'You killed her.'

He laughed. 'That's ridiculous.'

'It was the painting. She was going to tell Alan

and you had to shut her up.'

He stepped towards her with his arms open. 'Alice, my darling, just listen for a moment—'

'Get away from me.' She avoided his brotherly embrace and turned for the door.

He had to keep her quiet and charm wasn't going to work this time. Unless he stopped her now she'd soon be pouring her poison into the ear of Harry Giles.

He caught her by the reception desk and punched her in the stomach to silence her—only temporarily, of course, but it gave him time to find the things he needed as she lay winded and helpless on the floor. He fastened her hands with his belt and lashed her ankles together with his tie. He wadded her mouth with tissues from the box on the desk and sealed the gag with parcel tape.

As he worked he told her he'd not had any choice about Claire—not if he wanted to keep the money from the picture and make partner in the business and keep his tight-fisted brother onside. Then he told her was sorry he was going to have to kill her.

And he was sorry. She wasn't like those snivelling little jockeys—or even her selfish, gold-digging sister. But he couldn't think about that. He'd gone too far already.

He made for the door quickly. He reckoned he had ten minutes before Liz showed up, which made it bloody tight. But there was time to drive his car round to the side and load Alice into the boot—he'd give her something to keep her quiet. Then he'd dump her where she'd never be found.

He crossed the forecourt to his car, his thoughts buzzing. He knew a mineshaft on the moor the

327

other side of Sheffield.

He never heard the car coming until it was almost on him.

*   *   *

This time Gloria seized her chance, aiming the Range Rover at the tall figure striding across the car park. At the last moment he turned and looked at her.

There was no fear on his face. Just surprise. And irritation. The kind of look that said don't bother me now, I'm busy. The kind of look that Robin had directed at her all too often recently. She jammed her foot down harder.

The car hit him around the hips, flipping him up in the air. He bounced down onto the bonnet, obscuring her view for a few seconds before he slid off.

With a howling screech of tyres she yanked the big beast round in a curve.

The man in front of her was on his hands and knees, struggling to get to his feet.

This time he did look at her as she came back at him. She had his full attention this time.

Her only regret, in the ecstasy of the moment, was that the road kill beneath her wheels was not her husband.

EPILOGUE

If it had been left to Alan, the Claire Scott Memorial race at Doncaster would have been cancelled. But Alice told him that cancelling would be an insult to the memory of his dead wife. And this year, more than any other, Claire's memory should be honoured, now the truth of her death was known, albeit to only a few.

They knew now that Robin had killed Claire because she was on the brink of exposing his theft of the painting to Alan. And Robin had killed Mark and Eddie so the sighting of the third car at the scene of the accident would not come out.

It had taken a bit of persuading for the police to come to the right conclusion but Alice's certainty that Robin had borrowed his brother's car that night was a start. Then they'd found that the tyre tracks outside Eddie's factory matched Robin's vehicle. Gloria had supplied the last damning evidence. In her lurid testimony to the wrongs of Robin Scott she had included minute details of her recent encounters with him. Including an account of shaking the wardrobe in his bedroom until a white plastic carrier bag had fallen out and rolled across the floor in a manner that identified its contents as bottle-shaped. The assistant in the store on Crackington Road had recognised Robin's photograph. That Robin had planted the bag in his brother's car was among the most despicable things he had done, in Alice's opinion.

All the same, life without his familiar presence was strange. However, the hole he left in her world

329

was nothing to the one that gaped for Alan. He'd grown up with his brother's faults and loved him despite them. The pair of them were going to need some kind of therapy to see them through. She had a few ideas about that and they didn't involve a psychiatric couch. Surely there was a fair chance she could persuade Alan to give a good home to a puppy?

Alice watched the race with Alan on one side and Harry on the other. The two men appeared to be on remarkably good terms considering that one, albeit for a brief period, had thought the other capable of murder. Alan appeared to consider his arrest and short period of suspicion the least of his troubles. It was the one topic he made jokes about, at Harry's expense.

Luke had offered to withdraw from riding Don't Touch—he said he had expected Alan to prefer another rider. After he'd talked it through with Alice, Alan had taken a different view.

'Do you think it would be so bad to keep him on the horse?' he said. 'I mean, if Claire knew all the facts, do you think she'd object?'

'Do *you* object?' asked Alice. It was the only question that mattered.

'His crime was standing by his friends. I don't think loyalty is too bad a fault in a boy of sixteen.'

Luke had been overwhelmed when Alice had told him he was still required. 'I'm going to win that race,' he vowed. And watching through her binoculars as the runners rounded the top of the bend with Don't Touch going well she had the feeling that he might.

The previous Saturday she'd kept her word and invited Harry to accompany her to Grovelands to

330

meet Edwin. They'd taken a particular item with them, carefully wrapped and loaded in the boot of the car.

Dr Huntley had greeted her as usual and conducted the pair of them to Edwin's basement studio. The old man, dressed in a blue overall, stood poised over his latest work like a heron over a pool. He did not stir until, at Alice's request, Harry unwrapped the painting they had brought with them and propped it against the wall in front of the painter.

Huntley said, 'So, you've brought that back, have you? He did enjoy it last time.'

So it had been here before. Alice wasn't surprised.

'Who brought it then?' she asked.

This was important. She didn't know how she would feel if he said, 'Mrs Scott.'

But he didn't. 'Robin Scott,' he answered.

So Robin had been the sole architect of the scheme to fleece his brother. It was a relief for there to be no uncertainty.

Then Edwin, unprompted, filled a palette with the colours of summer and began to recreate the painting by Peter Rawdon. He worked quickly to produce a fast, loose image—like a concert pianist playing a lightning exercise to loosen up.

'Amazing,' Harry said. 'I didn't know he could paint like that.'

'He likes to copy,' said Huntley.

'He's always been a magician,' Alice said. 'It's just that he doesn't believe there's any value to this kind of painting.'

Which was a laugh considering he'd made a reproduction that could have passed for a picture

331

worth over £600,000. She supposed it was how you defined value.

On the way back, they bought an evening paper which contained an intriguing item: a photograph of a burly fellow with an earring being congratulated by an older man in a suit. 'Stanley Sheriton, manager of Splash nightclub, congratulates employee of the year Billy Chesil. Mr Chesil, whose delivery van was involved in the hit-and-run accident that claimed the life of stable girl Jeannette Presley, spotted the joyriders responsible at a Splash under-18s night. Due to his quick thinking, the club security guards were able to detain two youths who were also in possession of considerable quantities of crack cocaine. "Thanks to Billy," Mr Sheriton said, "we have not only been responsible for catching two wanted criminals but also for keeping Splash free from the scourge of drug-dealing."'

After they'd finished reading, Harry had grinned and murmured, 'Good karma.'

For a policeman, Harry had his moments.

The horses were at the beginning of the home straight now and Don't Touch was a length down on the second-placed horse—not a dissimilar position, Alice remembered, from the race at Beverley when he'd finished third and Luke had spotted his breathing problem.

Now Don't Touch cruised past the second horse as if it wasn't there and moved up onto the shoulder of the leader—Seb Stone on one of his future father-in-law's expensive animals. Seb Stone who'd been in the car that had been involved in Claire's accident. She couldn't hold that against him now.

'Luke's got him this time,' cried Alan.

He had, too. As Luke on Don't Touch bolted past Seb to win on the line, Alice reckoned that, after everything, he deserved it.